A Broken Marriage

With Hidden Secrets

An Inspirational Novel
Written by: Lakisha G. Louissaint

Prologue

S ingleness had become a thorn in her flesh until she met the man of her dreams; however, her impatience brought more than she bargained for. The secrets from their past creeps back into their lives with vengeance that threatens to rip them apart. Will the counselor heal their marriage or will they allow divorce to defeat them?

Chapter One

Mounted with frustration, Janelle's thoughts drifted back into memories of her past.

"I'm so confused.

Out of all of my friends, why am I the only one who's still single?"

In her late twenties, singleness had become a thorn in her flesh. Raised as a church girl, she was familiar with the frequent wedding announcements and had become weary of always being a bride's maid, but never the bride. She looked up as Pastor Peter smiled as he walked in.

"Hello daughter. Can I bother you for a moment?"

She slid her notebook aside.

"Of course, pastor."

He stood a few inches over five feet tall with a bald head, thick black brows, light brown skin, and brown eyes brimmed with long lashes.

She smiled.

"I didn't know you were here. Are you about to leave?"

He sat down.

"Yeah, in a few minutes. I just wanted to peek in and see how you were doing."

She picked up the Bible from her desk.

"I'm just going over a few scriptures so I can be ready for our meeting tonight."

"Janelle, I remember when I first ordained you to teach and I must say that I'm very proud of you and your spiritual growth."

She smiled and slightly titled her head.

"Thank you pastor, but you know I mess up a lot and it really hurts when I don't—"

His brows met as he interrupted her.

"Let me stop you right there before you allow those thoughts to consume and condemn you... We all mess up, including myself. If we were perfect, there wouldn't have been any reason for Jesus to die on that cross for our sins."

He stood up and patted his pockets to check for his keys.

"Well, I'll let you get back to your lesson for tonight. Focus Janelle and let God use you. Grace and mercy are sitting right next to you cheering you on."

She smiled.

"I appreciate you coming in before leaving. Oh, and thanks for the talk. I really needed it."

He looked back and nodded.

"That's what I'm here for Janelle."

She watched as he walked away.

"Be careful."

She leaned her head back, prayed, and reached for her Bible once more.

"Lord, please help me teach this lesson tonight."

Shortly thereafter, her best friend gently tapped on the door before peeking in. She looked up.

"Hey Sandra."

She smiled.

"Am I disturbing you?"

"No, come in."

She placed her purse on the desk.

"So, how's your day going?"

"Good... Other than this lesson frustrating me."

Sandra frowned.

"Why?"

She reached for her coffee and glanced down at the bracelet on her wrist as memories of her ex crept into her mind. She looked back up.

"Please don't tell me you're still thinking about him."

"Girl stop... I was just pondering on how to teach this lesson when I'm struggling with loneliness myself."

Sandra shook her head.

"Janelle, I may not be at church every Sunday, but I know that sometimes God gives us a word for ourselves through our own experiences, then we're able to teach others. When you look at it that way, you see things from a different perspective."

She smirked.

"I've also come to realize that we're never alone because God is always with us."

"Huh, that's easy for you to say. You have a husband."

She pointed to her ring finger. "Do you see a ring on this finger?"

Sandra reached for her purse and leaned towards the desk.

"You're married spiritually to God first. Seek ye the kingdom... Yeah, you know the rest."

She stared at her with furrowed brows.

"Well, at least you're married."

Sandra shook her head.

"Janelle, Janelle, Janelle. I learned this the hard way. I wish someone would've told me this good old fashion information, then

I wouldn't have to deal with this knuckle head of a man that I'm married to now. Marriage is a job you volunteer for."

She chuckled.

"And guess what, the minimum wage is free."

She stood up.

"So, stop thinking you need a man in your life and wait on the Lord."

She leaned back in her chair and folded her arms.

"Sandra, I'm serious."

"I bet you are and so am I."

She pointed to Janelle's notes.

"Well, I'll let you get back to your lesson. Remember, you're studying for you, not just them. You'll be fine."

A few minutes later, Janelle. She gathered her things and went home. Later that evening, she arrived at the church and noticed that some of the ladies were waiting in the parking lot. She got out of the car and playfully greeted them.

"Good evening ladies. Ya'll early."

Ms. Lula smiled as they walked into the sanctuary.

"And you aint late tonight."

Janelle smiled and shook her head as she walked to the front. After everyone had arrived, she slid the podium to the center of the sanctuary for her Bible and notes. She opened her Bible.

"Good evening ladies."

Ms. Lula adjusted herself on the pew.

"So, what's the lesson about tonight?"

She looked up and smiled.

"How to wait on The Lord."

Ms. Lula nodded her head.

"Uh... This should be interesting."

She turned and winked her eye at the ladies.

Janelle shook her head and prayed a short opening prayer. She stared down at her notes tapping her fingers on the edge of the podium.

"Well, I must say, it took a lot for me to teach this lesson tonight. I've been single for some time now and you know how some single women try to rush into relationships without waiting on the Lord for confirmation... So, I'll be soaking up all of this information for myself tonight."

She smiled.

"I have a lot of scriptures for tonight, but I'll only go over a few. My main focus is Jeremiah 29:11. It says, 'I say this because I know what I am planning for you, 'says the Lord. 'I have good plans for you, not plans to hurt you. I will give you hope and a good future.'"

She walked away from the podium, took a deep breath, and exhaled.

"Many times, we assume that what happens in our life is designed to hurt us and that's where I've messed up in my life. I assumed that I should've been married by now, but apparently God has better plans for me."

The ladies in the meeting held on to her every word as she continued. She walked back to the podium and flipped the pages in her Bible.

"Open your Bibles to 1 Corinthians 7:8-9. Ms. Lula, will you please read it for us?"

Ms. Lula's forehead wrinkled as she took a quick glance around the sanctuary and pointed to herself.

"Who me?"

Janelle smiled.

"Yes, ma'am."

She cleared her throat.

"Well, you're going to have to give me a minute or two. Baby, let me find my magnifying glasses so I can see what I'm reading."

While Ms. Lula fumbled through her purse, Janelle remembered how she selflessly became the mother figure she so desperately desired. Years before, Ms. Lula sat in the hospital at her mother's bed side and vowed that she would love and care for Janelle as her own. Being a woman of unwavering faith, Ms. Lula laughed at calamity. She had recently been diagnosed with Leukemia, but it didn't muzzle the joy that was in her heart. Janelle cherished every moment with her because she was a true definition of a faith walker. With her glasses hanging on the edge of her nose, Ms. Lula began to read.

"'But if they cannot control themselves, they should marry....'"

She closed her Bible.

"And that's why I need a husband. My hormones get the best of me sometimes."

She looked up.

"So, how am I supposed to wait on God? I've been waiting on Him to send me a man for over a decade now."

Janelle chuckled softly and stepped away from the podium.

"Well, Romans 8:25 tells us that although we are hoping for something we don't have yet, we're to wait for it patiently. So many people enter relationships today because of loneliness and in the end, it fails because neither of their hearts were in it for love. I guess we got out l's confused. Believe me, I should know. Those people were basically void fillers. That's why it's vital that we wait on the Lord before entering a relationship or marriage. My friend once told me that marriage is a job that you don't get paid for."

Ms. Lula looked up.

"I don't know what you're talking about. You see, they pay me."

She chuckled.

"I mean my sugar daddies that is."

Olivia looked up at Janelle.

"But didn't the scripture also say, 'It's better to marry than to burn?' I'm not trying to burn, but I'm also not ready for marriage. So, how do I deal with that? I'm gonna to be honest, I still have needs, Janelle."

Janelle smiled.

"Ummm. I understand that we have needs, but remember, 'all other sins that we commit are outside of our bodies, but when we sin sexually, we sin against our own bodies.'"

She lifted her palms upward.

"Do you not realize there are people purposefully infecting others with HIV and anything else they can? I mean, one moment of pleasure can cost you a lifetime of regret and pain."

Ms. Lula squinted her eyes.

"Well... it looks like I need to head to the clinic then."

She shook her head.

"Uh uh uh. Why ya'll just now telling me this?"

A whisper echoed from the back of the sanctuary.

"Ms. Lula always joking. She know she aint—"

Janelle laughed.

"Ya'll know Ms. Lula is a jokester."

She tilted her head.

"Right Ms. Lula."

Ms. Lula smiled sarcastically as she continued.

"But seriously, many generations before us just didn't know and chances are no one taught them."

She held up her Bible.

"But it's right here in black and white. 1 Corinthians 6:12-20 to be exact. I mean I was shocked when I saw it for myself. But, it helped me to understand why I was saving myself for marriage. You know, when you're intimate with someone, you become spiritually connected to that person, right. Our bodies are temples where the Holy Spirit dwells and when we allow others to invade that personal space by entering inside of us, we allow them to interrupt a passion within us that burns for Christ. Then, we become so consumed with lust that a spiritual connection with God is no longer desired. Just a physical touch and a brief sexual encounter."

Ms. Lula giggled softly.

"Listen at you trying to sound all deep and stuff."

Janelle smiled as Sandra walked in and sat next to Ms. Lula listening attentively as she taught her lesson.

"My friend once told me that marriage isn't easy. It's all about what you're willing to put into it because that's exactly what you'll get out of it. I look at it this way. Our words and actions are like boomerangs. When we throw it out, eventually it comes back."

She looked up.

"Sandra, what do you think about people rushing into relationships and marriages?"

She smiled.

"Well, I wish I would've waited on the Lord before I got married. You know, I've been through a lot with men in my lifetime. My father was never there for me and my last relationship wasn't the best. I've been abused emotionally and physically."

She lowered her head as tears crawled down her face.

"I was broken, but I blame myself for rushing into relationship after relationship without being healed first from the others. Reality is I didn't want to be alone and I thought attention from a man was love. It took years, but, I realized that I only used that as an excuse to fill an empty void that only God could fill."

She looked over at Ms. Lula and smiled.

"I had needs of my own and I allowed men to use my body over and over for a moment of sexual pleasure while I was left in shackles with their spirits."

Ms. Lula patted Sandra on the leg and passed her a tissue as a tear fell from her eye.

"Baby it's okay. No one here has any room to judge you."

She wiped the corners of her eyes and continued.

"I grew up watching my mother allow my dad break to her spirit. As a child, I didn't understand why she allowed it. Eventually, those same patterns carried over into my life. It wasn't until then that I realized the cycle of avoiding confrontation and rejection had to be broken off of my life."

She lowered her head.

"My father called my mother everything but a child of God even when she did everything right. Instead of shedding tears, she squared her shoulders back, and took every venomous word he spoke over her life. It were as if she had become immune to the deadly poison in his tongue that constantly spewed out negativity towards her. Although he constantly disrespected her."

She shrugged her shoulders.

9

"My mother feared he would leave her, so she did whatever he demanded of her. There were days when he would tell her that no other man would ever want to put up with a woman like her."

She cleared her throat.

"He beat her in the head with those words until he molded her into a woman he could control. You know, I believe the fear of being alone paralyzed her. I honestly don't believe she understood the damage that her passiveness was doing to her or me. There were days I overheard my dad talking to other women on the phone while my mother was upstairs. I was so confused, but eventually it began to make sense. My mother stayed trapped in an unhealthy marriage until the day she died. In my mind, I just don't believe that God wanted her to be miserable like that. Witnessing all of that shaped me into a bitter woman who refused to trust men." My mother deserved better than that, you know. I always prayed that I would never repeat what I saw because of the pain it caused her. Reality is that I did, but only for a moment. I refuse to allow my husband to treat me the way my dad treated my mom. Don't get me wrong, I love my husband, but I wish I would've waited for God to heal me completely before saying I do. We didn't rush to get married, but when you bring two wounded people together, something is bound to come and test their faith. You know, some women are so impatient that they jump into relationship after relationship as I did just for a physical touch from a man that's only an illusion of true unconditional love."

Ms. Lula looked up.

"Well I'll be..."

The young lady in the back laughed.

"Ms. Lula, don't you say it. We in church."

She turned around.

"I was about to say she just taught the whole lesson in thirty minutes."

She smiled at Janelle.

"I'll be home in time to finish watching my shows.".

Everyone laughed as Janelle smiled.

"Ms. Lula, you're absolutely right. Sometimes, God doesn't need an hour to make His point. I feel that the lesson has been delivered."

She looked over at Sandra and smiled.

"Thank you so much for sharing with us tonight."

Janelle ended the women's meeting in prayer and dismissed. She locked up the church and caught up with Sandra outside.

"You have no clue how much you've helped me and there's no doubt that you helped the other ladies too. I was like, is that my friend."

She looked over at Sandra and lightly pushed her.

"As quiet as you are around people you don't know, I didn't expect you to share all of that."

She rolled her eyes and giggled.

"Whatever Janelle. Sometimes, we share things with others when God is ready for them to be shared."

She pushed her and laughed.

"I'll see you later. I got to get home and cook dinner for Brian."

Janelle got in the car.

"Be careful."

Sandra smiled.

"You too."

Chapter Two

A few weeks later, Janelle sat on her sofa feeling sorry for herself, but later decided on a girl's night out. She reached for her phone and called Sandra.

"Hello."

"Hey lady, is Brian working tonight?"

"As usual. What's up?"

"Well, I wanted to go to open mic night at De Wan Café."

A wide smile graced Sandra's face.

"Really? Girl, you haven't been there in months."

She took a quick glance at the bracelet on her wrist.

"I know right. I realized it's time to deal with this brokenness from my ex and move on with my life. I've been holding on to a lost memory for far too long."

She took a deep breath.

"I know that if God blesses me with someone else and I'm still hurting, I'll only take it out on him. Girl, I need a release and sometimes the flow of open mic night sets me free."

Sandra smiled.

"Girl, that's what I'm talking about. What time do I need to be ready?"

She opened her closet door.

"All I need is about thirty minutes to get dressed and I'll swing by and pick you up."

Sandra smiled.

"Okay, I'll be ready in an hour."

Janelle laughed.

"Whatever, you're trying to be funny. Just be ready."

Sandra hung up the phone and smiled.

"Lord, thank you. I thought this day would never come. Janelle no longer sounds pitiful, she sounds powerful."

As Janelle got dressed, she stopped, and closed her eyes as the words began to flow through her mind like a river of flooding water. She closed her eyes.

"I can't wait to hit the stage."

After getting dressed, she reached for her keys, and headed to Sandra's house. When they arrived at Den Wan Café, the parking lot was packed. As she glanced over and took a deep breath, Sandra gave her a reassuring smile and embraced the moment of finally seeing her friend hit the stage. When they stepped into the café, the MC eyes grew wide. He stood on the stage in his khaki pants and blue polo shirt with a fresh cut and nicely trimmed goatee. He gave a quick laugh and pointed to the back as Janelle signed her name to the list to take the stage. With a wide smile, he leaned in to the mic.

"Tonight, we have a very familiar face that will take the stage and serenade us with some of her amazing spoken word. I can only imagine what she has for us tonight. Ladies and gentlemen, I now introduce to you a very close friend and supporter of the café."

He paused and spoke in a deep dramatic voice.

"Janelle."

The MC hugged her as she reached for the mic. Taking no time, she began.

"When I first met him, it felt as though his eyes pierced through my soul down to the deepest part of me that no other man had been able to reach. Closing my eyes, I tried to escape this feeling, but it felt so good that I had to let him in. But then, I allowed him to get too close. He unlocked places I had hidden to make me appear strong, and once he realized he had my heart in his hands, he gained complete control of me. I became his love puppet and whatever direction he pulled my strings, I followed. It was not his physical touch, but his words were sharper than a martial arts sword and every time he spoke, it cut deep. His words were suffocating me. The screams and name calling beat me in my face as if I were in a boxing ring. Left hook, right hook, upper cut I was knocked out. His words knocked me down until I had low self-esteem. Now, I must redeem myself to get back to where I use to be. I began loving me again by refilling my thirst for attention with the love of God and the way He saw me. I embraced His unconditional love, knowing that He would never hurt me, but that He would heal the wounds afflicted by a wounded man who had yet to find himself. You see, although he hurt me, he taught me how to pray. Even when his words caused me tears, they gave me the strength to release myself from the imprisonment of his puppeteer strings. So, young man, thank you because you taught me to never allow another man to tear me down again because of his own insecurities. Today is my mental and emotional death of you. In the midst of all the pain, I gained a new definition of me; not the definition from you. I am no longer pitiful. I am powerful, strong, beautiful, confident, bold, and free! I am HIS (Jesus) And He is mine. And I understand that His love will never hurt me.... Thank you."

Janelle looked out as the crowd gave her a standing ovation. She handed the MC the mic and walked away. In a deep voice, the MC continued.

"She has done it yet again. Once again, the amazing, Janelle." Sandra looked over as she sat down.

"Girl that was more than a release, that was pure freedom."

She smiled at the fact that she had left her pain on the stage and walked into a new refreshing promise of love and peace.

Chapter Three

A few days later, Janelle heard a knock at the door. She stared through the peep hole.

"Who is it?"

Sandra smiled.

"Girl open the door and stop playing."

She opened the door and smiled as Sandra walked in.

"What's up Ms. Poetic?"

She rolled her eyes.

"You're always trying to be funny Sandra."

Sandra sat on the couch.

"I need to talk to you about something."

She reached for the remote and turned off the television.

"Okay, I'm all ears."

Janelle snapped her fingers as Sandra stared into space.

"Well, are you going to tell me or just sit over there smiling?"

She shifted her body towards her.

"Of course. Well, when I got home last night, I walked in the house and smelled food right."

Janelle hung on to every detail as Sandra continued.

"Brian was playing Forever my Lady by Jodeci, right. Girl, you that's my song. So, I walked in the kitchen and he had the table all fixed up with a candle lit dinner, chocolate covered strawberries, and two glasses of champagne."

She motioned her finger back and forth.

"You know; he hasn't done that for me in a while Janelle."

Clueless of Sandra's marriage being on the chopping block, she smiled.

"Uh, no wonder you walked through the door like a glowing light. Maybe one day I'll get to walk through your door and tell you all about my night too." Janelle chuckled and walked over to the refrigerator. "You want something to drink?"

"Nah, I'm good."

She grabbed a bottle of water and returned to the living room, sat down, and listened as Sandra continued to talk about Brian's surprise. Her smile slowly dwindled away.

"Sandra, please don't take this the wrong way. I don't mind hearing about your marriage. It's just that... I don't understand when my time will ever come. I truly just got over my ex a few weeks ago, but I'm still lonely and you know I–"

Sandra exhaled and interrupted her.

"Janelle, let me break this down for you yet again. There's no need of you feeling lonely because you're single... You have no clue what others go through in their relationships and marriages. There are so many people that are married, but yet their still single. Believe me, people show you what they want you to see, especially in public and let's not forget social media. Of course, their smiling and looking happy, but behind closed doors, some of them can't stand each other. Don't get me wrong, there are happy marriages and relationships out there, but none of them are perfect. I'm telling you Janelle, looks can be deceiving."

Janelle placed her hand on the side of her face.

"I'm just tired of walking into an empty apartment every day. I want love too, you know. I pray, but it seems as if God is not answering my —"

Sandra stopped Janelle with a sharp look.

"First of all, happiness begins within you. There's no man in this world that can make you so happy that he makes all of your problems go away."

She pointed towards her.

"God is the only person that can fill that empty little void of yours. It may seem like it's taking Him a long time to answer you, but He may just be preparing you for the husband he has for you."

She tilted her head.

"Need I remind you of how to wait on the Lord? When I looked over the notes you gave me from the part of the lesson I missed, the first scripture I saw was Jeremiah 29:11."

She smiled.

"Yeah, you remember that one. Girl, you better be patient and let him prepare you." She laughed. "You never know what kind of issues the husband he gives you might have and if you're not prepared, you'll wish you would've waited. God knows you better than you know yourself. Trust me, your day will come. So, don't rush it. There's no love that could ever compare to God's love for you. In due time baby girl."

She leaned over and reached for her hand.

"Janelle, you know my marriage isn't always peaches and cream, right. My marriage keeps me on my knees. There are days that Brian comes home and goes straight to the room without acknowledging me. So, when he does give me the love and attention that I deserve, I get really excited."

Janelle shook her head.

"I'm sorry, I didn't know."

She smiled. "Girl it's okay. But anyways, enough about me. I know this guy Brian and I went to college with and the last I heard, he's single."

She smiled.

"His name is Joshua."

Janelle laughed as she continued.

"He's a little over six feet tall, about two-hundred pounds, with hazel brown eyes and wavy hair. I think he has some kind of texturizer in his head or something. They just don't look like real waves to me." Sandra added "Oh, and he look aight."

Janelle laughed as Sandra continued.

"We can meet up and do lunch or something together one day. He's a character you know."

She reached for her purse.

"I gotta go because I have a meeting at work that I can't miss."

She got up and walked Sandra to the door.

"Don't forget to call me."

Sandra looked back.

"I won't."

As she closed the door, she frowned.

"Fake waves, possible texturizer."

Chapter Four

Sandra figured it was time for Janelle to give this dating thing a try again. So, she and her husband made arrangements for a double date. She grabbed her phone and texted Janelle.

Are you busy Saturday?

Janelle reached for her phone.

No. What's up?

Sandra smiled.

Well, Joshua agreed...

She sent the message, paused, and thought to herself.

Forget it. Let me just call her.

As the phone rang butterflies danced in her stomach.

"What's up Sandra?"

"So, we reached out to Joshua and he agreed to go on a blind date with you."

She smiled.

"The thing is, it's this Saturday."

"Really Sandra. Saturday?"

"I know. I didn't expect him to agree so soon and why does it sound like you're smiling from ear to ear?"

She rolled her eyes. "Whatever, Sandra. That'll work. I'm getting ready to go over to Ms. Lula's house. I haven't seen her in a while."

"Alright. Tell her I said hi. Oh, and I'll see you this weekend. We're eating at GinLou's Cuisine downtown... And Janelle please don't be late."

She chuckled.

"I won't."

On the way to Ms. Lula's house, Janelle let down the windows and opened the sunroof to enjoy the fresh air. Minutes later, she arrived and rang the doorbell.

Ms. Lula opened the door and frowned.

"Why you ranging my doorbell? And where's your key?"

"I'm sorry. I forgot it."

She smiled and hugged her.

"I just wanted to stop by and sit with you for a little while."

She stared at her.

"Janelle, you pregnant? Because you glowing honey."

"Um, no ma'am."

She walked into the living room and smiled sarcastically.

"What can impregnate me? Air?"

Ms. Lula sat down on the sofa.

"Lil girl you want something. I can just feel it all over for me."

"Not really, but since you asked, let me get your thoughts on something."

She looked over at Janelle with her chin resting on her left hand.

"Don't let this take up my whole day."

She smiled.

"My boyfriend will be over shortly."

Janelle shook her head. "Eww. That's too much information Ms. Lula."

She chuckled.

"Baby, I'm lying."

She shook her head.

"Ms. Lula, I was just thinking about you and the long talks we've had about me being lonely and hearing Sandra's testimony about waiting... She quickly changed the subject.

"Oh! Speaking of Sandra, her and Brian invited me on a double date and I—"

"Did you just say a, double date? Uh-huh. So how does he look?"

She smiled.

"Sandra said he was six feet tall with some kind of texturizer in his hair. I mean, I've never seen him before, but Sandra wouldn't try hook me up with someone outside of my taste. Well, at least I hope she wouldn't. She knows what I like."

"Lord have mercy on this poor child right here."

She laughed.

"What if he ugly?"

Janelle tilted her head and smiled.

"Ms. Lula, God doesn't create ugly."

"You right, but a nasty attitude can rub all them good looks away."

Janelle's smile slowly faded.

"Really Ms. Lula... I'm already nervous. I don't want to be anxious but I know me. You know, I do believe in love at first sight."

Ms. Lula mumbled.

"Love at first sight. Yep, that's how you got the last piece of trash you had."

"You say something Ms. Lula?"

She shook her head.

"Janelle, if you continue to live your life afraid, you'll never take a chance at love again and it'll pass right by you into the arms of another woman. Fear is not from God, but He gives us wisdom and common sense."

She leaned over and lay her head on Ms. Lula's shoulder.

"You know what Ms. Lula. You're so right. I guess it's time for me to get over this fear of being hurt again."

She smiled.

"Yep, that's pretty accurate. Anytime you want me to meet him, you can bring him over and I'll fix him a nice dinner."

Chapter Five

A few days later, with only three hours left, Janelle reached into her closet for something to wear. She lifted her eyes towards the ceiling and prayed.

"Lord, please let this work out for me this time."

She grabbed a pair of jeans and a blue top, stood in the mirror, and frowned. "Nah, this is too casual."

She reached for her green and white maxi dress.

"I forgot all about this one."

She smiled.

"This is it."

Rushing for time, she got dressed and pinned up her hair. Fumbling through the closet, she reached for her shoes, then put on her pink accessories and rushed to the door, but realized she forgot something. She ran back to her room, grabbed her phone from the nightstand, and realized Sandra had texted her. She quickly replied.

Sorry. I just saw your message, but I'm on the way 😊.

After minutes on the freeway, she pulled up to the restaurant locking her eyes in on Joshua as he stood with Brian and Sandra across the street. She remembered Sandra's description of his hair.

"Uh uh uh. He looks better than alright. He is fine."

Dreading that clumsy would be her first impression, she sat in the car for a few seconds to pull herself together. She took a deep breath and slowly got out of the car being cautious not to fall.

Janelle, get it together girl. Don't look so desperate.

Joshua admired her as she walked towards them. They shared a smile.

"You must be Janelle, I recognized you by your tardiness."

He extended his hand.

"It's nice to finally meet you."

She smiled.

"It's nice to meet you as well. I guess Sandra warned you about my tardiness."

Brian laughed.

"Better that he knows the truth now, rather than later."

Janelle squinted her eyes.

"Shut up Brian."

Joshua smiled and held the door as Janelle walked into the restaurant.

Brian laughed.

"Look at you being a gentleman."

Sandra smiled. "You should try it."

After moments of waiting, the waitress seated them at a round table overlooking the courtyard.

"Welcome to GinLou's Cuisine. My name is Sammy and I'll be your waitress this evening. What would you like to drink?"

Sandra and Janelle ordered water while Joshua quickly scanned the menu.

"I think, I'll have your sweet passion iced tea with a lemon on the side."

As they waited for Brian to order his drink, Sandra bumped his leg. He looked up.

"Oh, I'm sorry. I'll have a glass of water please."

As the waitress walked away, Brian playfully smacked Sandra on the thigh and laughed.

"Girl stop playing. You know we on a budget. Besides, you already knew what I was gone drink anyway."

Sandra looked at her husband.

"Brian shut up."

They ordered their food and laughed as Sandra, Brian, and Joshua reminisced on their college days. After about twenty minutes, Janelle gave a sigh of relief as she saw the waitress walking in their direction. The waitress reached for the plates.

"I have a smothered shrimp casserole with steamed broccoli, and glazed carrots."

Joshua lifted his hand.

"That would be me."

The waitress placed his order on the table.

"Baked tilapia smothered in sweet peppers, sautéed beets, and rice."

Janelle raised her hand.

"That's me."

Reaching for the last two plates the waitress smiled. "I have two orders of grilled chicken with cream of mushroom, one with no cream of mushroom, asparagus, and macaroni and cheese."

Brian looked over at the waitress. "My order is without the cream of mushroom."

The waitress handed them napkins and smiled. "Enjoy your meals."

They all ate, laughed, and enjoyed each other. Janelle leaned over and smiled.

"Joshua, I'm pretty sure that you've heard this before, but you have really good hair. Would that so happen to be a texturizer?"

Sandra cleared her throat as Joshua looked over at her.

"Let me guess. Nobody but Sandra said that. Actually, my mother is Puerto Rican and my father is African American." He rubbed his hair. "That's where this good hair comes from... No need for a texturizer. She didn't tell you that I was from San Juan, Puerto Rico?"

She smiled.

"No... she didn't."

He gazed into her eyes.

"But enough about my hair, I'm pretty sure that you've been told this before. Eres hermosa."

Her brows met.

"What does that mean?"

He returned a smile. "That means you're gorgeous. Including your natural hair."

She blushed as the waitress walked back over to check on them. "Would you like to order dessert?"

She pondered on his comment. "Yes... can I get your caramel brownie delight please?"

Shortly after finishing dessert, Joshua leaned towards Janelle and stared into her eyes.

"I've really enjoyed this date." He looked at Sandra and Brian.

"I had the opportunity to see old friends and make a new one. I haven't had this much fun in a while."

She smiled as he softly kissed her hand. After the waitress handed Brian the bill, he opened it, laughed, and looked over at Joshua.

"Now let's see who picks up this tab. My wallet too small for this one."

Joshua reached for the bill.

"I got it. That's the least I can do since Sandra thought enough of me to introduce me to a new friend." He looked towards her.

"Ms. Janelle that is."

As they all walked to the front entrance, Janelle and Joshua exchanged numbers. Sandra looked at Joshua as he got ready to walk Janelle to her car. She tapped her on the shoulder with a smile.

"It must've been that kiss that got you smiling like this."

Chapter Six

J anelle lay in her bed staring at the ceiling. When her phone rang, but she wasn't compelled to answer. Her voicemail interceded.

"You have reached Janelle Richards. Please leave a message and I'll get back to you."

"Hi Janelle, this is Joshua. I couldn't stop thinking about you so, when you get a moment please call me."

An hour later, Janelle checked her messages, smiled, and returned his call.

"Hello."

"Hi Joshua. Sorry I missed your call. Are you busy?"

He smiled.

"Not too busy to talk to you."

"So, how have you been?"

He looked out of his living room window.

"I've been fine. Just thinking about you. So, let me get straight to the point."

Her brows met as he continued. "I believe in honesty. So, it's important that you know that I was in a previous relationship and she and I have a lot of history together... I was a little unsure if I wanted to take another chance at love. So, I decided to wait before I called. I didn't wanna to be that guy that would lead you on. And besides, I'm too old to play games."

She wondered if she should play Russian roulette with her heart again; especially after him speaking of his ex. Her brows met as thoughts of Ms. Lula's words of wisdom gathered in her mind.

Remember, love will pass right by you into the arms of another woman who is willing to take another chance at love.

She took a deep breath.

"So, how long has it been since you and your ex called it quits?"

He sat down on his sofa.

"Well, we actually stopped dating about eight months ago. She's a great person, but we just weren't meant for each other."

She stood by her bedroom window in deep thought. Joshua realized she was quiet.

"Janelle, are you still there?"

"I'm sorry Joshua, I'm still here."

She didn't want desperation to be the cause of another broken heart and the thought of Joshua and his ex having so much history frightened her. She took a deep breath.

"So, do you still communicate with her?"

His forehead wrinkled.

"Actually, we don't."

"So, Joshua are you sure that you're really over her?"

He responded with confidence. "Yes."

Caught off guard by her questions, he quickly changed the subject and slightly smiled.

"So, can you cook?"

A wide smile visited her face.

"Why of course, I'm something serious in the kitchen."

He reached for his remote. "Since you're so serious in the kitchen, when will you invite me over for lunch or dinner and a movie?"

A frown visited her face followed by a smile.

"First off, don't think that a kiss on my hand and compliments are going to make it that easy for me to invite you over." She walked back towards her bed. "By the way, I don't invite men over after meeting them once. It's way too much going on in this crazy world, you know?"

Flipping to the sports channel, he smiled.

"I understand that, but you see... I'm that guy, 'That likes to imagine the outcome before I make a decision.' I read that quote on IamLakisha.com... And besides, I really like you. It's just something about your personality that just clicks with me."

She smiled.

"How about I cook you dinner next week?"

He leaned back on his dark brown leather sofa. "Sounds great to me. Hey, I don't mean to rush off the phone, but someone's calling from the office."

She sat down on her bed.

"Okay. I'll talk to you later."

She leaned back on her pillow and smiled.

"Oh wow. His voice sounds even better over the phone. It can make a girl fall in love."

But, she realized that if you've been in love with someone, it's not that easy to get over them. What she didn't know was there was more to this previous relationship than he disclosed to her.

Chapter Seven

A week later, Janelle cleaned the apartment and got ready for Joshua to come over. Before she could put on her socks, the doorbell rang. On the way to the door, she hit her foot on the edge of the couch. She stopped, rubbed her foot, took a deep breath, and opened the door with a big smile.

"Hey Joshua, come in."

He playfully looked inside of the apartment and smiled. "It sounds like you're having fun in here. Is that jazz music?"

She chuckled.

"Yep."

He leaned over, kissed her on her cheek, smiled, and walked through the door.

"So, I don't smell any food cooking. Is that a sign that you really can't cook?"

She laughed.

"Whatever Joshua. The food is in the kitchen. I was waiting for you to get here... I figured we could cook together."

As they walked in the kitchen, she walked over to the sink and held up a red snapper.

"I hope you like seafood, because it's the only meat I eat."

"Interesting... I'm a pescatarian too."

As they prepared the food, Janelle looked over at him and pointed towards the kitchen counter next to the stove.

"Joshua, can you grab an onion, and the sweet peppers, and slice them thinly for me?"

His nose wrinkled.

"Do you not realize the damage onions can do? Let me guess, when my eyes start watering, you're gonna take a pic and upload it to social media and lie about making me cry, right."

"Whatever... I don't post all of my business on social media."

She smiled.

"There's something called a private life you know."

He reached for the onions. "Sure, anything for you."

After dinner was ready, he looked over at her and back to the plate.

"Uh, stuffed red snapper, glazed carrots, and sautéed asparagus. I wonder if it tastes as good as it looks."

After dinner, they walked into the living room and sat on the sofa. Joshua sat close enough to Janelle that their knees touched.

"Man Janelle, dinner was great."

She leaned forward towards the coffee table.

"Thank you. I rented a movie. You wanna watch it?"

"Sure. What kind of movie?"

"One action and one comedy."

"Alright. Those are my types of movies."

She got up to put the movie in and tripped on the corner of the couch. He reached out his hand to catch her fall and laughed.

"You good?"

She laughed.

"Whatever."

He gestured for her to sit next to him. She sat down and pressed play. After the movies were over, he leaned in for a kiss, but she smiled, leaned back, and shook her head.

"I'm sorry, but this goes against my promise to God. I know it may sound cliché, but I promised myself and God that when He sent me the man of my dreams, this time I would make it special. For me, a kiss would be going too far."

He lowered his head and leaned back. "No, no. Janelle, it's nothing like that, I promise." He licked his lips and rubbed them together. "But if a kiss is tempting you, then I won't overstep my boundaries. I respect you for keeping your vows to God."

She was relieved as they both laughed, but she started to worry.

I wonder if he'll still call me since I didn't let him kiss me. She shrugged her shoulders. *Oh well.*

After he left, she walked into her room, fluffed her pillow, and sat on the side of the bed. Hearing her phone ring, she reached for it, looked at the number, and smiled.

"Hey, I thought I ran you off."

He laughed.

"It's not that easy to get rid of me. I had a great time. I really would love to see you tomorrow. Oh, and I should remind you that the meal you cooked tonight was on point."

She blushed.

"Thank you. So, what time do you get off of work?"

He rubbed his face.

"Um, I'll be leaving the law firm about three."

Her brows met.

"Law firm?"

He smiled. "Yeah, do I get brownie points for that?"

She shook her head.

"Whatever. What about five tomorrow evening? I'll only be in the office at the church until twelve."

He paused and looked at his clock.

"Five is good. Hey Janelle, it's getting late and I really need to get some sleep. I got a long day ahead of me in the morning, but I look forward to seeing you tomorrow."

"Okay. I understand."

"Good night"

"Good night Joshua."

Chapter Eight

J anelle's attention and heart grew closer towards Joshua. His hazel brown eyes put her in a trance every time he gently gazed into her eyes and his deep voice serenated her ears as it arrested her attention. She finally allowed herself to fall in love once more.

After seven beautiful months, Janelle and Joshua were inseparable. While looking through clothes in her favorite store, her phone rang.

"Hey Josh."

He tapped his fingers on his desk. "Are you busy tonight?"

"No what's up?"

"Well, I spoke with Brian earlier about a double date and I wanted to see if you wanted to go. I was thinking about Olive Garden."

She smiled.

"Sure. You know they have the best salads ever."

He smirked.

"That's why I chose the spot this time."

"Hahaha. I bet. What time tonight?"

He looked over at his clock.

"About 6:30... Hey babe, let me call you back in a few. I need to finish up this paper work before I leave."

"Okay. I'll see you then. Love you."

"Love you too Janelle."

He texted Brian. *Hey man. We're all set for tonight. Can ya'll be there at 6:15?*

Brian replied. *Aight man. We'll be there. You got the bill, right?*

Joshua looked at the text and shook his head. *I got the bill last time. You so cheap, but yeah, I got it.*

Brian laughed and replied. *Lol. You know me. I'm on a budget. We'll see you then.*

He leaned back in his chair. *Whatever Brian. I'll see ya'll in a few.*

Hours later, Joshua realized he was pressed for time. He reached for his briefcase, walked towards the door, took a quick look in the mirror, and locked his office. As he walked towards his car, he shook his head, ran back into the office, and grabbed his phone.

Lord please don't let me get a ticket. I have less than thirty minutes to get to the restaurant.

His phone rang.

"Hello."

"Are you close man?"

He looked at the time.

"I'm running late. Give me like twenty minutes and I'll be there. Just stall for me. Please."

Brian laughed.

"I got you man. See you then."

At about 6:15, Janelle arrived at the restaurant. She looked around.

"I guess I'll go in; I don't see Joshua's car yet."

She smiled when she saw Sandra and Brian.

"Hey. I should've known ya'll would beat me here."

The hostess walked over to them.

"Good evening. How many?"

37

Sandra wiggled her fingers and smiled.

"We need a table for four please."

The waitress pointed.

"This way please."

Janelle looked back for Joshua, but he still hadn't made it. So, Brian did what he knew best, stalled for more time.

"So, Janelle, I see you got a new hairstyle."

She rolled her eyes.

"Shut up Brian. You've seen this style before."

He snapped his fingers.

"You know what, you're right. I was trying to give you a compliment though."

"Whatever Brian."

She looked over at Sandra.

"Don't you look cute today?"

"Thank you love." She shook her head. "Don't pay Brian any attention.".

Joshua smiled as he stood in his black dress pants and tan button-down shirt with a fresh hair cut admiring Janelle from afar. He took a deep breath, exhaled, and walked towards their table with a box in one hand and a dozen roses behind his back. Sandra and Brian smiled as he gently tapped her on the shoulder.

The waitress smiled.

"Your fourth party has arrived."

She slowly turned around as he got down on one knee and cleared his throat.

"Janelle... I never thought I would be saying this so soon, but you really mean the world to me." He took a deep breath. "Will you do me the honor in saying yes to this ring?"

Tears escaped from her eyes as she placed her hand over her mouth.

"Oh, my God... Yes."

Everyone in the restaurant smiled and applauded the newly engaged couple. Brian looked up.

"Aight enough of all that mushy stuff. It's time to order our food and celebrate."

Joshua frowned as he looked over at Brian.

"Seriously man you gotta stop being a hater."

Brian laughed.

"Whatever."

The waitress walked over, pointed to another table, and smiled.

"The lovely couple sent a bottle of Champaign over with their congratulations."

Janelle leaned towards Joshua.

"I love you so much."

She looked over at Sandra and pointed to her ring.

"Girl. I'm getting married."

Chapter Nine

A few months later, Janelle walked into the suite admiring the perspective mirrors on the wall and the angelic statues in a room created for a queen. Ms. Lula walked into the room and looked at the ladies.

"Look, don't ya'll mess up nothing in this room." She pointed to the furniture and statues. "Because we can't pay for none of this."

Everyone admired Ms. Lula and although she was a jokester, her wisdom demanded the attention of everyone's ears. Her presence alone would light up a room. Janelle's friend Amy stood next to a chair and gestured for Janelle to sit down.

Sandra looked over at her.

"We decided to get you something. It symbolizes our friendship, bond, and love for you."

She opened the gift and gazed down at the pearl cuff bracelet.

"Thank you so much ladies... I love it. It matches my mother's pearl earrings."

She reached for a kleenex to catch the tears as they escaped from her eyes.

Sandra looked at her, smiled, and shook her head. "You should be happy that I'm a makeupologist. Get over here so I can fix your face. You have thirty minutes left until you become Mrs. Richards."

Minutes later, Janelle looked at the clock then, over at the ladies, and smiled.

"I truly love ya'll, but I'll see you at the altar."

Sandra cleared her throat.

"Janelle." She paused and playfully stared at her.

"Who gone help you get into your dress?"

Ms. Lula snapped her fingers and pointed.

"Lil girl, don't act like you don't see me standing right here." She gently pushed her towards the door. "Let me help you out."

"Alright, alright Ms. Lula. I'm leaving."

She looked at Janelle and smiled.

"I'll see you at the altar."

Janelle walked over to the closet and pulled out her dress.

"Ms. Lula, when I bought this dress, I was happy, but yet torn because my mom would never get to see me in it. I really wish she were here."

A tear slowly crept down Ms. Lula's face.

"Baby, your mother would be so proud of you."

She wiped the corner of her eye with a kleenex.

"Now, I'm too pretty to be messing up my makeup, especially since I just put Sandra out. So, go ahead and put that gorgeous dress on so I can zip you up."

"Ms. Lula, I pray that I'm doing the right thing."

Her brows met.

"Baby, what's that supposed to mean? Is Joshua beating you?"

She gave a gentle smile.

"No ma'am. Joshua is a gentle giant."

"Is he cheating on you?"

"No ma'am."

She shook her head.

"Well, stop wasting my time and get in that dress."

"Ms. Lula, I don't remember much, but you remind me so much of her."

Her eyes smiled at the thought that she was about to be a wife. She slowly stepped into her dress and motioned for Ms. Lula to zip her up. Ms. Lula smiled as she walked towards the mirror and took a deep breath. Janelle turned around in her Embellished French lace fitted dress, with a modern trumpet and silhouette enclosed by an embodiment of tulle with draped strands of pearls. Although she was mesmerized by the beauty of her dress, the secret buried in her heart interrupted her joy for a moment.

Ms. Lula smiled. "Baby they're waiting on you. Don't you hear the music playing? You better go down the aisle and marry that man before I marry him for you."

She softly exhaled and reached for her bouquet. Ms. Lula popped her hand.

"Let me get that for you baby. I don't want you making any sudden movements in that beautiful dress."

She tittered at her sincere gestures.

"Ms. Lula, I love you."

She smiled.

"I love you more baby."

They walked out of the room hand and hand until they reached the doorway... She took a deep breath and exhaled deeply. She looked over at Ms. Lula and squared her shoulders back.

"Well this is it. I'm about to become Mrs. Richards."

Ms. Lula gently rubbed her hand.

"Baby, is there something you need to tell me?"

She wanted to release her secret, but instead she smiled and swallowed it along with her fears.

"No ma'am. I'm just a little nervous."

"Baby, put that nervousness to the side and go down the aisle and marry that man... unless—"

"I'm okay Ms. Lula. I promise."

As the doors opened, she scanned the room admiring the white silk balls that hung from the ceiling and the white ruched spandex covers that dressed the chairs draped with red bows. Her eyes met his gaze as he and the groom's waited at the altar. He stood confidently in his white Bartlett tuxedo with a smile that made the thought of her secret disappear once more.

She looked over at her favorite cousin Mark as he began to sing. When she reached the altar, tears slowly crept down her face. Joshua cleared his throat and wiped the corner of his eyes as Pastor Jordan turned towards their families and friends.

"Today, we will not commence as a traditional wedding ceremony. The couple has prepared their vows from the depths of their hearts as their declaration of love for one another... to share before family, friends, and in the presence of the Lord." He looked over at Janelle. "You may begin."

She stared into Joshua's eyes.

"I remember how I would cry myself to sleep praying and asking God to send me the man of my dreams... And now I'm about to spend the rest of my life with you. I don't regret the bucket of tears I've cried and the countless hours I've prayed for this day to come. Joshua, my friend, my lover, and my answered prayer... I vow to work through the hard times and pray through all indifferences. I vow to not lose faith in the love you have for me, but if fear creeps in, promise to hold. And as you hold my hand, I trust you to lead me as God leads you. I vow to always love you."

He stared into her eyes as they shared a smile.

"Janelle... I'm about to marry the woman of my dreams. A woman who accepts me for me. A woman with the strength to hold on. A woman that will pray with me through the storms. And finally, a wife to start a family with. Trials will come, but they'll only make us stronger. We're the ship and Jesus is our sail and as long as we're united in Christ, nothing will take us under. Remember, what God put together, no man or woman can tear it apart."

Pastor Jordan smiled, reached for the rings, held them up, and blessed them. "With these rings, a bond will be formed. It represents a union between two individuals who are now one in Christ. Joshua and Janelle, do you accept these vows that will bind you two together from this day forward?"

They slid the rings on one another's ring finger.

"We do."

Joshua caught the tear as it escaped Janelle's eyes and turned his attention back to the pastor. With a wide smile, Pastor Jordan glanced over at Joshua.

"You may now kiss your wife."

He slowly reached his arm around Janelle's waist and gently pulled her close to him. At the touch of their lips, two souls joined as one. Joshua's mother smiled as she caught the tear that escaped from her eyes. Pastor Jordan looked out at the families.

"I now present to you, Mr. and Mrs. Richards."

Chapter Ten

Three years later, Janelle sat on the sofa-wondering why her husband insisted on withholding his love and attention from her. He was a pro at pretending to love her in public while neglecting to love her behind closed doors. Walking in from work, he closed the door, and walked pass her without speaking. She looked over at him and chuckled.

"You are yet the phoniest person I know."

"Janelle, you're no angel."

She walked over to him and looked at him with gentle eyes.

"I never said I was."

He walked towards the kitchen.

"You're constantly pretending as though you have no part in the issues we have in this marriage. I'm tired of you on the phone with your friends making me look like I'm the bad guy. You always talk about what I do wrong, but what about the things I do right?"

She glanced around the room.

"I'm still looking for the things you do right."

He walked towards the door.

"So, let me guess, you do everything right in this marriage... Right." He shook his head. "I'm out. I don't have time for this."

She calmly walked behind him.

"Wait. Are you serious? No, I don't do everything right. I mess up a lot. It's like every time I try to tell you the truth, you leave or start an argument. Why can't you handle the truth? Do what you do best and walk away. The funny thing is, you look like a man, walk like a man, talk like a man, but yet you act like a little boy. I thought the Bible said when you become a man, you're to put away childish things. Well, you're holding onto those childish ways a little too tight Joshua. Can you please grow up?"

With his fist clenched tightly, he punched the wall.

"I'm so tired of you calling me a little boy."

"Start acting like a man then. We're not kids Joshua."

He laughed.

"Janelle, it's not my fault that we have issues, but why would I want to display that to the world?"

She rolled her eyes.

"I've asked you to go to counseling but you refuse to go. I'm tired of pretending for people. I'm tired of being married and lonely. If I wanted to be lonely, then I would've stayed single. Don't you get it Joshua?"

Reaching for his phone, he looked up at her with a smirk on his face.

"Little Ms. Perfect, can you tell me one thing? Is that the Godly way of doing things?"

She shook her head and chuckled.

"You really want to bring up the Bible? Every single time I tell you the truth about yourself, you attempt to assassinate my character, but it's okay. I'll let you have that one."

She wiped the tears from her eyes.

"Joshua, we need counseling and that's that. Oh, and to answer your question, calling you stupid may have been the wrong thing. Forgive me... But telling you the truth surely lines up with the Word of God to me."

He reached for the door.

"Whatever."

She walked behind him.

"And I quote, 'thou shall not lie.'"

He slammed the front door and walked to his car, put on his seatbelt, and reached for his phone.

"Man, where did I go wrong?"

After moments of thinking, he called his ex hoping it would help him escape from the reality that he was in a broken marriage.

Chapter Eleven

A few days later, Janelle lay across the bed contemplating ways to tell Joshua that she would never be able to give him a family. She feared he'd abandon her if he knew she couldn't conceive a child and with the constant arguing, she figured it wasn't the right time to tell him. In the middle of intense emotions, she picked up the phone and called Sandra. Her stomach knotted as the phone rang.

"Hello."

"Sandra... I really need to talk to you."

"What's wrong? Did something happen?"

"Do you remember when you went to the doctors with me and you decided to wait in the waiting area?"

"Yeah. I briefly remember. Why?... Janelle, please tell me you told Joshua about that already?"

She exhaled.

"I didn't because it wasn't on my mind until a week before the wedding and lately he's been pressuring me about having a family."

"So, Janelle what are you going to do about it?... "Janelle."

She lowered the phone to her chest.

"Hold on Sandra. I think I heard Joshua come in. He's supposed to be at work." She rushed over to the window. "Never mind. I thought I heard the door open and close."

Joshua quietly walked down the hall to his bedroom with a dozen of roses in his hand to make up for the days before. His brows met when he heard his name. So, he walked closer and listened as she continued.

"Sandra, how do you tell your husband that you're unable to have children?"

He quickly pushed the door open.

"Janelle, please tell me I didn't hear what I thought I heard?"

She dropped the phone and turned towards him.

"Please, let me explain... I wanted to tell you, but I was trying to wait for the perfect time.... Joshua, please let me explain."

He threw the roses on the floor.

"There's nothing to explain. I'm your husband. I should've known first, instead of you telling someone else."

She walked towards him.

"I was going to tell you but I —"

He turned away.

"I can't believe you sold me a false dream. No wonder you were always so hesitant about having a family."

She gently grabbed his arm.

"What does that mean? Joshua, I was going to tell you. I only called Sandra because I didn't know what to do."

He pulled away.

"For what. I'm your husband, not Sandra. Is that registering in that manipulative little mind of yours? Janelle that was plain out selfish of you. I wanted a family and you knew that." He walked towards the bedroom door. "I tell you what. I'm gonna to let you think about that."

He walked out of the room and slammed the door. She rushed out of the room behind him crying.

"Joshua, please wait."

He turned and stared at her with pain in his eyes.

"I have nothing to say to you."

Tears slowly crept down her face.

"Joshua, just stop and listen. You're overreacting."

His nose flared as he mocked her.

"Overacting. Little Ms. Perfect has secrets. I never would've thought you were capable of having secrets being a church girl and all."

She walked towards him.

"I'm sorry. I found out about five years ago and I locked it in the back of my mind and threw away the key because I didn't want that to be my reality." She softly exhaled. "A week before the wedding, I had intentions of telling you, but all of the last minute planning threw me off."

He scoffed.

"Janelle, I can't talk about this. I don't even want to look at you right now."

He looked at her with disappointment in his eyes and walked away, but she reached out to him once more.

"Joshua, please wait."

He snatched away and slammed the front door. She stood in disbelief that her secret had finally been exposed, but she never wanted it exposed like this.

Chapter Twelve

Held captive by anger, he got in his car and sped out of the back yard. He reached into his pocket for his phone as he pulled up to the stop light. Before getting on to the main road, he called his ex. She looked down at her phone and smiled as she answered the call.

"Hey Josh."

He glanced to the left before turning.

"Are you busy?"

"Not really, what's up?"

He took a deep breath.

"I can't believe she lied to me."

She frowned.

"Who? And what are you talking about?"

He deeply exhaled.

"I just found out my wife can't have children."

"Whattt, you have got to be kidding me."

His forehead wrinkled. "Can you meet me somewhere?"

Although, his ex sympathized with him, to her, she saw an opportunity to get back with her ex.

"Sure! Where do you want to meet?"

Sitting at the light, his phone slipped out of his hand and dropped onto the floorboard. He reached down for his phone, but his foot slipped off the brakes. The smell of burning rubber filled the air. He looked up as cars frantically honked their horns.

Swerving into oncoming traffic, he hit a car head on. His body sprung forward and back as the airbag knocked him unconscious. At the sound of the collision, his ex yelled.

"Joshua, Joshua, Joshua."

But there was no response. A witness from another car stopped her vehicle and ran over to him. In panic, she reached for her phone and dialed 911.

"Sir are you okay? Sir." There was no response.

"911 where is your emergency?"

She looked up at the street sign.

"There's been an accident on 54th street."

The dispatcher calmly asked.

"Is everyone okay?"

The lady panicked.

"No. The driver is unconscious and he's bleeding."

"Were you involved in the accident?"

She responded anxiously.

"No. I wasn't. Are you sending help, this man is bleeding?"

"Is he breathing?"

Frustration leaked through her voice.

"Yes."

The despatcher called for an ambulance.

"We have an accident on 54th street with injuries. A witness is with the injured driver. He's bleeding and unconscious."

Frustration gripped the witness.

"Are you sending someone?"

"Ma'am, remain calm. The ambulance is on the way."

She kneeled next to Joshua and closely monitored him until the ambulance arrived. She heard a distant voice.

"Hello, hello."

She grabbed the phone.

"Hello."

"Hello." His ex-responded in panic. "Who is this?"

She looked over and wiped the blood from Joshua's face.

"Ma'am, I'm sorry. There's been an accident." She looked across the street. "The ambulance is on the way."

His ex panicked. "Oh, my God."

Within minutes, the ambulance arrived, checked Joshua's vital signs, and transported him to the nearest hospital.

Fifteen minutes later, Janelle ran over to the phone, thinking it was Joshua.

"Hello."

"May I speak to Mrs. Richards?"

Her brows met.

"This is she."

"This is nurse Henderson at Clara B Medical Center. Your husband has been in a car accident. He's stable now, but he does have a minor concussion, bruises, and a few stitches."

Her voice quivered.

"Oh my God. I'm on my way."

The nurse confidently reassured her.

"Mrs. Richards, don't worry he's okay. Find someone to drive you here because you don't need to drive from the way you're sounding."

She quickly called Sandra.

"Hello."

"Sandra, I need you to take me to the hospital right away. Joshua was in a car accident."

Sandra sat up on the sofa.

"What?"

Slowly pacing the floor, tears rolled down her face.

"Sandra, please hurry. I feel like it's all my fault."

"I'm on my way right now."

She grabbed her keys and got in the car.

"Lord please don't let me get a ticket."

She pulled up and blew the horn. Janelle rushed out of the house and got in the car. Sandra backed out of the driveway.

"Janelle, what happened?"

She fumbled her words. "I knew that I heard the door open. I knew it."

Sandra frowned. "What are you talking about?"

She looked towards her. "Joshua walked in and overheard me talking to you about not being able to have children. That's why the phone hung up."

Sandra's eyes grew wide "Oh my God. I was wondering what happened."

"He went off. I've never seen him like that before. Not even when we argue. He refused to talk to me."

Tears swelled in her eyes as they passed the accident site.

Sandra glanced over at her.

"Janelle, it's okay. He's gonna be fine. Where's your faith?"

She shook her head. "This never would've happened if I would've just told him the truth. I love him so much and I don't blame him if he leaves me. I never should've entered this marriage with secrets."

Sandra reached over and comforted her.

"Don't say that. Joshua loves you. You're beating yourself up for nothing. Snap out of it. It's not like he's about to serve you divorce papers as soon as he gets out of the hospital."

Arriving at the hospital, Janelle rushed inside.

"Can you please point me to Joshua Richards's room?"

The nurse searched the database.

"May I have your name please?"

She stared at her intensely.

"My name is Janelle Richards. My husband Joshua Richards was transported to this hospital."

The nurse pointed.

"Oh, yes baby, I'm sorry. He's in room 3A. It's right around the corner."

Sandra looked at the nurse and smiled.

"Thank you."

The sight of her husband caused her stomach to stir as she walked into the room to see him laying in the bed with stitches over his left eye and a bruised face. With intensions to lighten up the moment, Sandra walked in, and looked over at Joshua, and smiled.

"Okay, I knew they should've never given you your license. From day one when you drove us to our first college party, I knew it was a mistake."

He smiled.

"Whatever Sandra, you're always joking about something."

"Ha, I knew I could make you smile."

She looked over at Janelle.

"I'll be in the waiting area if you need me."

"Okay."

Silence held her captive as she turned towards her husband. He looked over at her and brushed his nose with his finger.

"Baby, I'm sorry, I know you. You're probably blaming yourself for this, but it's not your fault. I'm a little beat up, but I'm okay. I should've stayed home and dealt with the issue, rather than running from it."

A tear escaped from her eyes.

"Joshua I'm sorry. Knowing your still alive is all that matters to me right now." Her eyes brightened as she walked over to his bedside.

He reached for her hand. "Their supposed to release me in the morning. They just want to make sure that all of my x-rays come back normal."

Before she could respond, the nurse walked in and looked at Joshua.

"I'll let the nurse see about you. I'm about to walk down to the snack room to grab a juice and some chips to take something. My head is killing me."

"Okay... Remember, I'm okay and it's not your fault."

As she walked out of the emergency room area, the nurse stopped her.

"Excuse me Mrs. Richards. Here's your husband's cell phone. I'm pretty sure he wouldn't mind me giving it to you. A witness gave it to the ambulance crew."

"Thank you."

She walked to the waiting area.

"Sandra, can you walk with me to the snack room?"

She got up from the chair.

"Really. Why wouldn't I?"

As they walked towards the snack room, Janelle bumped into a slender young lady of medium height.

"I'm so sorry. I need to pay attention to where I'm going."

The young lady smiled.

"It's okay. I should've been paying attention to where I was going myself."

She looked back down at her phone and walked away. Sandra looked back at the young lady and smiled.

"Girl, I like how she accented that dark brown hair with those blonde streaks. Ya'll natural hair sistas make me sick."

Entering the snack room, Janelle turned to Sandra as she put the money in the machine.

"Girl, my nerves are getting the best of me right now and this headache is killing me."

Sandra deeply exhaled. "I know you heard your husband tell you that he was okay... because I did. Girl, you have got to stop stressing so much. The good news is that your husband is alive."

She sat down and rubbed her head.

"Sandra, I try so hard to give my problems to God, but sometimes it's hard. I'm just being real."

"Look Janelle, as your friend, I want you to understand that life is too short to be stressing. You better cast your cares on God and let him take care of you."

"You're right. So are we—"

As they headed back to the room, they phone rang and interrupted them. She reached for her phone, but her purse continued to vibrate as her husband's phone rang. She reached in her purse for his phone.

"Hello."

When the phone hung up, she frowned, stared at the phone, and placed it back down in her purse.

"Why would they hang up?" She shrugged her shoulders. "Oh well."

After seeing the young lady Janelle bumped into on the way to the snack room standing at Joshua's bedside, they paused, then entered the room. Joshua's eyes grew wide as they walked in and stood behind her.

Janelle smiled.

"Hi. Have we met before?"

The young lady turned around and extended her hand.

"Hi. My name is Patrice. We've never met but... I'm Joshua's ex-girlfriend."

As his ex introduced herself, his eyes grew wide. He couldn't seem to speak as wrinkles formed between his wife's eyes.

She thought to herself. *So, this is his ex-girlfriend.*

Unsure of what to do, he looked at his wife from the corner of his eyes being sure not to make eye contact with her. He listened attentively as his ex continued. The lies rolled off of her tongue like a pro.

"My grandmother is on the 2nd floor and my brother came up to get me when he saw them bring Joshua in on the stretcher."

Sandra respectively intervened.

"Hi, my name is Sandra. Joshua's college friend." She touched Janelle on the shoulder. "And this is Joshua's wife Janelle; my best friend."

Joshua attempted to lean up as his ex glanced at Sandra and forced a smile.

"She just came in a few seconds before you baby."

Janelle smiled.

"It's nice to meet you."

His ex nodded with a partial smile.

"It's nice to meet you as well."

Janelle turned and walked towards the door.

"I'll give you guys a minute."

She walked out the room and reached for Joshua's phone from her purse. Sure, that it was his ex who called and hung up, she pressed redial. Hearing the phone rang, she glanced over at Sandra and back to the room.

Patrice glanced at the incoming call, looked over at Joshua, closed her eyes, and slowly shook her head. Sandra and Janelle looked each other with wide eyes. Janelle took a deep breath, walked back into the room, and stood at Joshua's bedside.

"You've got to be kidding me."

Patrice stood paralyzed in fear.

Janelle smiled.

"Patrice, I want to thank you for checking on my husband. Could you allow us to have a moment together please?" She extended her hand. "Again, it was nice meeting you."

Sandra walked Patrice to the elevator.

"I hate that you had to be caught in the middle of this."

Patrice lowered her head. "I really meant no harm. It's nothing like that with Joshua and I."

Sandra smiled.

"I understand."

She turned and walked into the waiting area as Patrice stepped into the elevator. Back in the room, Janelle looked over at Joshua.

"Apparently you were on the phone with your ex during the time of the accident. What's going on here?"

Before she could utter another word, the nurse stepped inside the room and walked towards Joshua with a needle in her right hand.

She smiled.

"Good afternoon. Mr. Richards, how are you feeling right now?"

He looked over at the nurse.

"I'm feeling okay."

"Well good. There were no abnormalities with your x-rays. So, you're set for discharged sometime tomorrow after the doctor sees you. We just want to watch you through the night to make sure you're okay due to the concussion."

She pressed the button on the Dinamap to check his blood pressure. "I'm going to give you this medication through your IV so you can get some rest..." She held up the needle. "Okay."

Janelle leaned up.

"Excuse me. Am I able to get a pillow for tonight?"

She walked towards the door.

"Yes baby. I'll bring you one back in a minute. Does your friend need one?"

She smiled.

"No ma'am. Actually, she's about to leave."

Sandra walked back into the room and over to the bed.

"Joshua be sure to get some rest. I'll let Brian know you're in the hospital and that you're just fine."

She looked over at Janelle.

"And you need to get some sleep. I'll see you in the morning."

Janelle got up from the chair.

"I'll walk you to the elevator."

Sandra looked over at her.

"I'm so sorry that this happened to you, but don't let it get the best of you."

She forced a smile.

"I'm good."

Sandra looked at Janelle.

"Look, be positive and wait until your home to deal with this."

She stepped on the elevator. "I'll see you in the morning."

She mumbled as she walked back to the room.

"Lord help me because I don't know what to do. The words that want to pour out of my mouth, don't exactly line up with Your Word."

She walked in and stared at Joshua as he slept. She looked at the door as the nurse walked back in.

"Hey baby, here's your pillow." She pointed at the lever on the side of the seat. "The chair you're in reclines."

She smiled.

"Thank you so much."

Before the nurse walked out, she looked back at Janelle.

"You're welcome. Get you some rest while your husband is sleeping."

She opened her eyes periodically as the nurses came in throughout the night to check Joshua's vitals. Tossing and turning, she thought about Patrice and wondered if her husband had more secrets. The next morning, she smiled as the nurse walked in.

"Good morning. Am I able to get a tooth brush, tooth paste, and a towel please?"

She smiled.

"Sure. Give me a minute after I check his vitals."

After checking his vitals, the nurse walked out of the room. About five minutes later, she walked back in and handed Janelle the toothbrush, tooth paste, and towel. Shortly thereafter, the doctor came in.

"Good morning Mr. Richards. How are you feeling?"

He smiled.

"I'm better."

He checked his vitals.

"We're happy everything checked out fine, so, you'll be discharged today." He shook his hand, but before he walked away, he looked at him. "Make sure you're connected to your blue tooth before using your phone next time. This could've ended another way. Thank God the woman in the other vehicle walked away and only suffered the loss of her car."

The doctor looked over at his wife.

"And you would've left this beautiful woman behind."

Joshua nodded.

"Yes sir. You're right"

Twenty minutes later the nurse returned.

"Now, Mr. Richards you need to relax for the rest of the day and get some rest. Here is a prescription for your pain."

Janelle forced smile as the nurse handed him the discharge papers and waited for his signature. She thought to herself.

He had the nerves to throw a fit about me not being able to have children, and yet he's still secretly talking to his ex.

The nurse smiled.

"Are you ready to go home?"

His forehead wrinkled.

"I may as well be ready."

Janelle looked at Joshua with a smile.

"Honey, are you ready?"

He closed his eyes and leaned his head back on the pillow.

With a bright smile, she looked at him. "Let me help you, honey."

He thought to himself. *I know she's mad. I mean, she just caught me talking to my ex. Why is she smiling?*

Unsure of her state of mind, he shook his head.

Man, I just went off on her for hiding her secret about not being able to have children and now I'm caught red handed in my own secret. He looked around. How the hell I'm supposed to get out of this?

The nurse walked towards the door.

"I'll be back with the wheelchair."

Sandra walked into the room.

"You need any help Janelle?"

"No, I'm okay, but can you go down and get the car and wait for us in the pickup area?"

Sandra looked at her.

"Sure."

"The nurse will be back in a few minutes with the wheelchair."

She went to get the car while Janelle waited in Joshua's room for the nurse to return and take him down to the pickup area. Ten minutes later, the nurse came back in and smiled.

"Mr. and Mrs. Richards, what a lovely couple. Are you ready to leave?"

"Yes ma'am, we're ready."

Joshua shook his head as they got in the car and started on their way home. Janelle sat in the car praying silently.

God please help me because I feel like I'm going to lose my mind. He's had his own little secret all this time. I wonder does he even have the ability to be faithful. At least I wasn't talking to my ex.

Chapter Thirteen

M inutes later, Sandra slowly pulled up to the house. As Joshua got out of the car, she tried to lighten the mood once again.

"Okay Joshua, let me know when you're ready for some driving lessons."

He laughed. "Whatever."

He caught on to what Sandra was doing and joined in on her humorous efforts. He slightly touched her as if to say thank you.

Sandra giggled.

"Feels like college days all over again. Only now you're not drunk, you just got beat up by your car this time."

She turned and walked over to Janelle.

"Wait until you have completely calmed down before you talk to him. Oh, and if you need me, just call."

Janelle smiled and walked Sandra to her car.

"Thank you."

After Sandra left, Janelle walked back into the house and to the bedroom to check on Joshua.

"Do you need anything?"

"Just some water to take my pills, please."

He held up the bottle of pills. She stared at him for a second, screaming within and forced a smile. Minutes later, she returned and handed him the glass of water.

"Honey, sit up so that you can take your pill."

"Look Janelle, you don't have to be so nice... I know you're angry with me. Can we at least talk about it?"

"Joshua... Love covers."

She smiled.

"Baby, you really need to rest."

He placed the pill on his tongue and took a few drinks of water.

"Do I need to sleep with one eye open?"

She laughed softly.

"If it were me, I would." She looked back at him with a smirk on her face. "Honey get some rest."

He watched as she leisurely walked out of the room. Before closing the door, she glanced back at him and smiled.

He mumbled.

"My wife has lost her mind."

Before long, the medication kicked in and he was sound asleep. Still hurt and a little confused, she sat down at the computer and pulled up his phone bill studying it like she studied the Bible. Highlighters in one hand and a permanent marker in the other. As she printed out the last four months of the bill, she scratched out every number she recognized with a permanent marker and highlighted the numbers that were called most frequently. After an hour, a number finally stood out. She pushed away from the desk.

"Are you serious?"

Tears escaped from her eyes as she tried to pull herself together. She grabbed her phone and called Sandra.

"Please answer the phone...please pick up."

After a minute or two, she hung up the phone.

"Lord, I'm so confused right now. I don't understand how this happened."

She stood up. "He had the nerves to tell me he doesn't have time to play games, and he's been talking to his ex for the last four months."

The longer she looked at the bill the angrier she got, but she remembered Ms. Lula's words.

The enemy will consume your mind with negative thoughts, but you have to stay focused on The Word of God. The enemy hates unity, but loves to cause division. He loves divorce because he knows being on one accord, there is power.

She lay down on the sofa to get some rest, but she tossed and turned pondering over Joshua and his ex. An hour later, she drifted off into a deep sleep and began to dream.

Joshua slowly kissed his ex on the neck. Inch by inch slowly easing up to her lips. He gently ran his fingers through her hair.

Janelle woke up in a sweat.

"Joshua..."

She got, eased into the bedroom, and sat in the chair next to the bed and stared at him as he slept. The dream of his infidelity rehearsed over and over in her mind. He woke up startled and looked over at Janelle.

"What the hell! Girl what's wrong with you? What... You thinking about killing me or something?"

She sat speechless as tears ran down her face.

"No. I don't have time for that. It takes too much energy."

She got up and walked towards the door. Pridefully, he looked at her.

"Janelle, why don't you just curse me out or something and get it over with. Stop playing these mind games with me. I know you're angry. Let's just deal with it."

She turned around and took a step towards him.

"Joshua, yes I'm angry, but that doesn't mean that I have to react to my emotions like you did earlier... I know I kept a secret from you, but my secret wasn't about infidelity. I wouldn't dare cheat on you. Yes, I should've told you that I couldn't have children, but that doesn't justify whatever you're doing with your so-called ex."

She shook her head.

"You're playing a dangerous game by walking back through the doors of your ex's heart. Women take that as love and when your actions don't line up with your words, revenge begins to flow through their veins. Then she'll begin exposing all you've said and done because you tampered with her heart."

"Janelle, I'm not sleeping with her. You're acting like I had an affair."

She reached for his glass.

"You may as well have had one from the way she was looking at you. Do you know how it felt to see this woman standing at your bedside at the hospital? It's obvious that you two have had some type of reconnection... People don't just show up at hospitals for exes they're no longer interested in."

He rubbed the top of his nose.

"I can explain that."

She walked out of the room.

"No explanation needed."

"Really Janelle. You're just going to walk out."

She reached for the door knob and glanced over her shoulder.

"I don't have the time or energy for this right now. My mind needs to rest and so does yours. If you need me, I'll be in the living room. Good night."

Chapter Fourteen

A week later, Joshua sat in his office reading a few text messages between he and Patrice wondering if their friendship had gone too far.

He shook his head.

"Man, why am I thinking about her like this?"

Clueless that their soul ties were never broken blinded him to the fact that calling his ex during he and his wife's marital conflict fueled her love for him. He was enslaved in his mind from the memory of pressuring her to have an abortion years before and she used it to her advantage. He feared any sudden disconnection would cause her to tell his wife the truth although they weren't sexually involved. In his eyes, he thought of their relationship as a friendship without benefits, but his ex had other plans. He knew if his wife found out about his previous engagement to Patrice, it would devastate her. So, he tucked the secret away praying that she would never find out.

His phone vibrated from a text notification.

I hope I didn't start any trouble. I just wanted to make sure you were okay. I'm sure your wife understands. It's not like we're in love or sleeping with each other.... Right 😊*.*

He stared at the text and placed his phone on his desk.

Patrice saw an open door back into Joshua's heart, so, she pretended to care about his marriage getting better. Knowing of Joshua's wife's barrenness, his ex knew that giving him the family he desired would push her away. She was waiting for her moment to expose his secrets. Patrice got pleasure in knowing she could taunt Janelle just like Hannah taunted Peninnah. Reality is, she was dealt the perfect hand when Joshua entered into his marriage with so many secrets. And now since her identity was no longer hidden, she knew it was time to eliminate Janelle from the equation. In the meantime, Janelle sat on the couch, thinking to herself.

I'm fed up with all of the nonsense in this marriage.

She reached for her phone.

"Forget it, I'm calling a counselor."

After moments of surfing the net, she found a counselor in their area and dialed the number.

"ND Counseling 101. How may I help you?"

"Good morning. I would like to make an appointment. My husband and... I mean I'm seeking marriage counseling."

"Great. The first thing we need to do is take down some information. What's your name and your husband's name?"

She twisted her lips.

"Janelle and Joshua Richards."

She typed in their information.

"First of all, I would like to congratulate you Mrs. Richards for not giving up on your marriage. Our top priority is to restore marriages through biblical counseling and intense sessions to get to the root of the problem or problems."

In a soft-spoken voice, she responded.

"Great. I want my marriage to work. I just hope it's not too late."

"That's we love to hear here at our office... The one thing we ask all of our clients to do, is to remain prayerful and come to all sessions with an open mind."

"Yes ma'am. Of course."

The secretary took a quick scan through the calendar.

"We have an open date for next week. How does Monday at 2:30 that afternoon sound?"

She paused as if thinking.

"That works out great. Thank you."

"I have you penciled in. Thank you again Mrs. Richards. We'll see you and your husband on Monday."

She worried about how to get her husband to agree with going to the session, but she eventually fell asleep. An hour later she was startled from the sound of the door opening, got out of bed, and slowly walked into the living room. Nervousness caused butterflies to dance in her stomach.

"Hi Joshua."

He sat his briefcase down.

"Hey."

"Can we talk?"

"Really? Janelle, I just got home."

She looked at him with gentle eyes.

"Yes."

He sat down on the couch and leaned back.

"I'm all ears."

She looked over at him.

"I know that we've had our moments and things seem to be getting worse, but I really want this marriage to work. I'm tired of watching the devil wreak havoc in our home and marriage. Remember, we vowed to work through times of confusion and anger."

He leaned forward.

"Yeah, but we don't expect problems and secrets to catch us by surprise like this. I mean, what husband expects his wife to bring secrets into a marriage?"

She looked at him in disbelief.

"Are you serious? Let's not go there because you brought secrets to the altar as well. Don't blame me because of your lack of faith. God never said that He wouldn't bless us with a child, but that's neither here nor there. It still didn't give you an excuse to continue talking to your ex. He did it for Abraham & Sarah. Doctors don't have the last say so you know. Where's your faith?"

He leaned back.

"Seriously. Are you really talking about two old people in the Bible like that's supposed to make me get over the fact that you lied to me?"

She shook her head.

"That's just like you to use reverse psychology and subtract yourself from the equation as if you're innocent. Look, I contacted ND Counseling 101 and scheduled a session for us. I know we—"

"That's what I'm talking about. You should've talked to me about that first? Stop making decisions for me."

"Joshua, I'm sorry that I didn't consult you first, but I thought that my prayer was answered when I found them. I was only trying to help the situation, not hurt it or us. I just don't like sweeping things under the rug. I like dealing with issues head on."

He shook his head.

"Little Ms. Perfect should be your real name. That's funny, you didn't seem to deal with your infertility head on."

Her lips parted.

"Wow. Devil you are a liar. I accept my part in this marriage, but what about you?"

He chuckled.

"I don't know what you're talking about... Little Ms. Perfect. Oh, I mean Janelle."

She smiled and held up her hand.

"All I was saying is that we need help or this marriage isn't going to make it."

She shook her head.

"And I refuse to sit here and allow you to blame me for your mistakes. I came into this marriage with only one secret and I had all intentions of telling you, but I dismissed it from my mind when I got caught up in the moment of all of the wedding planning."

He frowned.

"Yea, whatever. Janelle, you had three years to tell me."

He held up three fingers.

"THREE YEARS—."

She interjected.

"Your secret relationship with your ex had nothing to do with me. You made that choice. You had a free will just as I did and we both messed up." specifications

As he walked out of the house, he looked back.

"Whatever."

She looked towards the ceiling and shook her head.

"I'm tired of this childish mess. I'm tired of being in a loveless marriage."

Joshua stood on the porch and gathered his thoughts, he reached down and patted his pockets, but realized that he left his keys in the house. He deeply exhaled as he went back inside. His frown faded when he saw his wife crying. The ice enclosing his heart slowly melted away. He walked over to her with a heavy heart.

"I'm sorry Janelle. I'm so confused right now. I've always wanted children and the thought of you not being able to give me that hurts like hell."

Tears formed in her eyes.

"Joshua, don't you think it hurts me just as much as it hurts you, but throwing a tantrum isn't going to make God work any faster. We need counseling and a baby can't fix the issues we have. Besides, I wouldn't want to bring a child into this home right now and be affected by our unresolved issues... That wouldn't be fair. This is not the type of environment a child should be raised in."

He leaned forward and wiped the tears from her eyes.

"Janelle, I don't feel comfortable talking to strangers about our problems. I need a moment to think about it. I'm gonna go drive around the block. I'll be back in a bit."

He softly kissed her on the forehead before he grabbed his keys. He looked back before walking out the door.

"You know what, you're right. No child needs to be raised around so much animosity. You can call and confirm the session."

He opened the door.

"I'll take off Monday."

Chapter Fifteen

T he next week, Joshua sat in the car as Janelle walked into the office. He nervously fumbled through his phone deleting old messages between he and Patrice. Uncomfortable with airing their dirty laundry to a counselor they didn't know, he reached in the glove compartment for his liquor bottle and took a drink to calm his nerves. As he opened the car door he threw a few mints in his mouth to cover the smell of alcohol. Seconds later, he entered the office and sat next to Janelle on the sofa across from the secretary's desk. A Caucasian woman a little over five nine with brown highlighted hair walked out of her office in a black pencil dress and silver heels. She walked over to them.

"Mr. and Mrs. Richards, you may come back now."

He looked over at his wife.

"Janelle, I thought the lady was black."

She cut her eyes over at him.

"Marriage counseling has no color. It has tools to help us with things we can't figure out ourselves."

Walking in the office she smiled as she admired the big window overlooking the beautiful dogwood trees. As they sat down, the counselor smiled and shook their hands.

"My name is Mrs. Chambers. I'm so happy that you both have decided to honor your vows by not giving up on your marriage. Here at ND Counseling 101 we strive for marriages to be Christ centered. We also strive to see couples leave with a new outlook on life and marriage by the end of each session."

She lifted a finger as she reached for her note pad and pen.

"Oh, and during our sessions, it is a must that we allow the individual speaking to complete their thoughts. So... how long have you been married?"

Janelle took a quick glance at Joshua. "Well, we've been married for three years now and it seems as though the minute we said I do everything changed."

Joshua looked over at her and let out a short laugh.

The counselor jotted down a few notes, glanced over at Joshua, and smiled.

"Okay Mr. Richards, what's your take on this?"

He adjusted himself on the sofa.

"Well, lately sometimes I feel that no matter what I do, it doesn't make her happy. She's always wanting to talk about things. Don't get me wrong, I love my wife. It's just that we're not always on the same page when we converse with one another about issues we have."

The counselor observed Janelle's body language and turned her attention back to Joshua.

"Mr. Richards, it's all about perception. For many women, communication is vital. Can you be a little more specific?"

He looked up as if thinking.

"Well, she's always saying that I don't spend enough time with her, but that's not true. We live together. I see her every day."

The counselor smiled and reached for her tea, took a sip, and glanced over at Janelle.

"Mrs. Richards, what do you mean when you say that your husband doesn't spend enough time with you?"

Janelle cleared her throat.

"In the beginning of our marriage, my husband gave me so much of his time. We went out together, we watched movies, and my favorite shows together. He made me feel important and after a while, it all stopped–."

"Are you serious right now?"

The counselor intervened.

"Mr. Richards, during counseling, it is vital to allow your wife to get her point across without any interruption as stated before we began."

He leaned back.

"I'm sorry. It's been a long day and having to hear this all over again is frustrating to me."

The counselor placed her tea on the table next to her.

"So, Mr. Richards, your wife has mentioned this to you before."

"Many times."

She tapped her fingers together.

"Sometimes, when a woman feels that she isn't being heard, she will repeat herself until she sees that you're truly listening to her. I think your wife is really crying out for your love and attention any way that she can. It's almost like a child that will do anything for attention. It's learned behavior."

She looked over at Janelle.

"By no means am I calling you a child; however, sometimes we have to give relatable examples to eliminate any possible confusion."

She turned her attention back to Joshua.

"I'm here as your mediator to catch what you both would overlook due to a mental, physical, and spiritual disconnect in your marriage. I want to reestablish a respectful relationship between you and your wife. Somewhere along the way, it seems as though the barrier of communication was broken and so was the respect."

The secretary knocked on the door.

"I'm sorry to interrupt, but you have a call on line three, it's your husband. He said it's important."

"Thank you, Lisa. Please excuse me for one second."

She walked over to her desk and answered the phone.

"I'm in a meeting at the moment, is everything okay? Okay, look behind the picture on my desk and there's an envelope with the information on it. I'll see you in an hour."

She smiled.

"I love you too."

She walked back over to her seat.

"I'm so sorry, but I had to take that call."

She sat down and crossed her legs.

"Our mission is to establish where your marriage was broken and fix it through biblical counseling. And this requires walking one another through doors of hurt, unforgiveness, and division so that you both can close them. Never to enter them again."

Janelle stared out the window. It seemed as though her mind had drifted away from their session. The counselor looked over at her.

"Mrs. Richards."

Joshua softly tapped her leg.

"Janelle."

She looked over at the counselor.

"I'm sorry, it just looks so peaceful outside."

"Is that what you want?" The counselor asked. "A moment of peace?"

She smiled.

"Yes. I mean at times I feel like I'm in this marriage all alone. Every time I tell my husband how I feel, he cuts me off leaving me frustrated. I want him to be a man and accept his role in this marriage..."

She wiped the tears from her eyes.

"He acts like everything is my fault and he never takes responsibility for his actions and lack thereof."

The counselor passed her a box of kleenex and jotted down more notes.

"I understand what you're saying; however, your husband's perspective of him not being a man may be totally different from yours. It may actually be misread as an insult."

He leaned up with his elbows resting on his legs.

"Exactly. She has this thing with calling me a little boy and that does something to me."

The counselor nodded.

"Mrs. Richards, those words can be gut-wrenching to a man. You know, honesty during all session are vital. Being called a little boy is one of the things frustrating your husband. No man wants to be belittled and feel as though his wife is his mother and vice versa. You have to be willing to allow him to take you there so that you both can close that door and pray for God to allow you both to come to a mutual agreement that he is the head of the household and a man who simply makes mistakes, just as we all do."

"I understand."

"Mr. Richards, do you feel as if you give your wife the attention that she deserves?"

He smirked.

"Actually, I do."

The counselor adjusted her glasses.

"Is that a true statement?"

His smirk faded away.

"Well, maybe not every day, but she knows that I love her. So, why do I need to show her how I feel every single day. I'm tired when I come from work and all I want to do is sit down and relax. I don't always feel like hugging and kissing."

The counselor smiled.

"Actually, love is not about just hugs and kisses. There are so many forms of love that have yet to be discovered. Forgiveness is love. Patience and kindness is love. Understanding one another is love. Praying and reading together for spiritual growth is love. The list could go on and on... Mr. Richards, showing love is so much more than a physical touch or spending money."

She tilted her head and smiled.

"The question now is, did you show her love and affection before you married her?"

His forehead wrinkled.

"I showed my wife plenty of attention. There were times I would buy her roses, clothes, and shoes just because I wanted to see her smile. On my way home, I'd stop by the store and buy a simple card that said I love you. Throughout the day, I'd send her random I love you or I'm, thinking about you texts. But after a while, I felt as though she knew that I loved her."

He shrugged his shoulders.

"So, I stopped and kind of drifted away from it."

"Mrs. Richards, is this what made you fall in love with your husband?"

She slightly smiled.

"Yes. It was those things that made me feel appreciated, loved, and respected. Seeing his number and hearing his voice brought a smile to my face almost every day. I still remember the times before we married when he would come over after work and just kiss me on the cheek and tell me that he loved me. We always communicated back then. Even when we watched television, he would find a way to give me attention."

She smiled.

"He used to rub my neck or pinch my toes and smile."

She lowered her head.

"I miss those days. I want that Joshua back, not this distant person he's become."

The counselor slightly nodded as she glanced at both of them.

"Now we're getting somewhere. Mr. Richards, how does this make you feel hearing your wife say these things?"

With sorrowful eyes, he turned towards his wife.

"I'm sorry. That wasn't my intention to become so distant from you. Please know that I do love you. I've just been so stressed at work lately. I didn't realize I had become that person."

The counselor intervened.

"What I see here is an emotional disconnect that is fixable if you both want your marriage to work. I think this is a good place to stop and pick back up on your next visit."

She walked over to her desk and took out a calendar.

"I would like to schedule another session for next Wednesday. How about 4:30 pm?"

Looking at each other, they agreed that next Wednesday would be fine.

Mrs. Chambers looked up with a smile.

"I would like for you both to think about everything that we spoke about on today and determine whether or not you're serious about saving your marriage. I must tell you, it will take participation from you both for this to work."

They looked at one another and nodded. The counselor smiled once more.

"Have a wonderful evening and I'll see you both next week."

Janelle looked over at Mrs. Chambers.

"Thank you."

Joshua opened the door for his wife as they left the office and walked to the car. She couldn't stop thinking about him opening up in counseling, while he refused to talk about their issues at home. She got in the car and glanced over at him as she reached for her seat belt.

"Joshua, I think the session went great. How about you?"

He shook his head.

"I'm not comfortable talking to this counselor, but I'll go along with it for now. She's digging up things that should stay buried."

"Joshua, that's what counseling is for. We can't keep sweeping issues under the rug. If we don't somehow deal with our issues, they'll bury our love for each other so deep, that we forget how and when we fell in love in the first place."

While they were stopped at the red light, Janelle watched an older couple walk along the sidewalk hand in hand crossing the streets. She closed her eyes and cried within.

God when will I have that again? I'm dying on the inside and my husband doesn't even notice. He's so cold... I feel like I made the wrong decision to marry him. Lord, please help me and he's for me, help us.

During the ride home, you could feel the tension in the air. Joshua periodically glanced down at his phone while driving. He attempted to send a text. Signaling to turn left, he hit the brakes. Janelle's body jerked forward.

"Joshua... pay attention to what you're doing and put your phone down. I guess you still haven't learned your lesson."

He frowned.

"I got this Janelle."

Minutes later they arrived home.

"Looks like you made it home safely. A little whiplash won't kill you. Let me guess, you're going to mention that in counseling too."

She got out of the car and slammed the door as Joshua walked up behind her. He laughed and held up the keys.

"Looking for these?"

When he unlocked the door, Janelle walked inside and went to the bedroom.

He called out to her.

"Am I allowed to sleep in the room later tonight or do I need my pillow?"

She stuck her head out the bedroom.

"God loves you Joshua and so do I."

He sat on the couch and looked towards the ceiling.

"Here we go again. I thought counseling went well."

With tears in her eyes, she gently closed the bedroom door. She heard her phone rang.

"Hi Ms. Lula."

"Are you okay baby? You don't sound so good?"

She held the phone for a minute.

"Ms. Lula, I just don't understand where things went wrong in my marriage."

"Girl stop tiptoeing around this conversation and say what you have to say. It's me you talking to."

"Okay... Ms. Lula I never told Joshua that I was unable to have children and he overheard me talking to Sandra. And of course, you know about the accident and the ex... Well, we started counseling today and he made me angry all over again on the way home while he was on the phone texting and driving as if he didn't learn from the accident. I can almost guarantee he was texting her."

Ms. Lula squeezed her lips together.

"Baby don't let the sun go down on your anger. Just pray about it and let God deal with it. Stop all of that stressing. There's no person in this world, not even me that you need to be stressing over."

Tears flowed down her face.

"But Ms. Lula, she came to the hospital when he was in the accident and when I walked back into the room, he was smiling."

Ms. Lula shook her head.

"Baby... you can't blame this girl because Joshua could've stopped this a long time ago."

Janelle rolled her eyes.

"I'm not blaming her. I don't feel a need to. I married him. He's the one not honoring his vows. My question is why did God have to make my wound barren? If only I could have a child, maybe he wouldn't be this way."

Ms. Lula frowned.

"Wait a minute, don't you dare start blaming God for this. A child aint gone fix this marriage or ya'll issues."

Uncompromisingly Ms. Lula continued.

"You both gone to have to work this thing out. Have ya'll prayed together?"

"No ma'am."

"Well ya'll need to and besides... where's your faith? God still works miracles. A doctor's word aint final. God has the last word because He is The Doctor... your Healer. And with faith, anything is possible."

"Yea, but the doctor told me that—"

"Lil girl. I don't know who your doctor is, but my doctor is Jesus. So, if it aint faith talk, I don't want to hear it."

She looked down.

"Yes ma'am. I understand. I really do... We have another counseling session next Wednesday."

Ms. Lula scratched her head.

"I hope this is biblical counseling because the world didn't put you two together. You can't take worldly counseling into a marriage unified under Jesus Christ. That's how a lot of marriages don't survive because they take God out of it. Live the life of Christ before him and eventually The Word of God will cut all of this division out like a double edge sword and bring unity back into your marriage again."

Janelle rubbed her lips together.

"Yes ma'am."

She shook her head.

"I know that just flew straight over your head. It'll register in your brain before the end of the night. Just read 1 Peter 3:1-7 every day. And don't go blowing my phone up either."

She smiled.

"I love you Ms. Lula."

She laughed.

"I love you too baby, but look I got to get off this phone. You know it's movie night for me and I need to head to the theater, my boyfriend Denzel just dropped a new movie. I'll talk to you later."

"Okay Ms. Lula. Don't forget to keep us in your prayers."

"Baby, God has this under control. Aint no need to worry."

Chapter Sixteen

A t their next visit to the counselor's office, Janelle sat down and glanced out the window. The counselor reached for her notepad.

"Good afternoon. Are you ready for the next phase of your sessions?"

Joshua looked at her.

"I guess so. May I ask what today's session is about?"

The counselor studied Janelle's body language and cleared her throat.

"Mr. and Mrs. Richards, today's session will open doors to soul ties that's apparently ripping your marriage apart."

He looked over at his wife wondering if she had mentioned his ex to the counselor.

"Soul ties? What do you mean by that and just out of curiosity, what does the ND stand for?"

She smiled.

"I'm glad you asked. A soul tie is when an individual becomes emotionally and spiritually connected to something or someone who is not their spouse through physical touch, an emotional connection, sexual contact, or unresolved past relationships."

She chuckled.

"I saved the best for last. The acronyms stand for No Divorce Counseling 101."

He smiled.

"That's clever. I like the hidden message."

Janelle looked over at her husband thinking of his ex and their possible soul ties. The counselor smiled.

"Welcome back Mrs. Richards, you seemed to have drifted away for a minute there."

"I'm sorry."

"Are you ready to begin finding the open doors that need to be closed?"

They nodded as the counselor smiled.

"Mr. Richards, I would like for you to begin."

He rubbed his leg.

"Well, it all started when I overheard my wife talking to her best friend Sandra."

He looked over at his wife.

"She was telling her that she was unable to have children."

Janelle frowned.

"I—"

The counselor interceded before she could utter a word.

"Mrs. Richards, this is not going to be an easy session. You're going to have to hear the truth so that your husband can finally close this door that's apparently being used by your true enemy... You can find him in Ephesians 6:12. Please allow your husband to finish."

He looked over at his wife and back to the counselor.

"Thank you. As I was saying, I had taken the time to come home and surprise my wife with roses and an early lunch date. When I overheard her conversation about not being able to have kids... I was furious that she knew this."

He held up three fingers.

"She knew this for three years and never told me. My issue is she knew that I always wanted a family."

"Mrs. Richards, how does this make you feel to hear your husband say this?"

She twirled her ring around her finger and looked at her husband.

"I'm sorry, but every time I wanted to tell you, I thought about you leaving me."

He stared at his wife.

"But Janelle, don't you think that was selfish?"

She shook her head.

"Are you serious right now. You're still communicating with your ex."

The counselor intervened.

"Mr. Richards, the rules apply to you as well. Please allow your wife to continue without interrupting her."

She turned her attention back to Janelle.

"Mrs. Richards, how do you know this?"

She folded her arms.

"He seemed to tell you my secret, but he neglected to inform you of his." She rolled her eyes at him. "We got into an argument after he overheard me talking to my best friend and he left. His little secret was exposed when he got into a bad car accident. And guess who visited him at the hospital?"

The counselor looked over at him, then back at her.

"Please continue."

"Hi ex. Apparently, the soul ties between them were never broken because they still communicate. I could understand if they had children together, but they don't and it hurts like hell knowing that he would rather run to his ex to discuss our marital issues than come to me."

She shifted her body towards him.

"You have no clue how bad that hurt. There's nothing like being married to a man and all you see is the face of his ex. You proposed to me. I'm your wife."

He leaned his body over on the arm of the chair with a smirk on his face.

"I'm sure you have male friends. It's obvious that you do."

The counselor intervened once more.

"Counseling requires for you to listen to one another's heart. Understanding one another's emotions and pains is vital in a marriage. Marriage is sacred and I want you both to understand that if you're unwilling to listen to each other and live together in an understanding way, you yourselves hinder your own prayers according to 1 Peter 3:7 that is... It's vital that you don't allow miscommunication to stop your prayers."

She shook her head.

"It's just not worth it. Mr. Richards, I think that if you eliminate the sarcasm from your disagreements, it will diffuse many future arguments. God never calls for us to aggravate people with sarcasm or belittle one another."

She smiled.

"That's just not one of His Fruits of the Spirit."

He looked over towards the counselor.

"I understand how I may have hurt her, but she's reading too much into it. I don't see these sessions going anywhere because when we leave, the tension is thick."

He shook his head.

"With that said, this will be my last session... So, Janelle make sure you get it all out today."

She shook her head.

"Mrs. Chambers, this is what I have to deal with. If he's not willing to work with me here, then it's pointless."

The counselor leaned forward.

"Mrs. Richards, if you're willing to continue to work on you and your marriage, here are three things you can do."

Before she could finish, Joshua got up.

"I'll be waiting in the car."

A tear crawl down her face as the counselor walked over and comforted her.

"You remind me so much of my younger self. I had to do my part in my marriage and it wasn't always easy. So, when I tell you these things, it comes from a place of experience. The three things you need for your marriage to work are prayer, confidence in God's Word, and loving your husband even when you want to hate him. The enemy is going to fight to tear you both apart. But what God puts together no man or woman can tear it apart."

She held up a finger.

"Unless you choose to give up."

She shook her head and smiled.

"This is what the 1st Peter 3 woman is all about. She shows her husband the love of Christ even when his actions demand her to hate. Her love covers his hurtful actions in the midst of God working on him."

She smiled and pointed to her.

"He needs to see Jesus Christ in you... So that he may be won over without you saying a word. Let God do it, not you. That's just too much work for any individual."

The counselor smiled.

"Move out of His way because He doesn't want us getting His Glory."

The counselor looked at her with sympathetic eyes.

"So, clean up your pretty little face and fight with love and pray that God softens his heart. If marriage was so easy, there would be no need for divorce and I wouldn't have the job that I love so much."

She pointed at herself.

"I went through some ugly challenges in my own marriage, but we succeeded so that I could help couples and most importantly, women like you."

Janelle wiped the corner of her eyes.

"Thank you so much for stepping outside of your profession to speak to me heart to heart. I will never forget this or you. Please keep praying for us."

The counselor smiled and handed her a business card. "I will. We were connected for a reason. Call me anytime."

Janelle reached for her bag, slid on her shades, and walked to the car ready to fight for her marriage.

Chapter Seventeen

T he next day, on the way home from the office, Janelle stopped by the market to pick up a few items. Shortly after arriving home, she began preparing dinner.

"I refuse to sit back and allow the devil to rip my marriage apart... Since I'm the only Bible my husband will read, I'm gonna try and make sure that I'm a darn good reflection of Christ."

She turned down the radio when she heard the phone ring.

"Hey Josh."

"Hey... I'm gonna be a little late. I have a few more things to complete before I leave. I'll see you around eight."

His secretary walked in and passed him a folder.

"Hold on Janelle. Thank you Monica."

She grabbed the salmon out of the refrigerator.

"Okay. Take your time, I'll be here. Love you."

"Love you too."

She placed the phone on the counter and glanced down at the chopping board.

"Well, I guess that means that I can take my time cooking."

She finally accepted that she was going to have to be the bigger person in the marriage and the example of love her husband so desperately needed. She stared at the phone as it rang.

"Who's calling me from a private number?... Hello. Hello... Well, I guess they don't want to talk."

Time dwindled away as she finished dinner and Joshua's favorite dessert. She peeped out of the window.

"I know he said he would be home at eight, what's taking him so long?"

She dialed his number, but it went to his voicemail. She tried again, but still no answer, so she left a message.

"Hey Josh. I was wondering if you were going to be home any time soon. Call me when you get this message. I love you."

Fifteen minutes later, headlights beamed through the kitchen window. With a wide smile, she walked towards the front door. As Joshua opened door open, the smell of liquor permeated through his pores. Her smile faded away.

"Joshua, where have you been? And please tell me you haven't been drinking?"

He closed the door.

"Janelle, last I checked, I didn't have a curfew and yes, I've been drinking. I had water this morning and hot tea this afternoon."

She rolled her eyes.

"I thought you were working until eight?"

He sat down his briefcase and walked into the kitchen.

"Look, I didn't realize you were my mother oh... and your eyes gone get stuck one day?"

She forced a smile and followed behind him.

"I decided to make you dinner. You ready to eat?"

He smiled.

"Is that my favorite desert I smell? I should've came home first instead of going to the bar. Oh well, I'm full, but it smells good. I had some fried shrimp and fries at the bar."

He reached for a spoon and tasted cobbler.

"That's what I'm talking about."

He walked pass her.

"You've outdone yourself tonight."

She took a deep breath and smiled.

"Sure Joshua... anything for you. Oh, and one more thing, I'll be praying for you."

He turned around.

"I don't need your prayers. You do."

Tears trickled down her face as he walked away. She glanced over at the food.

"No need to let this food go to waste."

She wiped her tears, poured a glass of wine, and ate. Minutes later, she walked into their room, sat on the side of the bed, and   whispered.

"Joshua, this makes no sense at all. I put so much love and effort into making that dinner. I don't understand what's going on with you. I'm trying, but it seems that I'm the only one who wants this marriage to work."

He opened his eyes.

"I may be drunk, but I'm not deaf."

She shook her head.

"Ignorant is bliss to a fool."

He rolled over and fluffed his pillow.

"I love you too, Janelle."

She sighed.

"Lord Jesus, I'm trying to be the wife you want me to be, but this is no walk in the park."

Chapter Eighteen

A few weeks later, Janelle lay her bed staring at the ceiling. "God, please make this migraine go away."

She reached for her phone.

"Hello."

"Hey Janelle. I haven't heard from you in three days, what's going on with you?"

"Hey Sandra. Sorry I haven't called, but I've been down with this migraine for the last couple of days."

Her brows met.

"Are you sure you're not stressed out? You haven't had that issue in years."

"I know right... You know what, I can almost guarantee its stress."

"That's why it's so important for you to stop letting your husband stress you like this. I've tried my best to stay positive, but it hurts knowing that you're dealing with this... It's just not like him. Have you at least been to the doctor?"

She reached for her a glass of water from the nightstand.

"No, but I really need to."

Sandra pulled into her driveway.

"I'm outside. Come open the door."

She got out of the bed, peeked out of the window, and smiled.

"That's just like you to come and check on me. Give me a second. Here I come."

She opened the door and as Sandra walked in, looked around, and whispered.

"Is Joshua here?"

"No, he went to work."

"Okay Janelle, get ready we're going to urgent care to make sure you're okay. I'm not taking no for an answer."

"Sandra, I pray that everything's okay."

"Girl, you'll be just fine. Where's your faith?"

She stood in the mirror and pinned up her hair.

"You know it's hard when you start having the same symptoms your mom had."

Sandra's brows met.

"Like I said, where's your faith?"

An hour later, they arrived at the Urgent Care Center. After signing in, Sandra glanced over at her hand, leaned towards her, and whispered.

"Where's your ring?"

She looked over at Sandra and held up her hand.

"I left it on the dresser. It's not like he cares, especially since he never wears his."

She shook her head.

"Okay, but you don't have to stoop to his level."

She folded her arms.

"You're right."

Twenty minutes later, the nurse came to the door.

"Mrs. Richards, you can come back now."

"Sandra, are you coming with me?"

"I don't even know why you asked me that silly question."

The nurse smiled.

"Good morning Mrs. Richards. Could you please verify your date of birth?"

She gave the nurse her date of birth.

"When was your last menstrual cycle?"

She chuckled.

"Menopause kidnapped it. I haven't seen it in years."

The nurse laughed.

"So, what brings you here today?"

"I've been feeling lightheaded for the last three days, not to mention this migraine. And it's been really tender underneath my breast."

The nurse placed the thermometer under her tongue.

"Can you slide your right sleeve up for me please?"

She wrapped the blood pressure cuff around her arm. Seconds later, she looked up at the sound of the beep.

"Mrs. Richards, I need to recheck your blood pressure."

The cuff firmly gripped her arm and beeped once again.

"Okay, that's better, but your blood pressure is still a little high. Are you on any medications?"

She looked up at the nurse.

"No ma'am."

"Okay ladies follow me this way. You'll be in room 3A. I hope you feel better. The doctor will be in shortly."

She smiled.

"Thank you."

Sandra stared at Janelle as she sat on the exam table.

"Janelle... you know stress is the number one silent killer... right?"

She nodded as Sandra continued.

"I know you're strong and all, but you've got to talk to someone. I mean seriously, you don't need to go around bottling up all of your pain. You better release that stuff before it kills you."

"I know, but every time I talk about it, it makes me angrier than I was before. I'm tired of arguing with Josh. No wife should have to deal with this."

"Janelle, I understand, but all marriages have issues. Besides, not all men have the right example to follow. Think about it, Joshua wasn't this bad until he overheard you talking to me. So, he may be wondering what else you're hiding. You never know what pass memories you triggered."

Janelle looked towards the door.

"There's nothing else to hide. As for him and his ex, I'm really wondering what's going on with them. When I looked at the bill, one number in particular was listed several times over and over and it was her number."

The nurse opened the door before she could continue.

"Mrs. Richards, we need a urine sample."

She pointed across the hall.

"The restroom is directly across from you."

She reached for the cup and went to the restroom. Once she returned, the doctor entered the room.

"Good morning, Mrs. Richards."

He shook her hand.

"My name is Dr. Numiader."

He glanced over the information in her folder.

"So, I see you've been having migraines for three days now. Are you on any current medications?"

Her brows met.

"No sir."

He placed the stethoscope on her chest.

"Take a deep breath in and slowly exhale."

He tilted his head.

"Have you been stressed lately Mrs. Richards?"

Sandra touched her on the leg.

"Yes sir, she has."

He looked at her.

"Mrs. Richards, give me a minute. I want to check a few things first so I want miss anything. The nurse will come in a take some blood because the blood reveals all things... I'll be back in shortly."

Shortly thereafter, the nurse came in.

"Mrs. Richards, I need to take some blood. Hold out your arm and relax. This will only take a minute."

The nurse gathered the bloodwork together.

"The doctor will be back in shortly. I hope you feel better."

After the nurse left out, she paced back and forth around the room. Sandra shook her head and gently grabbed her arm.

"Honey, please just sit down and relax."

Twenty minutes later the doctor walked in the room. Janelle forced a smile.

"Mrs. Richards, after reviewing your blood work and urine, we've discovered that..."

Time paused as tears swelled in her eyes. Dr. Numiaders words paralyzed her in disbelief. She quickly glanced over at Sandra as she walked towards her in tears.

"Mrs. Richards, it would be best if you got some rest and scheduled an appointment with your primary doctor. We will send over the results."

Chapter Nineteen

A few hours later, Janelle reasoned within herself as she sat down on the sofa.

"How am I going to tell him? How did this happen? I thought..."

Nervousness consumed her when she heard Joshua's car pull up in the driveway. A few minutes later, the front door opened and slammed shut. He slowly walked into the living room and sat next to his wife.

"Janelle, can we talk?"

"Sure. We really need to."

She turned towards him.

"Sandra took me to urgent care today and—"

He rudely interrupted her and stared at the floor.

"Janelle look, I'm not happy with you. I've tried."

He watched as tears slowly crept down her face.

"Well, maybe not as much as I should've, but I think it's time to call it quits."

Her brows met.

"What are you saying? What about counseling?"

She pointed to her husband and back to herself.

"I thought we were—"

"I had my lawyer draw up the divorce papers about a week ago."

He bit down on his lips and stared into her eyes slowly tapping the envelope in his hand. She stared at him.

"I took your advice. You need someone that's going to truly love you and I'm not that guy. I mean, you can't even give me what I want and that's a family. You know a child that I can... Truly love."

She rolled her eyes.

"Typical you. I never thought that you could be so selfish."

She smirked.

"It gives you joy to hurt me, doesn't it?"

Her thoughts drifted back to her visit to urgent care.

"Joshua, I'm sorry for my part and I forgive you for yours."

He stood up and frowned.

"Forgive me for what? I don't need your forgiveness Janelle."

She walked past him towards their bedroom. "Joshua, I don't want to argue with you, neither did I want to be in a broken marriage. You're not the man I fell in love with. I don't know who you've become." A smirk slowly visited her face as she sighed. "I guess God doesn't move fast enough for you, but it's okay."

She wiped the tears from her eyes, grabbed her keys, reached for the envelope from her nightstand, and walked back to the living room. She stared into his eyes and gently placed the envelope in his hand on her way out the front door.

"Since your mind is made up, read this on your way out. And please lock the door behind you. Thank you for showing me how you truly feel about me... And this marriage."

He watched as she walked out the door and slowly opened the envelope. As he read the content on the paper, time stood still. He ran out the door to catch her, but she was already gone. He walked back into the house and fell down on his knees.

"God, what's wrong with me? I didn't know!"

He slammed the side of his fist on the floor finally connecting with his true emotions. He got up holding his hands tightly above his head.

"I can't believe this."

Hours had gone by, but Janelle had yet to return home. Shortly thereafter, he saw headlights shining through the living room window and sat up on the sofa. Before she could unlock the door, he snatched it open.

She frowned.

"Why are you still here?"

He reached for her hand.

"Janelle, I'm sorry. I didn't know. Why didn't you just tell me?"

She looked at him in disbelief.

"Are you serious right now?"

She snatched her hand away.

"You walked into this house with news of a divorce and I didn't even know we were headed in that direction."

He lowered his head.

"I wasn't thinking straight. Baby, I made a mistake. I allowed my emotions to get the best of me."

"Don't call me your baby now. It was pointless of telling you anything."

She placed her purse on the sofa. "Your mind was already made up."

He reached for her once more.

"I'm sorry. Why didn't you just tell me?"

"Joshua, you had already given up on us and our vows we made before God."

He walked towards her and gently grabbed her arm. "Janelle. I'm sorry! Why couldn't you just tell me?"

She turned around and shook her head with tears in her eyes. "Tell you what?... That I'm pregnant?"

Chapter Twenty

D isappointed in himself, he reached for her once more. "But I overheard you talking to Sandra about not being able to have children."

With sorrow in her eyes, snatched her arm away, and handed him the envelope.

"Here are the divorce papers. I signed them."

She walked to the kitchen.

"I hope you're happy now."

He walked towards her.

"No! Wait Janelle."

He ripped the papers into pieces.

"Baby, I'm sorry. That's not what I really want."

She deeply exhaled.

"Earlier you wanted a divorce. Now, you want to rip up the papers, you had your attorney to draft up for me to sign."

She pointed towards him.

"And you had the nerve to personally deliver them to me yourself."

She rolled her eyes.

"Please! Instead of you talking to me and praying about the situation, you decided to take matters into your own hands and confidently barged in here with divorce papers."

She turned away.

"And the sad part is that you knew it was gonna hurt me. I know I was wrong for not telling you about the infertility, but I can't help and will not apologize for my faith that God could restore this marriage and give us a child... And I quote that you can truly love."

With gentle eyes, he reached for her hand.

"I don't wanna to argue with you Janelle. I'm sorry, but what I would like to know is, where do we go from here?"

She reached for a bottle of water and took a sip.

"I don't know. You tell me. You're the one with the divorce attorney." She smirked. "But, I do know where I'm going and that's to bed. Good night."

She grabbed her phone from the island and made a call as she walked towards their bedroom.

"Hello. This better be good girl, especially at ten o'clock at night. You messing with my beauty sleep."

"Hey Ms. Lula. I'm so sorry. I didn't even look at the time, but I really need to talk to you."

She walked into the bathroom and closed the door behind her.

Ms. Lula yawned.

"Uh huh. What is it?"

She leaned against the sink.

"I don't know what I've done so bad in this marriage for my husband to treat me the way he does. He feels like he can do wrong, apologize, and everything is just supposed to go away and be okay... Ms. Lula."

"I'm listening."

"Well, Sandra took me to urgent care earlier today and they ran a few tests. Surprisingly, I found out that I was pregnant and my husband—"

Ms. Lula sat up in the bed and loosened her head wrap.

"Jesus... Did I just hear that girl say what I think she said or is this head wrap too tight?"

She smiled.

"You said that you're what nah?"

"I'm pregnant."

"Well I'll be—"

"Ms. Lula."

She laughed.

"I can hear you smiling through this phone. Look at God. He knows how to shut the devil lies down."

Janelle sat down on the side of the tub.

"But that's not all Ms. Lula. He came home earlier and personally delivered me divorce papers before I could even tell him about the pregnancy."

"What you say? Now, I've tried..."

She lifted her hand.

"Jesus, Father. Uh uh uh. You know what I'm just gone pray. Baby you okay?"

"Yes ma'am. I handed him the results, walked out, and asked him to lock the door behind him, but when I got back home, he was still here and so were his things. I mean, he admitted that he was wrong and all and said he wanted to work things out. So–"

"Baby, I really hate that you're going through this. I know I joke a lot and God still working on me, but I could choke that boy right now."

She shook her head.

"Yesss Lord Jesus, please help me before I go over there and show out on him."

She pursed her lips together.

"Baby, the only thing I can tell you to do is pray and let God do the rest."

She rubbed her forehead. "Ms. Lula, it's like I don't even know who he is anymore. Who I live with now is not the man I dated or the man that proposed to me."

Ms. Lula reached for her house coat, slid her feet into her slippers, and walked to the kitchen.

"Janelle baby, that's normally how it happens. You date the fake."

She laughed.

"Girl that rhymed. But any way, then, when you're married and living together, the real person starts rearing his ugly head. Uh huh that sounds about right."

Janelle placed her hand on her stomach.

"I guess so."

Ms. Lula poured herself a cup of coffee.

"Aint no guessing. That's the ugly truth. But seriously, you're carrying a child now and you can't be stressing for nobody; not even your husband."

"I'll try Ms. Lula."

She walked back into her room, sat her coffee on her night stand, and sat on the side of her bed.

"Well, you have nine months to practice. So, by the time you have your bundle of joy, you should be a stress-free expert."

She laughed.

"Yes ma'am."

"Well, I'll be busy preparing for my cruise in case you try to call and can't get me tomorrow. Just know that I aint ignoring your calls."

She took a sip of her coffee.

"I need this vacation to celebrate complete remission of that old Leukemia. God is giving me another chance at life. My faith just wouldn't let me doubt Him and I want you to trust Him with your marriage too. Okay baby."

"Yes ma'am."

Ms. Lula lay back in her bed.

"You see, sometimes dark clouds seem to linger in marriages to expose issues that need to be dealt with so that you both can move forward and love each other the way God intended in the first place. Marriage is supposed to be a beautiful thing, but sometimes challenges surface to test them vows you know. You have to trust God in the storms and not just when the sun shines baby."

She smiled.

"Even after the storms, He leaves a special rainbow to remind you of His promise... God speaks even in the storms, you know. When the rain falls; He's just watering your seeds of faith. When the thunder roars; He's saying, 'Janelle hear Me and obey.' When the lightning flashes; His Son Jesus is saying, 'Stop worrying and keep your eyes on me. My child... don't you see me at work in your life?'"

She chuckled.

"Just look at it this way, when the doctors told you that you couldn't have children, you believed differently right."

"Yes ma'am."

"And look at what came from that... A baby." She shook her head and smiled. "I just preached my first sermon and I aint got no business in nobody pulpit. Watch out now! Baby anyways, you gotta learn how to change your..."

She placed her finger over her lips.

"What's the word I'm looking for girl?"

Janelle's brows met.

"I have no idea Ms. Lula."

"Hmmm."

She snapped her fingers.

"Perceptions. That's that big word ya'll be using trying to sound all deep and stuff."

She laughed.

"But Ms. Lula what about the earthquakes, tornados, tsunamis, and hurricanes?"

She frowned and shook her head.

"Girl that stuff come from the devil because them storms come to kill, steal, and destroy."

She laughed.

"Only you could think of that."

Ms. Lula adjusted herself in her bed.

"You laughing, but I'm dead serious."

"Yes ma'am. I understand."

Joshua walked towards the bedroom. "Janelle."

She looked over at the door.

"Ms. Lula. I'll call you before you leave. Joshua just walked in the room."

"Baby, you act real nervous when that boy come around. Is he abusing you?"

She shook her head and laughed.

"No ma'am. He may be a lot of things that I don't like, but an abuser he's not."

"Abuse aint just got to be him hitting you. It comes in all forms."

Her forehead wrinkled.

"I know."

"Okay. Just know everything you're going through right now aint just for you. It's a test; you hear me?"

"Yes ma'am."

"If you don't pass it now, it'll revisit you later."

"Okay. I love you Ms. Lula."

"Love you too baby. Good night."

Ms. Lula hung up the phone, shook her head, and began to pray.

"Lord Jesus, please teach these women how to love the hell out of their knuckle head spiritually blind husbands until their eyes are opened and their wives can finally see their prayers answered. Oh, and give them the strength Lord because I know for myself it aint easy."

She smiled and rolled over in her bed.

"I thank you in advance Lord. Amen."

Chapter Twenty-One

T he next evening, Janelle heard her phone ring. She rolled over and reached for her phone.

"Hello."

"This is an automated confirmation call from ND Counseling 101. To confirm your appointment for this Tuesday at 10:30 a.m., please press one. To cancel, please press the pound button."

She twisted her lips as if thinking and pressed the button.

"Thank you for confirming your appointment with ND Counseling 101. Where our goal is to help save your marriage. Have a great day."

She ended the call and walked into the living room to find her husband watching a movie.

"Hey."

He looked back at her.

"What's up?"

She walked around the sofa and smiled.

"So, you really want to work things out, right?"

He gestured for her to sit next to him.

"I really do. I mean, you're carrying my child."

She sat next to him.

"So, are you wanting to work on our marriage because you love me."

She pointed to her stomach.

"Or because I'm having your baby?"

Not expecting her to question his response, he gently scratched his chin.

"What do you mean by that?"

She stared into his eyes.

"Joshua, please answer the question and stop stalling for time. Let me ask you in a different way. If you didn't find out that I was pregnant, would you have gone through with the divorce?"

He lowered his head, then he looked at his wife.

"If I tell you the truth, will we still follow through with counseling?"

"Yes. "

"Look Janelle, after I overheard you talking to Sandra, I was in a place where I no longer wanted to be with you. Then, I called my attorney to file for divorce, but when you gave me the envelope and I opened it, everything changed."

"So, in other words, if I weren't pregnant, you'd be gone?"

"Baby look, I can't pretend that my wanting to work on us isn't because you're pregnant, but that doesn't mean that I don't love you."

"Well, since you're so sure that's what you wanna do... Last week, I scheduled another counseling session with Mrs. Chambers and they just called to confirm the appointment and I did."

He looked over at her.

"I don't mind giving counseling another try Janelle, but my only issue is that you never include me in the decisions that you make. It's almost like you decide for me without giving me a chance to voice my opinion."

He shook his head.

"I hate when you do that."

She twirled her rings around her finger.

"It's never my intention to make you feel that way. I'm sorry."

Before she walked away, she looked over at him nervously.

"By the way... our appointment is in the morning."

He took a deep breath.

"Janelle, I do have a job you know. I have to give advance notice that I'll be late or not coming to work."

With a clinched jaw, he asked one last question.

"What time is the appointment?"

"It's at 10:30 in the morning."

He shook his head.

"Janelle, in the future, please be considerate of my job and career."

She forced a smile.

"No problem. Can you please pick me up because my car has been giving me trouble lately?"

"Okay. I'll pick you up after I leave work."

As she walked back towards the bedroom, he called out to her.

"Janelle."

She turned around.

"Yeah."

He gazed into her eyes.

"I'm sorry about everything you know. I love you!"

She smiled.

"Me too."

The next morning, Joshua was awakened by his alarm. He sat up on the couch and reached for his lower back.

"Man, this sofa aint for sleeping."

Before getting ready for work, he walked in their room and admired Janelle as she lay sound asleep. Slowly pushing the door open, he walked in, grabbed his clothes, and shoes from their walk-in closet. Being sure to grab everything he needed, he walked by his night stand and reached for his silver rolex. As Janelle rolled over, he paused being sure not to wake her up. After realizing she was only adjusting herself, he left out of the room and used the guest bathroom to get ready. Still in shock that his wife was finally pregnant, he looked up.

"Thank You God. I didn't think this day would ever come."

He lowered his head.

"I thought you were punishing me for the abortion or something."

As time dwindled away, he rushed to get dressed for work. Standing in the mirror in his grey dress pants, and black button-down shirt, he brushed his hair. He walked towards the door and put on his shoes, reached for his briefcase from the side of the recliner, and left for work. As he got in the car, his phone rang.

"Hello."

It was his divorce attorney.

"Good morning Mr. Richards."

"Good morning. How are you?"

"I'm great. I wanted to inquire about the status of the paperwork for the divorce to make everything final. You said you wanted it done immediately. So, how's that working for you?"

"Mr. Togglier, thank you so much for everything that you've done at such short notice for me; however, I would like to hold off on everything right now. My wife and I are going to try a few things and allow divorce to be our last option. I just found out that she's pregnant."

"Congratulations! I truly understand. I'm happy that you both have decided to work things out. Although my job is to make divorces final."

He chuckled.

"And it pays well, you know. But I think you're making the right decision. You save more money like that because women are killing their husbands with child support these days."

Joshua laughed.

"I know right."

Mr. Togglier rubbed his dark brown and blonde neatly trimmed beard and continued.

"You know; people don't want to do the work to save their marriage these days. I guess they like to make people like me rich because I can give them the easy way out, especially at the rate of the couples in this generation. Not all divorce attorneys care about how things end or how it affects everyone else; especially the children because it's all about getting paid, but I do. It's like they don't try put themselves in their client's shoes and I feel some kind of way about that Mr. Richards. You know, it's two types of attorneys out here; the ones that work from their heart and the one's that work solely for the money and they heart aint nowhere in it."

He chuckled as he arrived at his office and got out of the car.

"Mr. Togglier, that's an interesting point."

He laughed.

"In this business, fools believe anything but wise people." He shook his head. "Man, they think about what they do first and how it affects the family. Now, if adultery was involved or you feel that you're what they call unequally yoked; that'd be different. But that's not your case. Oh, and since you're not emotionally or physically abusing your wife, I don't have to put you in a boxing ring and make you fight me like a man. But in all seriousness, I can't help but to express how happy I am that you've decided to work things out in your marriage."

He sat down at his desk.

"I truly appreciate it Mr. Togglier."

"No problem. You know at one point in my life this was just business for me, but when I see a couple that has a fighting chance, I can't help but to celebrate them. To me it's just the mere fact that their trying. I truly hope things work out for you and your wife."

Jokingly but seriously he said.

"But if it doesn't, you know you can always bring your money to me."

Joshua laughed.

"I'm happy that you get it. Again, thank you for following up with me Mr. Togglier. Your check is in the mail. Have a blessed day."

"You as well Mr. Richards."

About an hour and a half later, Joshua called to make sure that Janelle was up and ready for counseling. He glimpsed down at his watch as the phone rang.

In a soft-spoken voice, she answered the phone.

"Hello."

"Good morning babe."

"Morning."

"I just wanted to make sure you were up and ready before I left work to pick you up in about an hour or so."

She yawned.

"I'm up, but I wasn't feeling my best earlier, so I called the office to see if she had anything available this afternoon."

He gently stroked the left side of his face.

"You okay? You need anything?"

"No, I'm just gonna to lay back down for a while. I've already called Pastor to let him know that I wouldn't be in the office today."

"Okay. Did they give us another appointment?"

"Oh, yeah. It's at 3:30 this afternoon. Does that work for you?"

His brows met. "Yeah, that actually works better. I'll just work through lunch. Get some rest and I'll call you after one o'clock so you can have enough time to get up and get ready. Love you."

"Me too. See you then."

Chapter Twenty-Two

A few hours later, he called home, but there was no answer. About an hour and a half later, he left work to avoid traffic. He arrived home fifteen minutes later to find his wife still in bed asleep. He walked over to the bed and gently shook her.

"Janelle, babe, its two o'clock. Are you up for going or do we need to reschedule?"

She got up and rubbed her eyes.

"Oh my God. No, uh uh. Give me twenty minutes to get dressed."

"You sure? Because you know it takes you two hours to get ready."

She laughed.

"I promise. I'll be ready."

After a quick shower, she got dressed and walked into the kitchen. She reached for an apple and a bottle of water from the refrigerator.

He smiled.

"Dang, you wearing that dress baby."

She smiled.

"You so silly."

They walked towards the door.

"Josh, do you have your keys? My keys are somewhere down in this purse."

"You mean that book bag right."

She laughed.

"It's called a purse."

"Whatever you say. I still say it's a book bag. I'll lock the door."

Before heading to their session, he stopped by the gas station to fill up his car. Shortly at about 3:20 p.m., they arrived to their session on MartavJ Blvd. Janelle smiled and signed in.

"Good afternoon."

The secretary smiled.

"Mrs. Chambers will be with you shortly."

"Okay, thank you."

She walked over and sat next to her husband. He reached for her hand and smiled. Seconds later, a young man about six feet tall stormed out of Mrs. Chambers office. He slammed the door.

"I don't have time for this."

The counselor walked the man's wife to the door and handed her a kleenex.

"He'll be back, I promise."

The young lady slightly smiled and wiped her nose.

"Yes ma'am."

A few minutes later, she opened her door.

"Good afternoon. You both can come back now."

As they walked into her office, she closed the door behind them. Her heart smiled as she walked over to her desk. She sat down and flipped her hair from her face.

"Mrs. Richards. I'm glad you're feeling better."

She gestured for them to have a seat.

"Mr. Richards, it warms my heart that you've decided to join us again. Have there been any changes since our last session?"

He looked over at his wife.

"Well, I came home with divorce papers and she had papers, but, it was for something else."

She looked over at Janelle and cleared her throat.

"May I ask what type of papers you gave your husband Mrs. Richards?"

She smiled.

"Yes ma'am. It was the results from my pregnancy test."

A smile graced her face.

"Wow. You're expecting. Congratulations to you both."

He cleared his throat and smiled.

"Thank you."

She smiled once more.

"Well, the great thing is that something beautiful happened when an ugly situation demanded its presence to be acknowledged. What do you think?"

She looked over at her husband as he spoke.

"I like how you see what we don't see."

"Mr. Richards, it normally happens that way. Sometimes we can't see what others see because we're just too close to the mirror, but many times, it's just spiritual discernment."

She leaned back.

"So, I guess we can now began our session. Mr. Richards, I know that our last session seemed a little tough because you both had to hear things that may never have come up without counseling."

She tilted her head.

"But, I still stand firm on the fact that a baby will never make unresolved issues go away."

He squinted his eyes as she continued.

"Mr. Richards, I 'm sorry. I don't mean that in any disrespectful way, but it's my job to be brutally honest during these sessions in order to straighten out the crooked places in your marriage. It's also my job to magnify the good in your marriage to balance things out."

"I'm sorry Mrs. Chambers, I truly understand."

"No apologies needed. The session we'll have today and continue to have if that's what you both would like, will deal with how you both ended up in counseling."

She crossed her legs.

"What I need to know is, are you willing to complete the program together this time... no matter what?"

Janelle smiled and pointed to herself.

"I would love to complete the sessions."

Joshua slowly scooted to the edge of the sofa and looked at the counselor.

"I'm all in this time."

The counselor reached for her pen and notepad from her desk.

"Well, let's begin investing in your marriage."

She smiled.

"Typically, I wouldn't share my personal life with couples; but, this case is different. I won't go into any details; but, I want you both to understand that what I share with you doesn't just come from a degree. It comes from experience... Now, that's not to discredit counselors with a degree, but I'm convinced that when experience and scripture are incorporated in sessions, you can't go wrong. Many couples fail to realize that God is the glue to their marriage and when they leave Him out, their marriage eventually fails... I've been where you both are and it's not a fun place to be. If anyone told you different, it would be a lie."

She smiled.

"Mr. Richards, what were your thoughts when your wife told you that she was pregnant.?"

He shook his head.

"Actually, words can't describe how stupid I felt. You know, as a child, I was so used to getting my way, but I never expected it to have such a negative impact on my life and marriage now. So, in the beginning when my wife wasn't getting pregnant, I felt like her and God owed me something and when it didn't happen on my time, stubbornness and pride gripped me and wouldn't let go. I needed someone to blame and at the time, my wife was the only person constantly in my view."

She smiled.

"So, how did that work for you?"

His eyes grew wide.

"It didn't. You know, in hind sight I realized I just didn't have the faith she had. Now, I see why she didn't tell me. It wasn't that she was keeping a secret, she was just stepping out on this thing called faith that I was and I'm still confused about."

The counselor smiled.

"In other words, she didn't want your doubt tampering with her faith."

"Pretty much."

"Mrs. Richards, what are your thoughts now that your husband has opened up a little more?"

She smiled.

"It really helps me to understand a little of what was going on with him."

The counselor smiled.

"It does help, doesn't it?"

"Yes ma'am."

"Mr. Richards, I admire your bold honesty."

She reached for a folder from her desk.

"Communication is number one in a marriage or any relationship. I would like for you both to work on your communication skills by sharing your likes and dislikes respectively with one another; therefore, I have an assignment for you both to complete for your next session. It's unique but much needed for healing to begin to take place in your marriage. Do you think the both of you will be able to complete it?"

He looked over at his wife and back towards the counselor.

"May I ask what it is first?"

"Sure."

She reached for coffee mug with black bold writing that read *Your Marriage is Worth Fighting For* filled with hot Rooibos Chai tea and took a sip. She placed the mug back on the table and proceeded.

"In many cases, I've seen couples rely on the other for happiness instead of dealing with the real issue. Therefore, I would like for you both to take time to sit, think, and write a letter to each other admitting to the unrealistic expectations you desired from the other to fill a void that neither of you could ever fill and open up about secrets in your marriage—."

Janelle cleared her throat before the counselor could continue.

"Mrs. Richards, did you have something you would like to say?"

"Yes ma'am... Um, may I ask why we can't just tell each other?"

She smiled.

"Mrs. Richards, I'm so glad that you asked. One of my jobs as a marriage counselor is to provoke you to question why I ask you to do a thing and question what you don't understand."

She leaned back in her chair and intertwined her fingers as she tapped her thumbs together.

"I'm giving you this assignment because it makes you search your heart and motives behind your eagerness to rush into marriage and it opens your eyes to the true love that you both have for one another."

Janelle lowered her head.

"Okay. That makes sense."

"Mr. Richards, how do you feel about this assignment?"

He leaned up placing his elbows on his knees.

"I mean, it sounds great to me."

He smiled, looked at Janelle, and back at the counselor.

"I wouldn't have thought of anything like this, but I'll do it."

The counselor slightly tilted her head.

"Hmmmm, I forgot one thing. This assignment is to be done alone because I don't want any of your inner thoughts interrupted by the other person's feelings or how you think your honesty may affect them."

She got up and walked to her desk.

"I'm going to schedule your next appointment for next Monday. This will give you plenty of time to think. I will need for you to bring your letters to our next session where they are to be handed to me in a sealed envelope."

She checked her calendar to accommodate a two-hour session.

"How does 3:00 that Monday afternoon sound for the both of you?"

They looked at each other and nodded. Joshua smiled.

"Sure, that'll work."

"Well, I look forward to our next session where you both sharing thoughts that your hearts have held captive for so long."

The counselor stood up and shook their hands.

"Welcome back to ND Counseling 101 where it is my goal to save your marriage."

Janelle smiled.

"Thank you. We truly appreciate you."

As they left the office, Joshua walked over to the passenger side of his car and opened the door for his wife. He smiled as she got in the car.

"My stomach has been talking to me the whole time, like, 'Joshua what's up with some food?'"

"You want to stop somewhere and grab a bite to eat before we go home?"

She reached for her seatbelt.

"Yeah that sounds great. I'm starving anyway."

"Any place special?"

"No, not really. Well..." She leaned over on the door. "I want some Chinese food. Hmmm, some shrimp lo mein and an egg roll sounds delicious right about now."

"Okay. Chinese food it is."

Chapter Twenty-Three

L ater that evening, they ate and got ready for bed. After a long shower, Janelle walked into the room in white tights and her husbands oversized t-shirt. He walked into the bedroom still in his work clothes and sat on the black ottoman at the end of their bed. She reached inside of her night stand drawer and grabbed a pair of socks, but not before Joshua could reach for her feet. He gazed into her eyes while giving her a foot massage. She leaned her head back on her pillow.

"I so miss you giving me foot massages."

"I know you do."

"Joshua, you're too cocky. You know that right."

He shrugged his shoulders.

"Pretty much."

He smiled.

"Babe, I must admit... this feels so familiar. It reminds me of the first time I visited you."

"I know right. I'm happy we're able to spend time together and enjoy each other. All we need now is—"

"Some cookie dough ice cream."

She smiled at his effort to make things better. He got up, walked over to the dvd player, put in a movie, and leaned against the headboard next to his wife. She smiled and leaned her head on his shoulder. Twenty minutes into the movie, she fell asleep.

"Babe, get under the covers so you can go back to sleep."

He kissed her on the forehead as she got under the covers.

"Good night."

As the movie ended, his message notification went off. He looked over to make sure his wife was asleep.

Hey Josh. Are you busy? 😊

He stared as the notifications continued.

I just wanted to see how things were going for you and your wife. I heard she was pregnant.

He ignored the messages and continued watching his movie.

Let me guess, you're with her right now and that's why you're not responding.

He looked over at his wife and attempted to silence his phone, but the notifications continued one last time.

Whatever. I love you too. Oh, and Congratulations.

Without hesitating, he deleted the messages and thought to himself.

Momma always said, if you don't feed the love of another woman, eventually it would die. But for some reason, starving this woman of my attention aint working.

He grabbed the remote, turned off the movie, and got a shower. About twenty minutes later, he got in bed and fell asleep. Minutes later be began tossing and turning.

Patrice walked into the church, knocked on Janelle's door, walked over to her desk, and took a seat.

He woke up in a sweat.

"I got to tell Janelle everything before Patrice decides to tell her."

He looked over at her.

"Baby, I pray it doesn't hurt you."

Chapter Twenty-Four

T he next day during his lunch break, Joshua sat at his desk. He shook his head at the thought of the dream from the night before and pulled up a new word document to type out his letter. Slowly twirling his wedding band around his finger, he couldn't help but think about how his words would break his wife's heart all over again. He twirled his chair around and grabbed a bottle of water from his mini refrigerator, took a sip, and softly whispered to himself.

"Man, I never thought for a second that I would have to revisit this, but hey, there's no turning back now. No more secrets. I can't keep hiding things like this from my wife. I don't need anything else to come back and haunt me. I just hope she understands."

Twenty minutes later, he printed out his letter, sealed it in an envelope, and locked it in his desk drawer.

A few hours later, Janelle arrived to work, walked into her office and called her husband.

"Hello."

"Hey, I just wanted you to know I made it to work."

"Alright. I'm headed to a meeting, so, I'll call you later. I love you."

"Love you too."

Later that day, she walked over to her desk, sat down, and opened a word document. She wondered if Joshua had completed his assignment. She mumbled to herself.

"Come on Janelle. Get it together girl. Don't get distracted worrying about what Joshua's writing. Just let your heart speak. It can't be that hard."

She fumbled the pearls that graced her neck back and forth and began typing. A couple of hours later, she printed out her letter, sealed it as instructed, placed it in her purse, and met Sandra at her house.

In the meanwhile, on the other side of town at work, Joshua finished his paperwork for the day and headed home. Before getting on the highway, he stopped at their local pharmacy near the house and grabbed Janelle's favorite items. He reached for his phone and called her.

"Hello."

"Hey, I'm here at the pharmacy up the street. I grabbed some ice-cream—"

"I hope you got—"

He chuckled.

"Cookie dough ice cream and mango juice."

She smiled.

"You really think you know me don't you."

He walked towards the register.

"I do. I'll see you in a minute."

She looked over at Sandra.

"Hey, Sandra's here."

"Aint Brian off today? Never mind. Just ask Ms. Greedy is she eating ice-cream too?"

She laughed and looked over at Sandra.

"Ms. Greedy, are you eating ice-cream?"

Sandra laughed.

"No and tell Joshua to shut up."

"Josh, she said no."

"Alright, I should be there in about ten or fifteen minutes. Tell Sandra I need her to vacate the premises by the time I get home."

"See you then Josh. Be careful."

"Aight."

Sandra reached for her purse.

"Janelle, thank you for letting me borrow your ears. I really needed this."

"Girl, anytime. That's what friends are for."

Sandra walked towards the door and smiled.

"Let me get home so you can have some time with your husband."

"Girl stop... I'll call you later."

Sandra opened her car door, got in, and let the down window.

"Okay, I'm on vacation this week anyway."

A few minutes later, Joshua pulled up and saw Janelle outside in her car.

"You about to leave?"

"No. Sandra just left. I was getting my things out of the car and you pulled up just in time to help."

They grabbed the things out of the car and walked in the house and enjoyed the rest of the evening eating ice-cream and watching a movie.

Chapter Twenty-Five

T he next evening, Brian and Joshua decided to meet at the bar and catch up on life. Joshua looked over at Brian.

"Hey man. I called off the divorce. Janelle and I are back in counseling and I find it rather interesting."

Brian looked at Joshua and sucked his teeth.

"Man, aint nothing interesting about counseling."

He gently rubbed his chin.

"We had to write each other a letter admitting to relying on the other to fill empty voids... And we had to open up about any secrets we were hiding. I spilled out my heart man. I told her things thought I would never speak about again."

"Man, you a sucker, being all emotional and stuff. She read the letter yet?"

"Not yet. So, you telling me that expressing myself makes me weak. Brian, my wife pregnant man."

He laughed.

"Pretty much. All I'm saying is, you making all that money at the office. You can afford a little child support."

"You got to be kidding me right. I knew not to meet you at the bar."

"Man look, women cause us a lot of unnecessary stress. They always wanting to talk and I aint no counselor. You know, psychology is for the people that either talk too much or they just straight up nosey and I aint sign up for that."

"Brian, I'm learning how to communicate my likes and dislikes to my wife through counseling. You should try it."

"I'm gone try that."

He smiled.

"You pay for the sessions and I'll just learn from you."

Joshua laughed as Brian ordered his drink.

"Josh for real man, don't listen to me. I'm all about finding a reason to laugh."

He took a sip of his drink.

"That's the only way I know to deal with life without it stressing me out. You doing the right thing."

Joshua shook his head.

"I wasn't listening to you anyway. I called you because I needed a good laugh. So, whatever man. What you getting to eat?"

He scanned the menu and looked up.

"I don't know. It depends on who picking up the ticket."

Joshua pointed at him and laughed.

"I'm good. You got the ticket this time. Stop being so cheap."

He laughed.

"Let me see what they got on the kid's menu, because even they appetizers too high in here."

Joshua laughed.

"Hey man. In all seriousness, I was watching Joel Osteen the other night and decided to accept Jesus into my life."

Brian looked over at Joshua.

"Let me ask you something man."

"What Brian."

"Did you get saved for me too?"

He shook his head.

"You need help man."

Brian laughed.

"Nah man. I'm playing. I'm proud of you."

After ordering their food and eating, they sat at the bar for a few more hours laughing and watching the game. Brian's phone rang. He looked down at the phone and shook his head.

"Josh, I got to get home man. Sandra done started blowing up the phone. Every time I leave home, she start trippin."

"If you stop flirting so much, you wouldn't have that problem."

"Nah man, women expensive these days and when they find out you ain't leaving your wife, they start snitchin. I aint got no time for that. Sandra cause me enough stress by herself... No need to add more."

Joshua laughed. "Aight man. I'm about to get out of here too."

Chapter Twenty-Six

A week later, Janelle and Joshua got ready for counseling. As they were about to leave, she ran back to the bedroom to get her letter and put it in her purse. She got in the car, put on her seatbelt, and looked over at him.

"Hey, do you have your letter?"

He started the car and looked at her.

"Actually, I need to stop by the office really quick and grab it."

"Oh, okay."

She pulled out her phone to play Candy Crush. Ten minutes later, he pulled into the parking lot in front of his office and walked in to get the letter from his desk. He walked by the receptionist and smiled.

"Good afternoon."

The receptionist looked up.

"How are you today Mr. Richards?"

"I'm great. Have I had any calls today?"

She reached for her message pad.

"Yes sir, you have. A lady called, but she didn't leave a name. She just said that she would call you later."

His brows met.

"Okay. Did you transfer the call to my desk so that she could leave a message?"

"No sir, but her voice did sound familiar. She's called here before. I never forget a voice."

"Okay. Thank you."

He walked to his office, retrieved his letter, and walked back towards the front entrance. He looked back.

"Have a good day."

She looked at him suspiciously and smirked.

"You too Mr. Richards."

Ten minutes later, they arrived to their session early. He looked over at his wife.

"Are you nervous?"

"A little. Why?"

"Because I am."

"Oh."

Minutes later, they walked into the office, Joshua signed their name and waited nervously to be called. As Mrs. Chambers prepared for their session, she took the time to whisper a prayer.

"Lord Jesus I know that these letters can possibly cause a little turmoil. So, please intervene and take over their hearts and minds. Lock out all confusion and guide this session for me that peace rest upon all of our hearts. I know You can heal this marriage. In Your Son's name, Amen."

Moments later, the counselor opened her door

"Good afternoon Mr. and Mrs. Richards. You can come back now."

Holding hands, they walked in and took a seat. The counselor sat down, reached for her tea, and smiled.

"Well, I'm pretty sure the both of you are curious as to what the other had to say. So, I won't prolong your wait."

As the counselor crossed her legs, they looked at her and back at each other.

"So, which of you would like to begin?"

Janelle looked at her husband and shrugged her shoulders.

"It doesn't matter. I can go first."

She handed Joshua the letter from his wife.

"Mr. and Mrs. Richards, in order to complete this assignment, you must first be willing to listen to your spouse's heart and not just the words in the letter. Stay in the moment, keep an open mind, and of course no interruptions. Remember, this is a part of the process to help heal your marriage."

Joshua slowly tapped the end of the envelope, opened the letter, and began to read.

Joshua,

Before I begin, I want to thank you for deciding to give our marriage another chance. My heart broke into pieces when you handed me the divorce papers and it made me feel as though I had failed you and our marriage. Let me explain why. When I first met you, I was vulnerable, lonely, and just getting over my ex. I didn't understand why things didn't work for he and I, but I also knew that it wasn't in God's plan for me to be his wife. Although, I knew he wasn't right for me, I continued to deal with the disrespect until I was tired and fed up with it. I spoke to Sandra about how I felt and she reminded me that my relationship with God was more important than rushing into another relationship.

True enough, I teach The Word of God, but I struggled hard with being lonely until I met you. I tried to give you perfection, but of course I failed miserably. Everything you did and said made me so happy and I began relying on you for peace and happiness instead of God. *That was never a load for you to carry. He intended for me to give Him my heavy loads and burdens so that I could receive true happiness and peace from His Son Jesus and for that I'm sorry.* The hardest thing for me right now is admitting that I sought after you for happiness that you couldn't give me. When you didn't give me what my heart desired, I became so frustrated with you.

My expectations of you superseded human nature. I wanted you to become the cement to fill broken and empty places within me. Reality is, God gave you to me as my husband, not as my doctor, not to fill voids only He could fill, not to erase the pain from another man, not to satisfy my flesh, but for you to love me the way He intended for a husband to love his wife. I can admit that because you didn't hold us down spiritually the way that I expected, I decided to make you the neck and me the head instead of trusting God to guide you to make the right decisions for us. You know this was something I saw my grandmother do and I adopted this behavior as my own.

Although I knew counting your wrongs and unforgiveness were wrong, it felt good to constantly remind you of the hurt that you were causing me. I'm realizing that it takes a strong woman to let things go and a prideful woman to hold on to the past for dear life as if it were oxygen. I would hear God tell me that love covered a multitude of sin, but it pleased my flesh for you to see and feel the pain you were causing me. If only I had admitted to this in the beginning instead of ignoring my mistakes, we wouldn't be in this place now, but I guess everything happens for a reason and this is just another lesson learned for me. Forgiveness towards you is now my new solution to letting go.

God has been and still is teaching me how to submit to you as my husband and it hasn't been fun at all, but it has surely been a learning experience. Please know that God is making me to be the wife you need and the wife you can love. I want you to be okay with being honest with me without fearing that it will lead to an argument. I'm open to that now.

Reality is many times I will fail both you and I because I am a woman being molded and many times remolded by God so that I can be all that He created me to be. I thought I was hurting you with the silent treatments until Ms. Lula confronted me one day. She was like 'Janelle, do you honestly believe you're hurting that man when you don't talk to him? You know men get tired of hearing women talk anyway.' I laughed because I knew she was right. I wish that I could turn back the time and meet you all over again to do things the right way. But today, I vow to do better not only as a child of God, but as your wife. I look forward to seeing the ugliness in our marriage transform into something beautiful.

You no longer have to be my superhero.
Love Your wife Janelle

Chapter Twenty-Seven

S ilence held the room captive after he read his wife's letter and that's exactly what the counselor wanted. She wanted to prick their hearts with an honesty that would cause them to reevaluate their thoughts and love for one another. She turned her attention to Joshua.

"Mr. Richards, please hand your wife your envelope."

He was a little hesitant, but he handed his wife his letter. She opened the envelope and began reading.

Janelle,

Where do I begin? First off, I'm sorry for the way I've been handling things lately. You never deserved to be treated the way I've treated you. You've always given this marriage one hundred percent, but I always found a way to make you feel as if you didn't. I want to thank you for living a Godly life before me. Just know even when I don't tell you, I'm watching. Pride held my tongue and it didn't help when your humility fed it. I thought your humbleness was a sign of weakness, but now I know that it was simply your strength. I'm sorry for thinking you were trying to be prefect, when you were only trying to please God.

Janelle, I came from a broken family and I've always been embarrassed to talk about it, but I'm now learning that it's important to deal with generational issues when brining two different families together, so it doesn't enter our marriage and carry on to our child. I grew up watching the way my dad treated my mom and he would always tell me. "What one woman won't do, another will." So, I never learned how to properly and respectfully love a woman the way she needed to be loved. I watched my friends and tried to learn from them, but it's kind of hard trying to mimic what you see and it's not really in your heart.

I realize now that I'm an imperfect man displaying an illusion of perfect love. Baby, truth is, I don't know how to love you, but if you'll let me, I'll try hard to give you the love that you deserve. I heard you talk about the biblical love, but in my mind, that doesn't exist in the world we live in. You may be wondering did I ever love you and truth is when were engaged I lusted for you and confused it with love. My way of erasing mistakes was to do away with things as my father did and the way he taught me to deal with life, love, and marriage wasn't the best example. I'm pretty sure that someone taught him what he taught me. Truth is, I hated what I saw, but reality is the one person I didn't want to become, I see manifesting every day in my life. I just want to be able to break whatever negative cycle this is in my life that it doesn't flow to our child and so on. I never told you, so now is the time to let the secrets out of the bag since we're back in counseling.

My ex that you met at the hospital was once pregnant and we agreed to have an abortion. God gave me a child with her and we chose to abort it. So, I'm sorry for making you feel guilty during the time you couldn't conceive. I'm sorry that I shared our issues with her.

Janelle's lips parted as she stopped and looked over at him. He took a deep breath and looked down as she continued to read his letter.

I really thought that she had our best interest at heart until I realized that she was still in love with me. I wish I could erase all of the hurt in your heart right now, but I can't. I thought God was punishing me, but your faith is a faith that allowed me to see the manifestation of my prayers finally answered. Patrice and I were also engaged at one point and it was me who messed that up. I foolishly decided to cheat on her with my ex before her and my guilty conscious never allowed me to disconnect from her, so that's why you saw her at the hospital. I'm sorry that you had to meet her that way. I never expected her to show up, but she did. Janelle, baby I have NEVER cheated on you sexually, but emotionally, she fed me what I thought you couldn't.

Her conversations soothed me when I was angry with you. She made me laugh and I cherished that until I realized how it all was hurting you. I looked at it as a friendly gesture, but either way, it didn't make our communicating right. My conscience would always tell me that I was wrong, but I ignored it.

Janelle, I'm sorry for hurting you. A man who doesn't truly love himself can't love his wife the way she needs to be loved. Liquor and running has always been the way that I dealt with my issues. No one ever taught me differently and it seems as though everything in my personal life lately is spiraling out of control. Just please bear with me, I know I can get better.

I'm sorry that I allowed my father's past to creep into our marriage. I can no longer hold him and his examples responsible for my actions because it's taking a toll on our marriage. So, today I

141

forgive him for the way he treated my mom. I forgive myself for the way I treated her. I even pray that someday she can forgive me. My grandma would always say, 'The way you treat your mom is the way you will treat another woman.' The sad thing is that I didn't believe her until now. It hurts knowing that my mom never deserved the disrespect I had towards her. I am learning that although we are financially stable, that money can't take pain away, it can't buy love, and it surely can't mend a broken marriage back together again. Only Jesus can do that for us and baby I need for Him to be the glue that holds us together right now. I never want our child to experience living in a divided home. I don't want our child to ever disrespect you the way I did my mother and the respect has to first start with me. I want our child to feel love throughout our home, not conflict and division. Janelle baby, I know that when you love, you love hard and I thank you so much for loving someone as imperfect as me.

Love,
Joshua Richards

Chapter Twenty-Eight

T he counselor sensed the awkwardness and interjected.
"Thank you both for completing this assignment. I understand that it may have been challenging writing the letters and even more challenging reading them... I remember when my husband and I had to complete this assignment. So, believe me when I say, I know that it wasn't easy. My goal for this assignment was to interrupt every lie the enemy had planted in your minds and hearts about each other to rip your marriage apart. You see, we don't need to fight each other, because the thing you're both dealing with is spiritual and your letters were the spiritual fire extinguisher to put out every one of the devil's lies. Sometimes when you're going through things in your marriage your spouse seems to be the enemy instead of the one you can't see."

His brows furrowed.

"Mrs. Chambers, that was deep."

His eyes were finally opened to the manipulative words the enemy would whisper to him about his wife. He realized it was a trap designed to tear them apart. In fact, it was his past that the enemy wanted him to suppress so that he could be in the driver's seat of their marriage instead of God.

Mrs. Chambers took a sip of tea.

"Part three of this session will require digging past the pain to find love again; therefore, I would like for you both to visit the place where you first met or maybe take a walk in the park."

She walked towards the park.

"Mrs. Richards, remember, you're with child, so enjoy your husband and please don't dwell on the letters... That would only bring about stress and the spiritual fire you just put out will find a way to burn again. Just know that takes discipline."

"Starting right now."

She looked at her schedule.

"Will the same time and day work for you both next week?"

Joshua's brows met.

"4:30 p.m. works better for me, so that I won't have to leave work too early."

She looked down at her calendar.

"How about 5 p.m.?

"Yes ma'am. That will work just fine."

"Perfect. I look forward to our next session."

She smiled once more.

"When you leave, remember to enjoy your day."

Janelle looked back at the counselor.

"Thank you. Have a great day Mrs. Chambers."

"You as well."

She pointed towards Janelle and smiled.

"Don't dwell on the letters. Trust me, I've been in those shoes before."

Janelle smiled as they walked out the door.

"Yes ma'am."

After leaving their session, they drove in silence. So, Joshua decided to take Janelle out for dinner to the restaurant where they first met. He knew being in a peaceful environment would take her mind off his confessions for a while. Ten minutes later,

144

they pulled up to the restaurant. Getting out of the car, he heard someone call his name.

"Yo! Joshua."

Janelle tapped his shoulder as he scanned the parking lot. She folded her arms and chuckled.

"Lookie lookie whose hear Josh."

With a firm grip, he shook his hand.

"Man, what ya'll doing here?"

"Um, to do the same thing you about to do... Eat."

Joshua shook his head.

"What's up Sandra. You can't speak?"

"Hey Josh."

Brian looked at him.

"So, how about a double date? I need one because Sandra being real extra today because I worked late."

Brian pointed towards her and back to himself.

"She knows that she don't want us to be in the dark, so, she need to chill out. I got to work to pay the bills, right."

Joshua laughed as Sandra rolled her eyes.

"Sounds good to me. What you think Janelle?"

"If it's okay with Sandra. I don't mind."

Brian smiled.

"So, was that the look you were really going for today Janelle?"

She rolled her eyes.

"Shut up Brian."

She grabbed Sandra by the arm.

"Let's go eat."

After being seated and making their orders, they ate and laughed the evening away until Brian reached for the ticket. All eyes locked in on him.

"What ya'll looking at?"

He looked at Joshua.

"You know what Josh, I got the ticket tonight. I owe you one for saving my ears from an hour or so of hearing..."

He looked over at his wife.

"Sandra nag and complain."

He pointed to Joshua.

"You the man tonight."

She looked at Brian.

"You men kill me with saying that women nag. I bet you some bitter old man avoiding confrontation came up with that and now ya'll just running with it. Reality is what you call nagging is simply a woman repeating what she's said to you over and over again, but you insist on doing the same thing."

She looked to her right.

"Am I right Janelle?"

She laughed.

"Sandra, I thought I was the only person who felt that way, but I guess not."

Sandra softly tapped the side of her right temple. "Girl it's all about perception." She turned towards her husband. "Brian can I ask you ask question?"

"No."

"What do you mean no?"

He looked at Joshua and back to his wife.

"You see, Joshua told me that I need to work on communicating my likes and dislikes."

Her lips parted as she shook her head.

"What are you talking about? I only asked you a question Brian."

"I know. That's the problem."

He pointed his hand to his chest and back towards her with a smile.

"I'm trying to communicate to you that I don't like when you ask me questions all the time."

He laughed.

"You know you ask too many questions, right."

Joshua shook his head and chuckled.

"Brian, you stupid man. You know you gotta go home right."

"Whatever man."

Ending a night of fun and laughter, they arrived home a little after nine. Janelle yawned and looked over at her husband.

"I'm about to get a shower and go to sleep. I'm really tired."

He placed his wallet and phone on the end table.

"Okay. What time you leaving for work in the morning?"

"I might just leave at eight thirty or nine. I'm not sure yet."

Walking towards the bedroom, she turned around.

"Thank you for this evening. It felt like old times again especially with Sandra and Brian."

She smiled.

"Good night."

A smiled graced his face. "I enjoyed you too. Good night babe."

He rubbed his head as he walked away.

"Man, I dodged that bullet tonight."

Chapter Twenty-Nine

T wo days later, Janelle sat on the sofa thinking about Joshua's letter from their last session. She got up and walked into his man cave and sat next to him.

"Hey."

"What's up."

"Josh, I've tried hard not to think about your letter or even bring it up, but why couldn't you just tell me all of those things about you and your ex before we got serious?"

He adjusted himself in the chair.

"Because I knew it would hurt you. So, I never said anything... Besides, I didn't want to deal with it myself. I just wanted to forget about the broken engagement and the abortion and move on. I figured since it was in the past, it wouldn't affect our marriage."

She lowered her head.

"Josh, it wouldn't have hurt so bad had you just told me in the beginning. I remember our first conversation as if it were yesterday. You said you weren't the type of guy to play games. I know you remember that because I do."

He leaned over on the arm of the chair and looked over at her.

"I'm sorry. Babe that was over three years ago and you still remember it? I guess it's true that women don't forget anything."

"Really... I think it's funny that you say that. I guess I can say the same for you. The problem is you only remember what you want to throw in my face. You seemed to remember to remind me that I had three years to inform you of what you called my infertility."

He scoffed.

"Janelle, I don't want to argue with you or anyone else for that matter."

"I bet you don't and I'm not arguing. I'm simply communicating to you how I feel. I can't walk around as if I'm okay with everything you wrote in that letter."

His brows furrowed.

"Where is your spiritual fire extinguisher Janelle?"

She pursed her lips.

"Whatever. It hurt having to read about something you could've told me face to face."

She held up three fingers.

"Over three years ago."

"Babe, I'm sorry. I just want us to be okay. You're right. I should've told you and I'm sorry that I didn't."

A slight smile graced her face.

"I'm not trying to make you feel guilty. I just want you to see that had you told me before we were serious, this wouldn't even be an issue right now. Having to read that in a letter literally made my heart drop to my stomach. I've been hurt before, but it's different when you find things out the way I did from the man you married. I mean I accept your apology and forgive you, but I'm asking you from this day forward to be honest with me. Can you do that?"

He looked at her with gentle eyes.

"Okay. Since you said it that way, I get it. I don't want you stressing about anything. Let's focus on the baby right now. Can we do that?"

She got up from the sofa.

"You're right. I'm going to let you get back to your game."

He smirked.

"If you need me. I'll be right here in my supposed to be man cave."

She laughed.

"Okay."

Chapter Thirty

A week Later, they arrived to their next counseling session. Realizing they were five minutes late, Janelle walked into the office and signed in while her husband parked the car and fed the meter.

"Good afternoon. Please forgive us. We were stuck in traffic."

The secretary smiled.

"Mrs. Richards, it's perfectly find. Mrs. Chambers is on her way from a meeting. She should be here any moment now."

About two minutes later, Mrs. Chambers and Joshua walked into the office together. He looked over at his wife.

"Look who I found feeding the meter while I was parking the car."

Mrs. Chambers smiled.

"I do apologize for my tardiness. I see that we're all running a little late this afternoon. Traffic is pretty bad out there. You both can come back now."

She took a minute to put her things down and called for the secretary to bring her a cup of hot tea with a slice of lemon and honey. She hung up the phone, grabbed her note pad, and sat down in her chair.

"How are you both doing today?"

Janelle looked over at Joshua and smiled.

"Were doing great. Thank you for asking. How are you?"

She observed the couple as she put on her glasses.

"I'm doing great. I'm sure that you both will appreciate the insight that I will give you from today's session. Our last session was very interesting because you both had to read each other's thoughts and hearts from the letters you wrote. So, this afternoon I will begin with the head of the house and not the neck."

She looked over at Janelle and smiled.

"Mrs. Richards, it took guts to admit that."

She looked back at Joshua.

"Mr. Richards, I would like to ask you what is the one thing that your wife does that frustrates you?"

He looked over at his wife and thought to himself.

Why would she ask me this question and we're in a good space right now?

Mrs. Chambers got the response she expected.

"I know that you don't understand my counseling strategies, but every question that I ask has a purpose. Mr. Richards, I'm intrigued by thought provoking questions and how they expose things like your fear of confrontation. I've noticed that you constantly avoid conversing your dislikes with your wife, but want you to understand that if your wife is unaware of what frustrates you, she'll never know what to ask God to help her to change. It's like, if I call for my secretary to bring me hot tea and she brings me coffee, it will continue if I never say anything, right; however, if I bring it to her attention in a loving way, she'll see her mistakes and correct them. When I do this, I diffuse conflict and confusion before it takes root."

"Hmmmm. I never would've thought of it like that, but since you put it that way, I hate when my wife brings up the past. It's like when will she ever forgive me for my mistakes. She doesn't do it as often as she used to, but she still does it from time to time."

The counselor took notes and glanced over as Janelle gazed out of the window.

"Mrs. Richards is there anything that your husband does to cause you to bring up the past?"

She shook her head.

"Yes... like when he deletes messages from his phone. It almost makes me feel as though he has something to hide. And when I try to communicate how I feel about it, he interrupts me and turns it into an argument."

The counselor looked at Joshua.

"Every action causes a reaction... Mr. Richards, you have to understand that confronting issues aren't always bad, especially if there done the right way." She turned to his wife. "And Mrs. Richards, if you want your husband to let go of the past, you must do the same. Counseling can bring up some ugly situations, but it's only to bring your attention to the things that are potentially ripping your marriage apart. And communication is one of the problems in your marriage. Mrs. Richards are you willing to throw away your history book collection and trust again?"

She shrugged her shoulders.

"I guess."

She turned her attention to Joshua.

"Are you willing to communicate your feelings and be honest about things that are really bothering you?"

He rubbed his nose.

"I don't have a problem with that."

"If you do this, I see your marriage going far and all of the ugliness will become beautiful once again."

He looked at the counselor.

"So, how do you suppose we fix this?"

"Well for starters, I would like for you both to practice trusting one another again. Mrs. Richards give your husband your heart that he once had and Mr. Richards please explain to your wife why you continue to delete messages from your phone."

He smiled.

"Wait a minute. What makes you think I'm deleting messages?"

The counselor waited for her response.

"Well, the other night when you received a text message, you assumed I was asleep, but the notifications from your phone woke me up and I watched as you read and deleted them. And when you looked back at me. I closed my eyes."

"Mr. Richards."

He shook his head.

"But, I never responded to her."

Mrs. Chambers injected.

"Mr. Richards, who is her?"

He looked away.

"My ex."

Janelle shook her head.

"I already knew who it was."

The counselor observed Joshua's body language.

"Mr. Richards, avoiding things has become a norm for you, but in order for things to change, you have to confront the very things that you think will go away on its own. You've brainwashed yourself into believing that if you ignore a situation, it'll go away... You must be willing to break the negative cycles you witnessed growing up."

She crossed her legs.

"Have you asked your ex to stop all communication and respect your marriage?"

"Actually, I haven't. We have so much history and I don't want to hurt her."

His wife shook her head as the counselor continued.

"I see that history in this marriage is a big problem."

She took off her glasses.

"Each time you allow your ex to text you, it hurts your wife and your inability to respectfully demand her to stop, isn't helping. Playing with one's emotions, is a dangerous game. And your ex is your past. Scripture says forget the things of the past and look at the new thing He's doing. Mr. Richards, your wife is your new thing."

She chuckled.

"We have way too many uncertified historians in this world and I used to be one of them, but I decided that it wasn't worth it. So, I made peace with my past because it was affecting my mind, body, spirit, and marriage. And let's not forget that once I threw my husband's past mistakes away, it made marriage a lot easier. Letting go was a blessing in disguise."

She slightly tilted her head.

"You know division and a lack of communication actually blocks blessings."

She handed Janelle a kleenex and looked at her husband.

"Mr. Richards, if you would allow yourself to be completely honest with your wife, you'll discover a whole new level of happiness in your life and your marriage... You don't have to allow your past to win. It seems hard, but if you trust the process, I promise that things will get better."

She took a sip of tea.

"Just one more question Mr. Richards. Please tell your wife why you didn't respond to your ex."

He looked over at his wife.

"I didn't respond because I figured if I didn't entertain her, she would eventually stop and she did. Her messages can be kind of random at times."

He reached for her hand.

"Baby, I love you and I promise I haven't been responding to her messages."

She pulled her hand away.

"But Joshua, why is it that I have to hear all of the things you don't like about me, but you never say what you don't like about her? That's not fair... Or should I ask if you're hiding anything else?"

His brows creased as she continued.

"She has the right to hear the truth. You're playing a dangerous game and if I end up hurt because of you, it's going to be a big problem and I'm not sure if I'll be able to forgive you."

The counselor intervened. "Mr. Richards, do you understand the dangers of leading your ex on? You know... someone could get hurt if she's emotionally unstable."

"No. I didn't think about it like that."

Janelle looked at her husband.

"I need for you to think of possible outcomes and make the right decision. Either way, someone will end up hurt. Would you prefer it be me?"

"Babe no. Okay, I'll deal with it."

Mrs. Chambers brows met.

"If you handle it respectfully and the right way, it will work out Mr. Richards. You're going to have to pray and ask God for guidance on this one. We ran a little over our time today." She walked to her desk. "Your next session will be in two weeks. Is that fine?"

Joshua scratched his chin.

"I mean, back to back counseling seems expensive and I'm just —."

She interrupted him and tilted her glasses.

"Mr. Richards, before you interrupted me I was going to say that your next session will be on me. This is not about money."

She looked down at the schedule book.

"This is about saving a marriage from divorce and an unborn child from entering into a divided home. How does five-thirty sound?"

Janelle smiled.

"It's fine with me. I can meet my husband here after work since he's closest to you."

Joshua stood up.

"That works for me. By the way, I'm sorry for my assumptions"

She smiled.

"It's okay. One last thing. Your assignment tonight will be to go home, practice what we've discussed, make peace with your past, and lay them to rest. Don't give it the power to destroy you or your marriage."

She smiled once more.

"I look forward to your next session."

Chapter Thirty-One

J oshua opened the door for his wife. As he got in the car, she stared at him with concern.

"What? I know that look."

Her phone rang.

"Hello."

"Good afternoon. May I speak with Mrs. Richards."

"This is she. May I ask whose calling?"

He turned towards her and listened attentively.

"This is Ms. Retner with Dr. Somediv's office. I'm calling to schedule your appointment for your ultrasound."

"Okay."

His eyes penetrated her soul. He couldn't shake the fact that her answers were so short.

"We have an appointment available tomorrow morning at eight or ten. Would you to like to schedule for one of those times?

She smiled.

"Ten o'clock will work."

Joshua felt a sense of relief.

"Thank you. Please be sure to come thirty minutes early to complete your paper work. We'll see you then. Have a good day."

"You as well."

She ended the call.

"Why you staring at me like that?"

He laughed.

"I was trying to figure out who you were talking."

She smirked.

"Josh, could it be that your past is taunting you. I don't have the time or energy to entertain another man. That was the doctor's office scheduling my appointment for my ultrasound."

He started the car.

"Whatever! When is it?"

"Looks like I hit a nerve. It's in the morning at ten."

He mumbled.

"You trippin talking about my past taunting me."

"Did you say something?"

"Nope. But I won't be able to go because I have court in the morning? That's crazy. I won't get to hear my baby's heartbeat or see what we're having."

"Joshua it's okay. I just found out that I was pregnant a month ago, so we won't find out anyway."

"Ooooh. Okay."

"Josh, I promise it's okay."

"Okay, but next time I'm going."

"Alright. Can we stop by the seafood market to get some shrimp?"

"Sure."

Shortly after arriving home, Janelle changed and prepared dinner for later that evening. She yelled out from the kitchen.

"Joshua."

He yelled back.

"Yeah."

She opened the bag and put the shrimp in the sink.

"Can you come cut up the onions and peppers for me?"

"Alright. Give me a second. Let me change."

"What you say, I didn't hear you?"

He yelled from the room.

"Give me a second."

"Oh, okay."

He walked in the kitchen and reached for the onions.

"The red one or the sweet Vidalia?"

"Both."

He shook his head.

"You trippin."

She laughed as she cleaned the shrimp and reached over for the sweet peppers. Minutes later, Joshua heard his phone ringing and ran to the room to get it.

"Hello."

"What's up man."

"Nothing. Just helping Janelle prep the food for dinner."

"You think you can meet me at the bar?"

"Yeah. Just give me about thirty minutes."

She called out to her husband as she put the pasta in the boiling water.

"Josh."

"Yeah."

"Can you help me really quick?"

"Yeah, but I'm about to go the bar and hang out with Brian and have a few drinks."

Her lips parted. "So, Brian is more important than me?

"What you mean Janelle?"

"I'm about to cook and now I have to wait for you to come back from the bar. If you invested the time in me and your marriage as you do the bar and Brian, we'd be okay."

"Come on Janelle, do you really have to start this? Every time I want to go somewhere, you got something to say."

"Oh, and I thought you stopped drinking."

"I mean I have, I'm only gonna have one drink."

She deeply exhaled. "Whatever, just be careful."

He leaned in to kiss her on her forehead, but she moved away.

"I'll be back in time for dinner."

"Alright."

He got in the car and met Brian down at the bar. As he pulled up, he saw Brian get out of his car with the phone to his ear. It appeared that he was arguing. He hung up the phone as Joshua walked towards him.

"What's up man?"

"Women. I'm telling you, I don't understand them. I can't do anything right when it comes to Sandra."

"Man, tell me about it."

They walked inside and took a seat. Brian looked at the bar tender.

"Can I get two long island ice teas with double shots?"

Before the bar tender could bring their drinks, the man from the counseling session sat next to them. He looked over to make sure it was him. The guy turned to him.

"What's up."

Joshua's brows furrowed.

"You the guy from the counselor's office, right?"

Brian looked over, shook his head, and whispered to Joshua.

"So, you telling me... That all of us got women issues?"

They laughed as Joshua turned and looked at Brian.

"Man, whatever."

He turned back to the young man and pointed.

"That was you right."

He took a deep breath. "Yeah, that was me. That counselor was trippin. She was in there digging up dead stuff from my past."

Brian laughed.

"I may not go to church all the time, but it sounds like she pulled that Ezekiel on you and told them dead bones to live again."

Joshua laughed.

"Man, you stupid."

He looked back at the young man.

"I'm sorry man... Don't listen to him. What were you saying?"

The guy took a sip of his drink and shook his head.

"My wife is forever talking about God this and God that... I aint into to all that stuff. Too many fake Christians out here for me and I'm sick of hearing her nag."

Brian listened attentively as they continued. Joshua extended his hand towards him.

"My name is Joshua and this is my friend Brian."

"My bad. My name is Mike."

"Nice to meet you. So, how old are you?"

"Twenty-nine."

"Look, I'm not trying to change your mind about counseling, but Mrs. Chambers is a really good at what she does. I remember the first time I walked out on my wife during counseling."

Brian laughed and shook his head as Joshua continued.

"You should give it a try. I mean the first few sessions can be pretty deep, but after you get over that hump, it gets a little better."

Mike reached for his shot glass and took a sip.

"I feel you, but it was like she was speaking about stuff I thought my wife forgot all about. Like she asked. 'What brings you to counseling?' When my wife told her about the baby I have by another woman, I just flipped out. I don't even drink and I'm sitting here at the bar with ya'll."

Brian laughed and extended his hand to Mike.

"Welcome to the fraternity young brother."

Joshua looked over at Brian and shook his head.

"Look Mike, I know you may feel some kind of way about counseling and God. I did too at one point, but you know, He aint that bad."

"Who?"

"God... I mean, you can't let other Christians and what they do predict your relationship with Him. I mean I aint perfect, but I'm learning a lot from the counselor and my wife. I'm even learning to respectfully communicate my likes and dislikes with her. The key word is... learning. You should try it man."

Mike looked at him.

"So, you saved."

"Yeah and I wouldn't change it for the world."

Brian placed his hand on Joshua's shoulder.

"You know what man. I want to be saved too."

He moved his hand. "Man, you gotta joke about everything."

"Naw, but Pastor Josh, you just won my heart man."

Mike took a sip of his drink.

"I mean; I guess I can give the counseling thing another try."

"What about God?"

"What you mean?"

Joshua shrugged his shoulders.

"Don't rush it, but when you're ready, you should give Him a try. He's the glue to your marriage."

Brian smiled.

"And He gone save our souls from hell for sitting in here talking about our wives."

Mike laughed as he got up and firmly shook Joshua's hand.

"Thanks for the talk."

He looked over at Brian and extended his hand.

"And the laugh."

Brian smiled.

"Anytime man."

Joshua reached into his wallet and handed Mike one of his business cards.

"Aight man. Good luck."

Brian sat down and leaned back on the stool.

"So, you turning bars in to pulpit's now?"

Joshua smacked his lips.

"Man, please shut up."

Chapter Thirty-Two

Later that evening, Janelle sat at the table and talked to Joshua while they ate dinner. With her right hand, she twirled her fork in the pasta and opened wide attempting to put the noodles in her mouth, but a noodle along with a little Italian dressing escaped from her lips.

He laughed.

"I take it that you need a bib right."

She gently rubbed the side of her mouth with a napkin.

"Whatever Josh."

"So, are you excited about the ultrasound and hearing the baby's heartbeat for the first time?

He took a sip of tea.

"I mean, who wouldn't be? I just hate I can't go. You know, one of the contract lawyers at work said that nothing could ever compare to being able to see your child on the monitor for the first time. I really hate I'm gonna to miss it."

Her eyes smiled.

"Josh, you'll always have next time."

"If it's a boy—"

"If it's a girl."

They laughed as she got up from the table.

"You got the dishes tonight."

He winked his left eye.

"Anything for you baby."

She shook her head.

"Whatever."

She went into the bedroom, scanned the closet for something to wear, and yawned.

"Sleep is calling my name and I must answer. I'll find something to wear in the morning."

As she got in the bed, Joshua walked in the room.

"So, you just gone get in the bed without showering right."

She pulled the covers up.

"Really, I showered earlier."

"Let me smell under your arms."

"You really think your funny, don't you?"

He smiled.

"I am funny. There's no denying that." He pointed towards her. "Oh. Did you find something to wear yet? You know you."

She rolled over.

"No. Find something for me."

He looked at her.

"Oh, you just full sarcasm tonight huh."

"I learned from the best.... Did I get it right?"

He took off his shoes.

"Hey. You remember the guy from the counseling session that stormed out?"

"Yeah. Why?"

"He was at the bar tonight."

"So, did you talk to him."

"You know I can't break the man code. Men don't gossip. I can't be telling you all of that man business."

"What's that supposed to mean?"

"I can't tell you what was said, but I will say that I did talk to him about giving Mrs. Chambers and God a chance."

"Whatttt. Look at you."

"I must say, it felt good to encourage him to go back and fight for his marriage."

"I'm so proud of you."

"Oh, and I never even got a chance to have a drink either."

"Oh wow. You know God is looking down smiling at you, right."

He smiled.

"I got to get up early and you need to get some rest. Good night."

"Good night Josh."

Chapter Thirty-Three

T he next morning Joshua got dressed and prepared for the case he would be assisting one of the attorneys at the firm.

Janelle smiled.

"I guess I married the sexiest paralegal ever, huh."

He brushed his wavy hair and smiled.

"I guess so. Baby I got to get out of here. I got to be at the courthouse at eight."

"Okay. I'm gonna to head over to the office until it's time for my appointment."

"Alright. I love you."

She walked over and kissed him on the forehead while he sat at the end of the bed putting on his shoes.

"Love you too."

Shortly after nine, she headed over to the gynecologist office for her ultrasound. She walked in the office and smiled as she signed in.

"Good morning Mr. Richards."

"Good morning."

"We'll need a copy of your insurance card and i.d., please."

She reached in her wallet for her i.d., and insurance card, then handed it to the receptionist.

"Thank you. Please complete the highlighted areas and that will complete your process. If you don't finish by the time the tech calls for you, you can give it to her."

She smiled.

"Okay. Thank you."

She scanned the office and sat in the first seat she could find to complete her paper work. The lady next to her looked over at her with a smiled.

"Hi."

She returned a smile.

"Hi. How are you?"

"I'm great."

She looked over at Janelle as her heart smiled.

"So, what are you having?"

A wide smile graced her face. "I'm not sure. Today is my very first ultrasound. I just found out that I was pregnant a month ago."

"Oh, congratulations."

She looked towards the lady.

"Same to you. So, how far along are you and what are you having?"

"Today marks six months."

She smiled.

"And I'm having triplets. I chose not to know the sex of my babies because I want it to be a surprise."

Before she could respond, the ultrasound technician opened the door.

"Mrs. Janelle Richards."

As she got up and smiled, she looked over at the lady.

"Nice meeting you and congratulations. I pray there's only one inside of me."

The lady laughed.

"Have a good day."

"You too."

She handed the tech the clipboard as they entered the ultrasound room and sat on the table. The technician reached for the jelly. In her strong Kenyan accent, she looked over at Janelle.

"Good morning Mrs. Richards. This should be exciting for you since this is your first pregnancy."

She smiled.

"Yeah. I'm excited, but I'm also nervous."

"Well, you have nothing to worry about. Can I get you to lay back on the table and lift up your shirt to your breast please?

She slowly lifted her shirt.

"Do you think I'll know the sex of the baby today?"

She smiled.

"That depends on how far along you are and your child. Sometimes we get to see and sometimes they play with your emotions... I'm going to place this towel at the top of your pants and under your shirt so the gel won't get on your clothes. Are you ready?"

She smiled.

"I guess so."

She turned the ultrasound screen towards her and began.

"I'm going to start by taking some measurements and thennnn we're going to hear your child's heart beat for the first time."

Tears formed in her eyes as she looked at the screen, but it was the heartbeat that made her smile.

"Oh my God."

She rubbed her index finger underneath her nose.

The nurse handed her a Kleenex and smiled.

"I can feel your excitement."

"You know doctors told me this day would never happen, but look at God."

"Yes ma'am. God is amazing."

The ultrasound tech continued until the time to reveal the sex of the baby.

"Mrs. Richards, it looks like you're eighteen weeks and you're having..."

She pointed to the screen.

"Can you see?"

She placed her hands over her face and smiled.

"Oh my God. Joshua is going to freak out."

"Again, congratulations Mrs. Richards."

She fixed her clothes.

"Have a good day."

"You too Mrs. Richards."

She got in her car and smiled.

"How do I do this... Oh, I know."

She stopped by the store to purchase the items needed for the baby reveal and a card. After arriving to the office, she put some things in the trunk and walked inside. She sat down at her desk and began writing a poem in the card. A few hours later Pastor Peter walked in.

"Good afternoon Janelle."

"Hey Pastor. How are you?"

"I'm good. I just wanted to let you know that I'm leaving in about twenty minutes to take the Mrs to her appointment, but I'll be back shortly."

Her brows met.

"Okay. Is she alright?"

"Yes, she's doing better. You know prayer changes things."

"Yes sir."

"If you need me, just call."

"Okay."

Thirty minutes later, she went to the car, but it wouldn't start. She walked back into her office and called Joshua and thought to herself as the phone rang.

Hmmm. I could do the baby reveal now.

Before she ended the call, he answered with excitement in his voice.

"Hello. So, what are we having?".

"Hey. I need a jump off because my car isn't starting."

"How far along are you and what are we having?

She laughed.

"I want to tell you face to face."

"Janelle, you play too much. You got the jumper cables, right?"

"Yeah, but no one's here. Pastor just left thirty minutes ago."

"Okay. I was just leaving the courthouse, so I'll be there in five minutes."

Minutes later, she watched at the entrance as he pulled up. He got out of the car and looked at her.

"Hey babe get your keys and pop the trunk."

She looked at him and smiled as she pressed the button to open the trunk. When the trunk opened, pink and blue balloons escaped. He looked over at her.

"Girl or boy. Stop playing."

"I'll tell you when you jump my car off."

He reached for the jumper cables and hooked them to her car and then his. She walked towards him and handed him the card while she got in her car and waited for the battery to charge. He opened the card and read it aloud.

"I know that you are confused by the pink and blue balloons, but after Noah built the ark, he called them in two by two. I want to share with you the really good news. For our prolonged wait, we've been blessed with two. A girl and boy is what God has placed inside of me to give to you."

His eyes grew wide as he walked over to his wife, reached for her hand, and kissed her on the forehead.

"Baby. I love you soooo much."

She smiled.

"Babe, I love you too."

Chapter Thirty-Four

About a week later, Janelle sat on the sofa next to her husband watching television. When his phone vibrated, she looked down and saw the text from Patrice float across the top of his screen. She took a deep breath and looked at him.

"I thought we agreed that you would stop all communication with your ex."

He looked at his wife. "What?"

She frowned.

"Joshua don't play stupid. I just saw a text from Patrice float across the top of your screen and I quote she texted, 'What's up? Why you not answering your phone....'"

He reached for his phone.

"I mean come on Janelle. Why you watching my phone? I don't do that to you."

"Are you serious? Don't try to throw the ball back in my court. Why does she feel so comfortable questioning you about not answering your phone?"

He inhaled and exhaled deeply.

"Janelle look, I don't know."

She scoffed. "What I do know is, if you really wanted her to stop messaging you, you would change your number."

His brows met.

"Too many people know my number for me to do that."

"As usual, you're full of excuses. No, reality is—"

"Naw, you don't understand. I have too much invested in this number. Family, business relationships, and friends. I'm not about to give her that kind of power over my life."

Frustrated, she stopped and pointed towards him.

"You really want to hang on to the emotional soul ties you have with her. My whole thing is you're not even considering how it's affecting me and our marriage."

She pointed to her stomach.

"And let's not forget our unborn children."

"Janelle. I don't want to be with her and I don't want you stressing over a text that means nothing to me."

She got up from the sofa and walked towards the bedroom. He turned around.

"Janelle."

She looked back.

"Don't call my name, call Patrice."

"Babe, you being real petty right now."

"Stop the communication or I'll be filing for divorce papers. You're giving me my way out."

"How is that?"

"The other woman. Some men really don't get it. You know what go ahead and do you."

She slammed their bedroom door.

"Jesus help me."

Days went by and Janelle had no words for her husband. Her routine consisted of cooking cleaning, and work, but the sight of her husband discussed her. The mornings became harsh and morning sickness took over. She was clueless that stress was consuming her. The next day her phone rang.

"Hello."

"Hey Janelle. You've been on my mind, so I figured I would check on you."

"I'm just in a bad space right now. Patrice is still texting Josh and he doesn't seem to understand how it's making me feel. I told him that I was filing for divorce if the communication didn't stop."

"Janelle, I've seen this before, but you have to pray and ask God what His will is for your marriage. I know it hurts and what I'm saying doesn't feel good, but girl you have to pull yourself together for the babies and let God deal with him. I refuse to watch you allow the devil to use another woman to tear your marriage apart."

"Sandra, what would you do if the shoe were on the other foot?"

"The shoe is on the other foot, but when and if God releases me from my marriage, divorce papers will be served. Until then, my job is to love my husband and pray for him."

"Sandra, I'm sorry. I thought everything was—"

Sandra interrupted her.

"Yeah, just because we look happy together, doesn't mean that everything is okay. Again, as I have told you before, looks can be deceiving. My husband acknowledges me in public, but at home he's distant and cold. I tried talking to him about it but you know what, he did what he does best... Make excuses."

"Tell me about it."

They talked for hours and before long, Joshua pulled up to the house.

"Sandra, Josh just pulled up. I'll call you tomorrow."

"Alright. Work things out with your husband Janelle."

"I'll try."

Joshua walked in, put his briefcase down, and walked towards his wife.

"Babe can we please talk?"

She rolled her eyes and walked away.

"So, is that the way God would want you to handle this?

"You're absolutely right. He wouldn't want me to respond foolishly and that's why I need to calm down before I open my mouth and say something that I'll later regret. You can find that in the book of Proverbs. With that said, I need time to think before I speak."

She walked into the room and closed the door.

Chapter Thirty-Five

A few days later, Janelle and Joshua arrived to their session as scheduled. As they walked in, the secretary smiled.

"Good afternoon."

Janelle forced a smile.

"How are you?"

"I'm great. No need to sign in or take a seat, Mrs. Chambers is ready for you."

"Okay. Thank you."

They walked into the counselor's office.

"Good afternoon. How are you today?"

"I'm great and how are the Richards?"

Joshua sat down.

"We're good."

Janelle looked at her husband from the corner of her eye as the counselor put on her glasses.

"Well we're going to jump right in and get this session going." She smiled. "Today's session will cover unanswered prayers."

She reached for her Bible to eliminate any confusion and handed it to Joshua.

"Mr. Richards, please read 1 Peter 3:17."

He looked over at Janelle and scanned the page for the verse.

"'In the same way, you husbands should live with your wives in an understanding way, since they are weaker than you. But show them respect, because God gives them the same blessing he gives you, the grace that gives true life. Do this so that nothing will stop your prayers.'"

He speechlessly looked at the counselor as she elaborated.

"Mr. Richards, I wanted you to read this particular scripture so that you could understand that being a husband comes with great responsibility."

Studying their faces, she continued.

"Each individual plays a part in the struggles in their marriage whether they want to accept it or not. The way to get past something like this is for both individuals to deal with the small issues before it grows into something big."

Janelle cleared her throat.

"I'm sorry to interrupt you Mrs. Chambers, but if you have addressed the small issue, but the husband refuses to deal with it, what do you do?"

His eyes grew wide as he looked over at his wife.

"Well, Mrs. Richards, it depends on the situation. Please enlighten me."

"Well, my husband has continued to allow his ex to communicate with him via text, even after our sessions... It's kind of hard to trust someone who's unwilling to deal with a situation that's hurting me."

She pointed to herself.

"His wife. And then he has the nerve to embrace me for sex... I don't want him touching me because I feel like he's thinking of her. It's just the thought of it that sickens me."

"Mrs. Richards, you have a valid point; however, your body is not yours and vice versa. Biblically you're not supposed to withhold from your husband unless you both are fasting and have come into agreement to restraining from sex."

With wide eyes, he looked at the counselor.

"I didn't know that was in the Bible."

He pointed to himself.

"Besides, I didn't agree to none of that."

"Mr. Richards, you have to understand that this isn't easy for your wife and it doesn't give you a free ticket to continue to not do what's right. It's also vitally important for you to reevaluate your situation with your ex. Dealing with it allows you to find what's really in your heart for her. You have to try and understand how it affects your wife, so her heart can heal as well. As I said before, every action causes a reaction from your wife who is simply expressing to you how she feels."

"You're right."

Mrs. Chambers smiled. "You know, many marriages suffer due to a lack of communication and an unwillingness to acknowledge faults and most cases, eventually end in divorce."

She smiled.

"That's why it's not my job to show favoritism. It's my job to magnify the good in your marriage, and help you both identify the errors in your marriage."

Janelle adjusted herself.

"Mrs. Chambers, my biggest issue with Joshua is that his ex continues to text him and he has yet to use his spiritual fire extinguisher to put her out."

He leaned his head back and frowned.

"I didn't use mine because you refused to use yours. You just wanted to argue."

Mrs. Chambers interjected.

"Tit for tat never works. It only adds fuel to the fire. Mrs. Richards did you explain to your husband why you were angry?"

"Of course, I did, but he found every excuse not talk about it."

The counselor looked over at him.

"Mr. Richards, we discussed this during our last session and Ii know it's hard, but you're going to have to talk this out because if you don't, it's only going to get worse. What's keeping you from asking your ex to stop contacting you?"

He shook his head.

"It's not that I have feelings for her, but it's the guilt that controls me. She was a really good woman and I hurt her in more ways than one."

"I understand that you don't want to hurt her, but your actions are hurting your wife and leaving her confused. If you don't close that door soon, it will ruin your marriage... Mr. Richards, do you want your marriage to work?"

"Yes, because I love my wife."

"And what about you Mrs. Richards?"

She looked at her husband.

"Yes."

"Well, do the work. I'm simply a mediator walking you through the process of putting out the necessary flames to help you begin loving and trusting one another again."

She looked over at Janelle.

"I know you're angry with your husband, but if you're going to fight, then you have to fight the who's responsible for the confusion in your marriage and that's the enemy. His goal is to divide and conquer. He knows many can't see him because they're spiritually blind."

"Yes ma'am, but..."

"As I said before, you have minor issues in this marriage and once you both learn to respectfully communicate with each other, your marriage will get better. It's a must that you both come to a mutual agreement without arguing on how you're going to resolve this issue. I can give you suggestions, but it won't work until you put it into action... and it's not going to happen overnight because this is years of built up frustration. I wanted to spread out your sessions, but that wouldn't be wise at this point. Mr. Richards, is it okay with you if I schedule you all for next week?"

"As long as it's gonna help, its fine with me."

"I'll see you both in a happier place next week at five."

Chapter Thirty-Six

O n the ride home, Joshua reached for Janelle's hand.
"Babe, I'm sorry. I'm really trying and I want our marriage to work."

She looked over at him.

"Me too."

He put his right signal on as he approached the stop sign.

"As long as we do the work, it'll get better... Right."

She looked out the window.

"But you know doing the work requires you dealing with your ex, right. "

"I know. It's just complicated."

She smiled.

"Let me make it easy for you. You have my permission to call her with me on the phone and address everything. Then, if she continues to text you, I want have a reason to be angry because I know you tried."

Her brows met as a moment of silence gripped him.

"Josh."

He took a deep breath.

"You know what, you're right. I'll do it, but can you please give me some time?"

"How much time do you need?"

He tapped the stirring wheel.

"I promise; I'll do it soon."

"Okay, but for now, can we stop and get something to eat? I don't feel like cooking dinner... I just want to eat and get ready for bed."

He looked through his rear-view mirror to change lanes.

"Yeah. What you wanna to eat?"

She stopped as if thinking.

"A grilled tuna melt sandwich with sautéed onions and tomatoes."

His brows met.

"I can make that at home. How about I cook for you tonight?"

She smiled.

"I guess."

He reached for her hand.

"Mine is better than theirs any way."

Shortly after arriving home, he prepared dinner for his wife. As she walked into the bed room, he called out to her from the kitchen.

"Janelle."

"Yeah."

"Can you cut up the onions for me?"

She chuckled.

"No."

He smirked.

"Oh. It's like that."

"Yep."

He reached for the onion and thinly sliced it.

"You can come eat in about five minutes. I just need to sauté these onions."

"Okay."

Ten minutes later she walked into the dining room to a candle lit dinner.

"Soooo, what do you think?"

She smiled.

"You really know how to win a woman's heart."

He gazed into her eyes as she stood on the other side of the table and smiled.

"That's just who I am."

He walked over to his wife.

"And you deserve this. I just want you to know that I love and appreciate you no matter what we go through."

He pulled the chair from the table for her, placed a napkin in her lap, and softly kissed her on the forehead. As bad as she wanted to be angry, her heart wouldn't allow it. She reached for his hand.

"Lord thank you for this food. Please don't let it make us sick."

She laughed.

"Amen."

"Whatever, Chef Richards got skills in the kitchen."

She laughed as he continued. "Anyway, I know you like parakeets and giraffes, so I figured we could go to the petting zoo tomorrow. How does that sound?"

Her cheeks flushed red as she smiled.

"I'd love that. I guess you do pay attention to the things I like."

"I always pay attention to you. I'm learning how to be something I've never been before and that's a husband. So, all I ask is for you to do is to be patient with me. I'm really trying."

"Wow. I never thought about it like that."

"What?"

"That you're learning to be something you've never been before and that's a husband."

"Yeah. I mean neither one of us have ever been parents and we're about to have to learn how to be good mothers and fathers."

He held up two fingers.

"To twins. You get what I'm saying. It's not like I came out of my mother's wound with a manual on marriage."

She chuckled.

"I guess you just schooled me."

As they walked into the room to get ready for bed, he closed the bathroom door and realized he had his wife's heart back in his hands.

He pointed to his reflection in the mirror.

"You the man."

Early the next morning, Janelle walked into the bathroom to shower. Stopping to look in the mirror, she admired the changes that were taking place in her body. After showering, she wrapped the towel around her. As she untwirled her hair, Joshua walked behind her, and gently rubbed her belly.

"You know I got names already right."

"And so do I."

"Our son's name shall be... Camaro. You know after my car."

Her smile faded away.

"Joshua. No."

"What's wrong with that?"

"I want us to name our children for their future. You know if an employer saw that on an application, they'd toss it to the side real quick."

He laughed.

"That's funny. I can see our son in high school getting teased by the girls. Since you're a woman what would be your pick-up line?"

She smiled.

"I'd be like, hey Camaro, can you take me for a ride?"

He chuckled.

"Let me stop playing, I got to get to work. I'll see you later."

He slid on his shoes, grabbed his brief case, and left for work. As he got in the car, his phone vibrated. He stopped and looked down at the text.

Josh, we really need to talk. ASAP

The messages continued as he backed out of the driveway.

It's really important.

He continued driving to work without responding. Twenty minutes later, he pulled up to the office and walked in. The secretary reached for the notepad on her desk.

"Good morning Mr. Richards. Someone called, but they didn't leave a message."

He smiled.

"Thank you."

He tried to gather his thoughts before their meeting, but he couldn't shake the messages. He looked down at his phone and back towards the file on his desk.

"God this may be one of the hardest things I've had to do in a while. I pray Patrice understands."

He grabbed his things and walked down the hall to their meeting.

Chapter Thirty-Seven

A week later, Janelle and Joshua met each other at the counselor's office for their next session.

"Good afternoon."

"Hi. How are you all doing today?"

He smiled.

"Good and you."

The secretary smiled.

"Mrs. Chambers is running a little late, but she should be here shortly.

As they sat down, Janelle pulled out her phone. Joshua shook his head and looked at the secretary.

"How much do you all charge for Candy Crush therapy?"

She laughed.

"I really can't say much because I play it too."

She looked at Janelle.

"Mrs. Richards, what level are you on?"

She looked up and smiled.

"Five fifty-one. How about you?"

"Wow, you're way up there. I've been stuck on level three-twenty for about a month now. I wish they would create a candy pass for people like me that's been stuck on the same level for over a month."

She laughed.

"I know that feeling."

Fifteen minutes later, the counselor arrived.

"I do apologize for my tardiness, but I had to pick my son up from the airport."

"No, it's fine."

"If you could give me five minutes to get situated, that would be great."

She looked at the secretary and smiled.

"Could you please get me a hot cup of hot tea with honey and lemon please."

"Yes ma'am."

As she got up, she looked at Janelle and Joshua.

"I really enjoyed talking to you all."

Three minutes later, the secretary walked into Mrs. Chambers office with her tea."

The counselor pointed to the table next to her chair.

"You can put it there... Oh, and please send Mr. and Mrs. Richards back. Thank you."

The counselor walked out and smiled.

"Mrs. Chambers is ready for you."

Joshua smiled.

"Thank you."

As they entered into the room and sat down, Janelle noticed two workbooks in their seats.

"Thank you both for your patience. Again, I apologize for being late. How did your assignment go after our session from last week?"

Joshua looked over at his wife.

"I think it went well. I cooked dinner for my wife and discussed doing some things that she likes."

"Mrs. Richards how did this make you feel?"

"I mean, I really enjoyed my husband. He shocked me when he admitted that he's learning to be a husband."

The counselor smiled as she continued.

"He explained that he didn't come out of his mother's womb with a manual on marriage."

"Interesting analogy and I completely agree. Wouldn't you agree Mrs. Richards?"

She smiled.

"I do."

He sat back on the sofa, crossed his legs, and smiled as the counselor began their session.

"Well, as you can see, in your seats you will find a leather workbook that I have created that we'll work from on today. Is that okay with you?"

They both looked at each other.

"Okay. Let's get started. On page one, there are four important questions that I would like for the both of you to keep in mind throughout our session. Mr. Richards will you please read the first two?"

He opened the work book.

"Before your marriage, did you participate in any intense marital counseling?" He cleared his throat. "Did you pray for guidance as to the timing of your marriage or did you rush into it? If so, why?"

"Mrs. Richards, please read the next set of questions."

She looked down and began to read.

"Have you been patient with your spouse during the process of working on your marriage? When issues arise, do you and your spouse attempt to resolve them before going to bed or does it linger into the next morning, week, month, or year?"

Her eyes widened as she looked away from the counselor. Mrs. Chambers reached for her tea, took a sip, and placed her black mug with white writing that read I Can Do All Things back onto the table.

"Completing this workbook allows you both to begin the process of being honest with yourself and each other. So, what is your answer to the first question Mr. Richards?"

He lowered his head.

"Actually, we didn't go through premarital counseling. I never thought it was important."

"Hmmmm. A lot of married couples feel that way, so there's no reason to be ashamed. Premarital counseling is one of many ways that prepares couples for possible outcomes that could lead to divorce and so on. The questions in the workbooks are designed to open your eyes to how counseling could have helped. Premarital counseling would have also possibly decreased your desire to rush into marriage and it would have given you time to first put things in order. The workbooks that I have given you will guide you through a step by step process for the next three weeks. But as I've said before, you have to do the work."

Joshua looked up at the counselor.

"So, we won't have counseling for the next three weeks?"

"Correct."

Janelle adjusted herself on the sofa and looked at her husband.

"Hmm. That's interesting."

She gave a reassuring smile.

"Mr. and Mrs. Richards, I understand your concern; however, I call this The Process of Trust. You're going to have to trust God that whatever happens during this time, He will help you through it. Remember, my strategy is not for you to become dependent upon me, but that your dependence is solely on God. Remember, He's the glue."

She pointed to herself.

"Not me."

She smiled.

"I look forwarded to hearing some great news during out next visit."

Chapter Thirty-Eight

A fter leaving, they got in the car and talked about the work books. But before heading to her car, Joshua's phone rang. He seemed to have forgotten to disconnect his phone from the Bluetooth. Before he could reject the call, Janelle saw Patrice's name pop up on the screen.

She looked over at him with envy in her eyes.

"Why is she so comfortable calling your phone?" She scoffed, got out of the car, and slammed the door.

He got out of the car and walked towards her.

"Janelle, can we talk about this? I didn't know she was gonna call and you gave me permission to talk to her."

She walked hastily to her car.

"I asked you to tell her to stop contacting you. Besides, we were supposed to be together when you made the call."

Patrice watched from across the street as he rushed over to his wife as she got in her car. She slammed the door and pulled out barely missing his feet. He stood in complete shock as she drove off.

"This girl is wrecking my home."

He got in his car and with a clinched fist, he punched the steering wheel. He put on his seat belt and quickly drove off. Shortly thereafter, Janelle pulled up to Sandra's house. Before she could park, Brian opened the door to walk to his car.

"What's up Janelle?"

"Hey Brian."

"What Joshua do now?"

"Not today Brian... I'm not in the mood."

He shrugged his shoulder.

"Well, Sandra should be here in about five or ten minutes."

She deeply exhaled.

"Okay. I'll just call her later."

He stopped her before she could get back in the car.

"Janelle look, I know the last person you want to talk to is me, but your husband called looking for you. It's not my business, but whatever the situation is, running from it won't make it go away."

She stroked her forehead with tears running her face.

"I'm tired of this girl interfering in my marriage. Every time I think about her calling him, I get out of character."

His brows met.

"I know you're a Christian and all, but..."

She stared at him in disbelief.

"Brian, don't play with me."

He shook his head with concern in his eyes.

"Seriously, I'm not trying to be funny right now. Like I said, I know that you're a Christian and all, but you're also human. You think Christians walk around like robots and don't get angry?"

"No."

"Aight then. Just relax and when Sandra gets here, ya'll can do that woman to woman thing ya'll do. I kinda have an idea what's going on, but you gotta look at this as sensitive situation."

"Since you know how to handle it, what would you do."

He paused as if thinking.

"I would pray."

"Really Brian."

He shook his head and frowned.

"Just because I don't go to church and I clown a lot, doesn't mean I don't pray."

They turned and looked as Sandra pulled up in the driveway. She got out of the car and looked at Janelle.

"Hey. You okay."

She shook her head.

"Sandra, I really need to talk to you."

Before Brian got in his car, he looked at Janelle with sympathy in his eyes.

"I hope you feel better."

She walked towards Sandra and looked over at Brian.

"Thanks Brian."

He laughed.

"Oh, don't worry. The next meal on you."

She and Sandra laughed.

"Shut up Brian."

As they walked in the house, Sandra looked over at Janelle.

"Janelle, what's going on?"

She wiped the tears from her eyes.

"I'm so tired of the whole situation with Joshua's ex. My ex doesn't call me, so how is it right for her to keep contacting him?"

Sandra inhaled and exhaled.

"It's not right, but are you really going to allow another woman to bring this kind of tension in your marriage."

"Sandra, it's like he doesn't understand how this is hurting me. I guess the saying is true. 'Men are from Mars and women are from Venice.'"

Sandra chuckled.

"No, it's not true. They actually came from the dust and will return to the dust. As your friend, my job is to tell you to stop overacting."

Her brows met.

"How am I overacting?"

"Did you let him explain?"

"No, I drove off."

"My point exactly. So, what makes you think he knew she would call?"

She shrugged her shoulders as Sandra continued.

"Exactly, as I said, you overreacted. Janelle, I can't tell you what to do, but I can make suggestions. Your job is to pray, sit down, and work things out with your husband. However, God deals with him in regards to his ex, you let Him do that, but move your buts out of the way. But he this, but he that."

She looked over at her, sat back, and took a deep breath.

"I guess you're right."

"No, you know I'm right. Now, fix your pretty little face and stop letting the devil use this woman to get you all worked up. If your husband wanted to be with her, he would've done so by now. So, apparently he has his reasons for the way he's handling things."

"So, I'm supposed to just wait?"

"Exactly. You need to take care of yourself and worry about the babies you're carrying and not his ex."

After talking for a while, Sandra looked at Janelle.

"I guess it's time for you to head home."

She smiled.

"I guess so. Thanks for the talk. I don't know what I would do if you weren't in my life girl."

She smiled.

"That's what true friends are for."

She walked her to the car.

"Go home and talk things over with your husband."

"Alright. I'll see you one day this week. Love you Sandra."

Sandra waved goodbye. "Love you too Janelle."

Chapter Thirty-Nine

A bout two weeks later, Joshua sat on the flipping through the photo album of he and Janelle when they first met and their wedding day. Tears welled up in his eyes as he realized the moments they captured of their love and friendship had become less and less as the years had gone by. He realized that his inability to listen and communicate with his wife had created a wedge between them. Not to mention his constant sarcasm and his ex.

Knowing that Janelle was waiting for Ms. Lula's flight to land at the airport, he grabbed his phone from the charger and got in his car. As he drove, he decided to capture pictures of the place they first met, the park they walked through, the restaurant where he proposed to her, and the building where they were married. He later pulled up to the drug store and walked in to print them.

Walking over to the cards with a smile on his face, he searched for the perfect card to match the thoughts in his heart. An older lady who stood about four feet eleven inches with long flowing gray hair dressed in white stood next to him holding a cane with a cross on the tip of it. After about two minutes, she looked over at his big smile.

She leaned her cane against the shelf.

"She must mean the world to you? Your smile says it all."

He smiled.

"Yes ma'am she does. How are you?"

In a modulated voice, she replied. "I'm blessed, but I would be more blessed if I had my glasses to read these words on this card. I left them in the car and if I go back to that car for my glasses, chances are I won't come back in because it's hot out their baby."

He smiled with compassion.

"Please, allow me. I can help you. What's the occasion?"

She smiled.

"Well, today is my wedding anniversary and I wanted to buy a special card for my husband. He's been a little down since he's been in the hospital... He's been ill for a while now, but the love we have for each other is strong."

He looked at her with sympathy.

"Congratulations and I'm sorry to hear about your husband."

She laughed.

"Thank you and don't feel sorry for us baby. My husband and I have had our challenges in marriage. It wasn't always happy, but I must say that our last five years of marriage has been amazing compared to the first twenty years."

His forehead wrinkled at the thought of the first twenty years being horrible as she continued.

"God has a way of making a man and a woman deal with issues, you know."

She shook her head.

"And even their past so they can love like they never thought they could love when..."

She winked her eye at him.

"That is when they finally surrender to Him. Oooh weee, Jesus is a healer of all things including marriages and sickness. And if He decides to heal my husband in heaven, I'm at peace with that because our latter days together have been full of love, peace, and joy."

"Yes ma'am."

Joshua scanned through the cards.

"Ma'am here's a card that says it all."

He handed it to her.

"I really needed this talk. I guess I ended up at the right place at the right time to hear this from you."

"Ohhh yes. That's the kind of God we serve. A God that has that word we need at the right time."

She smiled.

"Uh, He does it all because He loves us; especially you. I know the one person you wish you would've heard that from never said it to you, but today God is saying it through me for your father. Oh, how He loves you. By the way, thank you sweetie."

His brows met.

"You're welcome. Have a good day."

"You too baby."

He stood in shock as time stood still and the old lady walked away. He looked over to see if the she had made it to the end of the aisle, but she was gone.

"Man, she quick to be an old lady."

He picked a card and looked on the other side as he headed to the register, but she wasn't there either. He handed the cashier the card.

"Did you see an older lady check out?"

Puzzled, the cashier looked at him.

"I'm sorry sir, but you've been the only customer to come in in the last thirty minutes."

He seemed taken back.

"I..."

He shook his head.

"Never mind."

He paid the cashier and left. As he started the car, the radio personality closed out his session with a scripture.

"Before I leave for today, I'll leave you with this. Be careful how you treat people because you never know when you're entertaining an angel." In a deep voice, he continued. "Signing off here on CJG200 radio, that's safe for all families to tune in to. Be safe and blessed out there ya'll. I'm your radio personality JL Cam'berry. Until tomorrow,

I'm out."

Chapter Forty

After sitting in the car for a minute, Joshua dialed Janelle's number, but it went to voicemail. He couldn't stomach the thought of losing his wife, so he scrolled through his contacts and composed a new message to send his ex. Before he could text her, his phone rang.

"Hey Janelle. I just tried to call you."

"I was trying to start the car, but it's not cranking. I'm here at the airport. Can you come see what's going on with it because I don't want to leave my car here."

"I'm on my way. Did Ms. Lula's plane land yet?"

"Yeah. We'll wait inside until you get here."

"Alright. Just give me about twenty minutes and I'll be there."

"Okay. We're parked on level one lot B in front of the airport."

She ended the call and looked over at Ms. Lula and Sandra.

"I can't stand my husband at times."

Ms. Lula shook her head.

"I bet you can't, but God has a way of humbling us. Then we have no choice but to talk to the person we've tried so hard to ignore. What he do now?"

Sandra looked over at Janelle and waited for her response.

"His ex keeps texting him and he still hasn't stopped all communication with her. He's worried about hurting her, but he's still hurting me. So, is that okay. I'm his wife. He—"

"Now Janelle, I understand that you're hurting, but what about her? Aint you supposed to be living the life of Christ before him? And yes, you his wife, but she's also his ex. Did it occur to you that maybe that young lady needs closure? Did he tell you how it ended with them?"

Sandra eyes followed the conversation as she ate her chips. Janelle slowly lowered her head and took a deep breath.

"Maybe she does and he cheated on her with his ex before her."

"Sounds like a pattern to me. Baby, some men don't always think the way we think. He already hurt the woman one time and I'm pretty sure he doesn't want to hurt her again. Does it make what he's doing right? No. Has he figured out that he's only making things worse? Probably not and that's why prayer is your best option. If you've already talked to him about it and he's still not listening, it's just gonna have to be a lesson he learns the hard way."

"Yes ma'am. I get it."

"Lil nosey girl. How's your marriage?"

Sandra pursed her lips.

"Shaky."

"Well, I guess you better unshake it with prayer too. Have ya'll thought about fasting together for ya'll marriages?"

They looked at each other and then back at Ms. Lula.

"No ma'am."

"Looks like you better get started then."

They ordered their food and waited for Joshua to check the car. Five minutes later, Janelle's phone rang.

"Hello."

"Hey I'm here. I have my set of keys, so ya'll can wait inside until I'm done."

"Okay. Just call me when you finish."

He popped the hood of the car and mumbled.

"I bet it's this battery again."

Just as he thought, she needed a new battery. For the time being, he jumped her car off until they got to an auto part store to purchase a new one. He called her phone.

"Hey. You got a bad battery, but I jumped you off again.

I'll follow ya'll to the nearest auto part store and buy a new one."

"Okay. Give us like ten minutes and we'll be out there."

"Okay."

As he opened the trunk, he remembered the baby reveal and leaned his head back.

"God, you got to help me here. I don't want to hurt my wife, but I also don't want to hurt Patrice. I don't know what to do."

Shortly thereafter, they arrived the auto part store. After getting the battery, Joshua walked over to the passenger side of the car.

"Hey Ms. Lula. How are you?"

She looked at him then at Janelle and smiled.

"Janelle, your husband gets finer and finer every time I see him."

She smiled.

"Hey there baby. I'm good and you."

He smiled.

"I'm good. It's good to see you back. Was your trip everything you needed it to be."

"Baby, it was all that and more."

He looked over at Sandra.

"What's up Sandra?"

"Hey."

He smiled.

"Janelle, I'm gonna head home. I'll see you when you get there."

"Okay."

"Ya'll be careful."

Ms. Lula smiled. "You too."

He got in his car and headed home, but decided to make one last stop by seafood market to order out. Shortly after arriving home, he set the table with a little slow music in the background, placed the roses in the vase on the table, and walked to the bathroom to get a shower. Five minutes later, Janelle pulled up and walked in the house. After hearing the music, she scanned the room and smiled.

"Okay."

Seconds later, Joshua walked in the kitchen and placed his hands on the island as she turned around.

"Babe. I'm so sorry for everything. You know, I'm not a fan of your silent treatments."

She looked away.

"Janelle, I love you and aint nothing is gone to change that. I figured we could discuss how I'm going to break it gently to my ex that we can no longer be friends or communicate. Is that fine with you?"

She walked over to the table and smiled.

"I guess so."

After talking for a few hours, Janelle agreed to everything, but her heart also hurt for his ex. She looked over at her husband.

"Thank you for ordering out"

He chuckled.

"Okay. You caught me."

"Josh, I really pray that this doesn't tear her apart."

"Me too Janelle..."

He leaned back.

"Me too."

Chapter Forty-One

T wo days later, Joshua sat on the sofa gathering his thoughts as he dialed Patrice's number. Excitement echoed from her voice as she answered.

"Hello."

He rubbed his forehead.

"Hi Patrice. How are you?"

She smiled.

"I'm good and you?"

She continued with a touch of sarcasm.

"Today must be Side Chick Day for you to grace me with your voice."

He shook his head and responded respectfully.

"Look, I don't want to hold you long... but I wanted to let you know that I can no longer communicate with you.... At all."

Her heart slid to the bottom of her feet as her worst fears had come true. Every memory from their past began to flood her mind. She thought to herself.

How could he do this to me? Why would he play with my emotions like that?... I deserve some answers, and he's gonna give them to me.

She rolled her eyes.

"And may I ask why?"

He shook his head once more.

"It's not right that I continue to disrespect my wife and marriage like this—."

"What do you mean? It's not like we're sleeping together." She placed emphasis on her words that would follow.

"We're just friends."

He glanced to the left and took a deep breath.

"Look, that's the problem and it has to stop today."

Taken back by his statement, she placed her hand over her chest as rage and jealousy pierced through her heart.

She laughed.

"Oh, so you think its gonna end like this and everything's just gonna to be okay... Boy you are something serious, you know that? Where did all of this come from?" Envy dripped from her voice. "Let me guess, your wife."

He smirked and replied calmly.

"My wife! Actually, it came from me. I'm a grown man. I can think for myself."

She frowned.

"Whatever... I guess you finally found your little princess that you could be faithful to huh? So, I wasn't good enough for you?"

He looked to the left again with wide eyes and shook his head as she continued.

"I was a good woman to you and you decided to cheat on me... You decided to play with my emotions."

She stood up and paced the floor.

"And it was you that decided to keep my heart longing for you when you informed me about all of your marital issues giving me false hope. I gave you five faithful years of my life. I gave you a family and you decided to ask me for an abortion.

Everything you ever wanted was inside of me. You made me think that we had a chance when you filed for divorce from your wife. And now, all of a sudden, you find out that she's pregnant and you want to run back to her. Boy... you lost your mind?"

He shook his head.

"Patrice look. I'm sorry that I hurt you."

She laughed mockingly.

"You think that's supposed to just make the pain go away?"

Sympathy spilled through his voice.

"I don't want to argue with you. I'm sorry. Maybe I should've handled this before you got attached again."

She pursed her lips.

"Maybe you should've and I bet your wife has no clue your talking to me right now. Does she?"

She chuckled.

"Since we're being so secretive, I have a little secret of my own. Remember, five years ago when I moved away and no longer contacted you?"

He frowned.

"Patrice what are you taking about?"

"Hmmmmm... I guess you don't. You forgot huh? Well, let me refresh your memory. Your daughter turned four last week."

He jumped up from the sofa in disbelief. "What? You had an abortion and I was there. Now you just being petty."

"So, you think. I guess you're not done with me after all."

He frowned as his thoughts raced back to five years before. He and Patrice pulled up to the abortion clinic. They got out of the car walking in hand and hand. Joshua looked over at her.

"Are you sure you want to go through with this? I don't want you to feel forced."

She looked over at him with tears in her eyes.

"It's for the best. Besides, we're not ready for a family."

As they walked in, she signed her name while he proceeded to pay. Once her name was called, she began walking to the back with the nurse. He reached out for her arm.

"Would you like for me to go to the back with you?"

She looked at him with tears in her eyes.

"Joshua, I'll be just fine."

He snapped back to reality and shook his head as rage echoed through his voice.

"Daughter? You told me you had the abortion."

She smirked.

"Yes, but I never went through with it."

Janelle's jaws clinched tightly as she quickly unmuted her phone. She turned and stared at her husband with envy in her eyes. A tear escaped and crawled down her face. She gathered herself and intervened in a gentle voice.

"Hi Patrice."

Patrice hesitated and chuckled.

"Seriously Joshua. Is this the kind of game you're playing?"

Janelle intervened once more.

"Patrice, I'm sorry that Joshua hurt you. I'm sorry that he even asked you about an abortion. You're a gorgeous woman and I know God has someone for you... Besides, I don't want any animosity between you and I."

Patrice's heart dropped as she held the phone in complete shock, confused as to what just happened. Janelle respectfully continued.

"I don't have all of the answers, but please let's not put an innocent little girl in the middle of indifferences between you and my husband."

She shook her head.

"This is not her fault."

Patrice scoffed.

"What makes you think you're so special. He's only going to hurt you the way he hurt me."

She paused and wiped the tears that slowly crept down her face.

"Patrice, to be honest he already has. My heart is hurting right now, after hearing everything you've said. Just knowing that he allowed you to text him hurt me, but I forgive him. You're both going to have to learn how to co-parent and co-exist for the sake of your daughter."

She looked at her husband.

"We all really need to clear our heads—"

Joshua interrupted with anger in his voice.

"Hell no. I want a paternity test. Only an evil heart can think of something like that. Who's to say this child is mine, especially since she moved away? If she is, all she had to do was tell me the truth—
"

Janelle calmly interrupted him. "Joshua, please don't disrespect your ex."

She looked over at him.

"And now possible baby mother while I'm on the phone. You didn't do it while you were sneaking talking to her behind my back. So, please don't do it now. We all really need time to think about this because a child may be involved."

Patrice snapped.

"Maybe—"

"I didn't mean it that way, but it's not about us anymore, it's about her."

She looked at her husband.

"Reality is, in the midst of my husband trying not to hurt you, he hurt the both of us. I'll let you talk back to Joshua. Again, I'm sorry."

Janelle placed the phone on the table and walked outside to get some air. Joshua watched as his wife closed the door and ended the call. Patrice smirked

"Hello. Hello."

She looked at the phone.

"I know he didn't just hang up."

A few hours later, he finally picked up the phone to call his ex again. Fury gripped her tongue as she answered.

"What do you want?"

He walked outside.

"Look, until we can have a paternity test, I don't think it's wise for me to speak to you or your; I mean our daughter, if she's mine. Anyway, I went with you to the clinic and paid $650.00. So, what happened to my money?"

"First of all, Joshua, I was only with you, but if that's what you want to think, then fine. I don't have a reason to lie. I was faithful, but I can't say the same for you. Secondly, I kept the money to take care of a child you didn't want. And one more thing."

She moved the phone from her ear.

"Ashely baby, someone wants to speak to you."

He froze as she handed her daughter the phone.

"Hello."

She turned to her mother.

"Mommy, no one's on the phone."
He took a deep breath and exhaled.
"Hey sweetie, how are you."

Chapter Forty-Two

S he smiled.
"Hi. I'm doing fine."
She looked at her mom and pointed to the phone. In her soft childlike voice, she continued.

"Who is this?"

He hesitated.

"This is uncle Josh. How you been?"

Her forehead wrinkled.

"I'm good. Ima about to go play with my friends."

A tear fell from his eye. "Okay baby. Be good okay. I just wanted to say hi."

"Okay, bye."

As she walked pass her mother to go outside, Patrice reached for the phone and rolled her eyes.

"Hello."

Joshua looked at the phone and ended the call. He looked over towards his wife in disbelief.

"Janelle."

She looked back at him.

"I can't talk to you right now. Your denial and unwillingness to deal with your ugly past has me caught in the middle of your mess."

As she turned to walk away, he threw his glass of water against the wall. She jumped and looked back at him.

"Seriously Joshua. It's not my fault that you screwed yourself."

He threw up his hands.

"Okay. I get it. But how was I supposed to know that she followed through with the pregnancy?"

She turned around and stared into his eyes.

"First of all, don't raise your voice at me... That's what happens when you tell a woman to abort a child that maybe she wanted just to fit your own selfish desires... So, don't get an attitude with me because your past finally caught up with you." Before walking away, she looked back at him. "Did you stop to think for one second why she continued to contact you?"

He looked at her with apologetic eyes.

"Babe, I'm—"

"There's no way that you didn't pick up on that. Your love for her blinded your spiritual discernment to the point that you couldn't even see why she wanted a friendship with you in the first place."

She pointed to herself. "Even I could sense that something wasn't right when I saw her at the hospital talking to you. At first glance, when we accidentally bumped into each other in the hallway, she seemed sweet and innocent. But, when I shook her hand, her eyes said it all. It were as if envy pierced through my soul... I typically pick on things, but Joshua, I never expected this."

As she walked away, he reached out to her.

"Baby, can we please talk?"

She attempted to hold back her tears, but they escaped from her eyes. She walked into the bedroom, leaned her back against the door, and made a call.

"Hello... Hello. Janelle, you there?"

"Sandra, this is so hard for me right now. I don't understand why this had to happen to my marriage."

She wiped the tears from her eyes.

"Janelle what are you talking about?"

"Joshua may have a daughter."

Sandra's eyes grew wide. "What?"

"I'm hurting so bad right now. I mean I don't understand what went wrong."

She wiped the tears from her eyes.

"Please pray that God will speak to both of their hearts so they can get the closure they need and for me to stay humble and out of His way because girl... my flesh wants to do the total opposite right now."

"Janelle, you know I got you."

He stood on the other side of the door heeding to the pain he had caused his wife, placed his hands in his pockets, and continued to listen.

Janelle cleared her throat.

"I pray that God covers this poor little girl who's being pulled in the middle of their mess because of their selfishness."

She buried her face in her hand.

"Sandra, I don't know what to do. I'm so angry right now and if God doesn't help me, I'm going to lose it."

He knocked and attempted to open the room door, but she pressed her back against it.

"Joshua don't."

He took a deep breath.

"Look Janelle, I know you don't have anything to say to me right now, but baby I'm sorry. I didn't know. I never meant to hurt you like this."

He tried to talk to her once more, but when she didn't respond. He walked away, reached for his keys, and left the house.

Sandra rubbed her head.

"Janelle, I know you're hurting right now but, there has to be some kind of explanation for all of this."

She walked over and looked out the window.

"You think."

"Just take a minute and calm down so you can think clearly and listen to God and not how you feel. Please... just do that for me."

Janelle watched as Joshua got in his car and slammed the door.

"I'll call you later Sandra."

"Okay. I'll talk to you then. I love you Janelle."

"I love you too."

Chapter Forty-Three

L ater that evening, Joshua and Brian met up at the bar. He slowly turned towards him in the maroon leather swivel stool.

"Man, you don't even understand how this bar gives me life... especially when Sandra get on my nerves."

He looked over at Joshua.

"What's up man?"

Joshua looked down at his phone.

"What's up."

He smirked.

"Josh, I know you aint at this bar crying."

He scratched his beard.

"Man, whatever."

Brian placed his hand on his shoulder.

"All jokes aside, I'm here for you man."

He shook his head.

"Mannnn, some women are so malicious."

Brian looked at the bar tender and the bar tender looked back at him.

"You want your usual Brian?"

"Nah, I don't want my usual. Let me get a glass of water."

The bar tender reached for a shot glass and gave Brian his usual.

"Here you go man."

Brian shook his head and turned his attention back to Joshua.

"I know I asked this dude for water and he gave me liquor anyway... This dude always trying to be funny."

Joshua shook his head.

"At least the things that you reaping is a good laugh or someone annoying you the way you do me."

His brows met.

"And at least your ex didn't claim to have an abortion and randomly tells you about your four-year-old daughter... after you tell her you can no longer communicate with her."

He clenched his jaws.

"Like it's a game of chess or something."

Brian turned towards Joshua.

"You playing, right?"

"Naw."

He laughed.

"Check mate."

Joshua smacked his lips.

"Whatever man. And the sad part is, I had Janelle on the phone with me and if looks could kill, I wouldn't be sitting at this bar with you right now."

Brian looked over at the bar tender who stood close by listening.

"Let me get a double round of my usual."

He pointed to Joshua.

"Because he gone need it."

Joshua held his hand up to the bar tender.

"Nah. I'm good."

Brian laughed, looked at the bar tender, and back at Joshua.

"He's been delivered from drinking, but he in bondage with his ex. Look man."

He held up his finger.

"Rule number one, when you got woman issues and you don't have a clue what the other woman gone say, don't have your wife on the other end of the phone."

He laughed and held up another finger.

"Number two, that was stupid, just plain out stupid man."

He looked over at Brian.

"Man, I don't know why I call you when I'm going through stuff."

Brian looked over at him and laughed.

"I don't know either, but you making me feel like I'm the best husband in the world right now. Keep encouraging me."

The bar tender interjected.

"I'm not trying to be nosey, but—"

Brian laughed.

"Oh, you being nosey because if you weren't..."

He pointed to the other end of the bar.

"You'd be down there helping them three old men on the other end."

The bar tender ignored Brian and turned his attention back to Joshua.

"Look, I was in a similar situation about two years ago and it took a minute for us to bounce back from it, but we prayed and before I knew it, my wife and I were on the other side of it."

A serious look graced Brian's face.

"So, you saved too."

The bar tender squinted his eyes.

"Just because I work at a bar, don't mean I aint saved Brian. I got bills to pay and this job was open at the time. Oh, and the best place for me to minister is right here where God has me; at the bar where men and women like ya'll come in and vent to they friends."

He smiled.

"This here... Is my pulpit."

Brian turned his head.

"Really."

The bartender smirked.

"Yes, really. Any ways, sometimes they ask me for my opinion and sometimes I'm moved to say something like in Josh situation."

He looked back over to Joshua.

"I'm telling you, it's gone be alright. My wife and I went to this counselor for a few months and she gave us this workbook that I kind of threw to the side until my ex told me about my son that she claimed to have aborted."

He smacked his lips.

"I'm telling you man, I picked that workbook and Bible up so quick, even my wife was confused." He reached for the towel and cleaned the area in front of him, smiled and slung the towel over his shoulder.

"Man..."

He reached for a glass.

"I don't claim to know it all, but God let certain things happen to get our attention. He aint trying to hurt us or nothing like that, but..."

He looked at Brian.

"You know we can be stubborn sometimes and when life knocks us down, He has our full attention again."

The bar tender turned back towards Joshua.

"Then, He picks us up, dust us off, and lets us know He got everything under His control. He knows how to make the bad stuff good, you know."

The older business men at the other end of the bar gestured for the bar tender. He smiled.

"Hey, let me take care of my customers before I get fired down here talking to ya'll. I need my job. You know business men tip real good."

He looked back at Joshua before he walked away.

"I'm telling you, it'll work itself out eventually, but you gotta trust God."

Brian patted Joshua on the back.

"I guess Jesus aint just on the throne and in the pulpit. He even at the bar."

Joshua snatched his shoulder away from Brian.

"Man shut up. Jesus everywhere. He even sitting her listening to you talk stupid."

Before leaving the bar, they stood outside for a minute talking. Brian looked at Joshua.

"I know you going through some thangs right now man, but you gotta find a reason to make your wife smile through it all... This is the time that you really need to make her feel like a queen."

He chuckled.

"I know right."

"Oh yeah, don't forget to pray."

He looked at Joshua and reached for his hands.

"Let us pray."

He closed his eyes as Joshua watched him with one eye open. Using a deep scratchy voice to imitate a pastor, he began to pray.

"Father."

He cleared his throat.

"Joshua done messed up and he in desperate need of your help." He looked up at him.

"Amen."

Joshua shook his head.

"Brian, you just don't stop do you."

He smacked his lips.

"I'll call you tomorrow."

Brian smiled.

"Aight. I'm telling you man, you need laughter in your life. That's why God sent me to you."

Chapter Forty-Four

Three days later, Joshua walked into the room as Janelle got ready for work.

"Good morning."

She walked pass him to their walk-in closet and reached for her shoes. He followed behind her as she walked in the living room.

"Janelle, can we please talk? It's been three days."

She refused to respond causing him to turn around and leave out of frustration. she continued to rebel against forgiveness as it gently tapped on her heart. Twenty minutes later after he left, she reached for her phone and made a call.

"Hello."

"Hey Ms. Lula. What you doing?"

She smirked.

"I was sitting on my couch minding my business until you called. What you doing?"

"On my way to work."

Silence gripped her tongue for a brief moment as she didn't know how to break the news to Ms. Lula.

Ms. Lula pursed her lips.

"So, you just called me to hold the phone right. You better say something or you gone hear this dial tone in five, four, three, two—"

She stopped at the light.

"Ms. Lula."

"I thought you'd say something. What is it child?"

"Joshua has a four-year-old daughter by his ex."

She shook her head.

"Well I'll be dog. Ya'll two. I tell you the truth. Who needs reality tv when I can watch ya'll marriage."

She smiled.

"Just full of drama, drama, and more drama."

The doorbell rang and interrupted her. She looked out of the window and saw the cable truck.

"Hold on child. I been waiting on these people to come fix my cable and they at the door."

Ms. Lula reached for her house coat and walked towards the door.

"Just a minute. I'm coming."

The doorbell rang again.

"Didn't I just say I'm coming? Don't be rushing me."

She looked towards the ceiling.

"Lord help me hold my tongue so I can be nice to these folks."

She snatched the door open.

"Oh, heck naw. What you want?"

She stood in the doorway.

"Janelle let me call you back. The devil just rang my doorbell and I didn't see him through the peep hole and opened it by mistake."

Janelle sighed.

"Okay."

She smiled as she stood at the door.

"Well, well, well. What did I do to deserve for you to rang my doorbell early this morning?"

The man smiled. "Good morning."

"Good morning to you too handsome."

She looked up and whispered.

"Jesus help me Father."

She pulled herself together.

"Come on in. How you doing this morning?"

"I guess I'm okay."

He walked in the living room behind her with his hand in his pocket. She sat down on the sofa and crossed her legs.

"I don't have all day Joshua. What is it?"

He lowered his head and adjusted his tie.

"I messed up big time Ms. Lula."

He leaned back on the couch.

"I don't know what to do because it's been three days and she still isn't speaking to me."

She chuckled.

"Oh yeah. You done messed up if she aint said nothing to you in three days. So, what you do?"

He looked up.

"She didn't tell you?"

She popped her gum.

"Yep, she surely did, but I want to hear it from you."

She turned off the television.

"I'm listening."

He leaned up and placed his elbows on his knees.

"When I decided to finally tell my ex that I could no longer communicate with her and disrespect my wife and marriage, she told me I had a daughter."

"Mmmm hmmm."

"Ms. Lula, I thought she had the abortion."

She shook her head.

"Baby, you can't kill what God desires to live. You know that right?"

He shook his head and frowned. "No, I'm confused. What do you mean?"

"Baby, what God wants to live... it shall live and nothing, I mean nothing can stop it. Not even an abortion. You know everything happens for a reason. Now as bad as I want to tell you a piece of my mind, I can't, because that was your past and Janelle is gone have to somehow pull it together and get over it. I know she hurt and all, but everything has a purpose in life. I mean everything."

He sat in shock that Ms. Lula didn't' take sides.

"I was prepared for you to go off on me."

She shook her head and smiled.

"I bet you were. Like I always tell Janelle, right is right and wrong is wrong. I just pray for your sake that you being totally honest with me."

His brows arched.

"I am. I mean, it's my fault that my ex felt comfortable talking to me and I can own that, but when I ignored her, it seemed to make things worse, especially when she heard that my wife was pregnant."

She shook her head.

"Well, what did you expect? It sounds like that girl was still in love with you and your refusal to give her the closure she needed pushed her over the edge."

He leaned back. "So, how am I supposed to handle this?"

"All I can tell you to do is pray. Child, can't nobody fix this but Jesus... You done got yourself in a world of mess trying to ignore your past and now a child is involved. Not to mention them babies your wife is carrying."

She adjusted herself on the sofa.

"Then there were six."

"Ms. Lula, where did you get six from"

She laughed.

"You, Janelle, the twins, your daughter, and I saved the best one for last.... Your baby momma. You know how to speak in tongues?"

His smile disappeared.

"No ma'am."

"Well, you might better pray for that gift because I bet you aint got the words to pray for the mess you in."

Relieved from her understanding his situation, He smiled.

"Thank you for taking the time to listen to my issues."

She smiled.

"You're welcome."

He smiled.

"I owe you big time Ms. Lula"

"Yesssssss you do and you can do that by fighting for your marriage. Now, get out my house."

He laughed.

"Yes ma'am."

She walked him to the door and pretended to speak in tongues. He looked back and frowned.

"What did you say?"

She laughed.

"Boy, I don't know. I don't have that gift." She pointed to the sky. "But He still hear my prayers."

He smiled and got in the car. Ms. Lula walked back into her house and sat down at the kitchen table.

"Lord, that girl know better than to let the devil get her stirred up in silence like that so he can talk in her head with a bunch of foolish mess."

She reached for her phone to call her, but got the voicemail.

Hi! I'm not available at the moment, but please leave your name, number, and a message and I will return your call within twenty-four to forty-eight hours.

She took a deep breath.

"I tell you what, I got your twenty-four or forty-eight hours. You better call me as soon as you get this message girl or else."

Chapter Forty-Five

A few hours later, Ms. Lula looked over at the phone, but didn't recognize the number.

"Hello."

"Hey Ms. Lula. I just checked my messages and saw that you called."

"Why you calling me anonymously?"

She walked over to the printer and reached for a paper.

"I'm calling from the church."

"Well good. While you there, walk to the altar and fall on your knees."

She frowned.

"Ma'am."

"You heard me. You should be ashamed of yourself. You need to be on your knees repenting."

"Ms. Lula, what are you talking about?"

"Your husband stopped by today and we had a long talk. What's with this three-day silent treatment you giving this man?"

She rolled her eyes.

"Ms. Lula."

Ms. Lula sat up on the couch.

"Don't Ms. Lula me. I want the truth Janelle."

She walked back over to her desk.

"I just feel like all of this could have been avoided had he just dealt with his past before we got married."

"Janelle baby, listen. You had a secret of your own. This is just as much your fault as it is his."

She sat down.

"But he didn't want counseling."

"Well, you shouldn't have said I do until he gave you what the both of you needed. Ya'll should've sat down and talked about everything instead of walking down a aisle for people and be in the place you in right now... In a troubled marriage needing God's power to fix it."

She leaned back in her chair.

"Ms. Lula, am I wrong for not talking to him?"

She shook her head.

"Yes, you are. You should never give a man that much power over your life to control your emotions because all you gone do later is have to repent girl. Now, my aunt once told me, the best way to handle a marriage is think before you speak. She also said, if you know what you say gone hurt the other person, keep it to yourself until love consumes your thoughts and take over your tongue."

She exhaled deeply.

"But it's so hard Ms. Lula and—"

She shook her head and interrupted her.

"You know it had to be hard for Jesus to die for us too. I know because He asked God to take that cup of tea from Him. But the great thing for us is that He did God's will instead of His own. He shut that flesh down girl. Do you understand what I'm saying to you Janelle?"

"Yes ma'am."

"Don't say yes ma'am if you're not willing to move past your feelings and deal with what's going on in your marriage. You ignoring that man aint right. And I won't tell you it is. You're better than that."

She reached for the stapler.

"I get it. I'll talk to him."

"And act like you got some sense when you do."

"I will."

She got up from the couch. "Well, I got to get off this phone and finish cleaning up so I can cook."

Janelle leaned back in her chair. "Thank you for telling me the truth Ms. Lula."

She laughed.

"Girl, that's all I give out. You know... it's the truth that set you free and it's up to the person listening to put what I tell'em to use."

Janelle smiled.

"You're right. Well, I'll let you get back to cleaning. I got to print out a few things and run some errands for Pastor. I love you."

"Love you too baby."

Chapter Forty-Six

L ater that evening Joshua arrived home, walked in the kitchen, and followed the smell of peach cobbler pie. He looked over at his wife and smiled.

"Hey. I see you've cooked my favorite dessert. Is it safe to eat?"

She looked over at him.

"Actually, I baked it for Ms. Lula."

"Oh."

He looked down at his phone, opened the text, smiled, and replied. He looked back up at Janelle.

"So, what time you headed to Ms. Lula house?"

She looked up at him.

"I'm about to leave in ten minutes. Why?"

He got a bottle of water from the refrigerator and took a sip.

"I just asked. Well, I'm about to make a run real quick, but I'll be back in a little while."

She walked past him towards their bedroom.

"Take your time."

"Awe, you actually care."

He smiled. "I'm about to take the pie to the car for you."

She sighed. "Okay."

She got her things from their bedroom and headed to the kitchen. Joshua reached for the pie and chuckled as she rolled her eyes. She grabbed her phone from the island and walked to the car.

He smirked. "Please... tell Ms. Lula I said hi."

She looked at Joshua.

"Okay, I will."

An hour later, he arrived at Ms. Lula's house, got out of the car, and rang the doorbell. Ms. Lula looked over at Janelle and leaned back on the couch.

"Baby, go get the door for me. I'm tired"

She slowly got up from the chair.

"Just a second."

As she opened the door, Joshua stood with roses in his hands and a smile that could melt anger from her heart. She looked back.

"Ms. Lula were you expecting Joshua?"

Ms. Lula looked back at her.

"Was I expecting you?"

She looked at him and rolled her eyes.

"Yes ma'am."

Ms. Lula turned back towards the television.

"Well, I was expecting him too."

He walked in, looked over at Ms. Lula, and handed them roses.

"Thank you for the invite Ms. Lula. I feel special."

She winked her eye at him.

"You're more than welcome. I even made sure Janelle cooked our favorite dessert." She looked over at Janelle and laughed. "We needed something sweet since she acting all bitter and stuff."

He laughed. "I smell food. Did you cook?"

They walked towards the kitchen.

"Yep. I cooked a nice family dinner for all of us. A little of Janelle's favorite, a little of my favorite, and since I didn't know what your favorite was, I created you one."

A smile graced his face as he looked over at Janelle.

"Ms. Lula, if you don't mind me asking, what did you—"

"I do mind you asking. So, please have a seat at the table."

She looked Janelle up and down.

"Oh, that means you too."

She walked in the kitchen, got the dishes, and walked back to the table. She smiled and looked over at Joshua.

"Baby, can you get that big pot out of the oven and sit it on the table for me?"

He got up from the table as she looked over at Janelle and pointed towards the refrigerator.

"Baby, get that sweet tea out of the refrigerator and my special glasses out of the cabinet."

"Yes ma'am."

She got up and reached for Ms. Lula's best drinking glasses and held one up.

"Ms. Lula, you mean these, right?"

She looked back at Janelle.

"Girl, you better stop playing and get them plastic cups. Them glasses is for special occasions."

Joshua looked over at Janelle and laughed as she shook her head.

"So, this isn't a special occasion?"

Her brows arched.

"Girl, get them plastic cups and come on. I done told you, you way to sensitive."

235

Janelle rolled her eyes and smiled. After the table was properly set, they sat down to eat. Ms. Lula reached out for their hands.

"Father, thank you for this food. We ask that you bless it to nourish our bodies and not make us sick. In Jesus name. Amen."

She pointed to the big pot.

"Joshua, baby open that up and slide it towards me just a little."

She smiled and wiggled her body.

"Now, this is what you call good seafood right here."

She reached for the spoon, dipped it in the pot, let some of the juices drain, and placed a big spoon of what was going to be Joshua's new favorite dish on his plate. He looked down at his plate filled with roasted crab legs fused with her special ingredients, red potatoes, and diced sweet peppers. She opened the dish next to her and placed a spoonful of her sautéed spinach and red onions on his plate. She pointed to him and smiled.

"Now, that's your new favorite dish."

He reached for his fork.

"Man, if this taste as good as it looks and smells, I'm gone need seconds."

She looked at Janelle and smiled.

"Now, baby what I have for you is the meal your mom always cooked for you."

She reached for her plate and placed a big piece of fried catfish on it. She opened the other dish and placed a spoonful of seafood rice, and french green beans on her plate, then handed it to her. She smiled as if she could see her mom handing her the plate.

"Ms. Lula. You have out done yourself. But what about you?"

"Oh, baby, don't worry about me." She reached over and opened the last two dishes.

"All I need is my chicken and homemade macaroni and cheese." She bit into her fried chicken and shook her head.

"Now, this is some good chicken right here."

She turned her attention back towards them.

"But anyway, the reason I have ya'll here tonight even in the midst of ya'll marital issues is because."

She took a sip of tea. "I want you both to understand the importance of coming together regardless of what's going on in your marriage."

She ate a spoonful of her macaroni and cheese.

"Janelle, I remember watching your mom and dad allow the devil to rip their marriage apart and I never opened my mouth to say a word."

She pointed towards her.

"Because I didn't want to get caught in the middle of they mess, but I refuse to keep my mouth shut this time. Now, the thing that you're in a uproar about is from this man's past. Regardless of if he continued to talk to her or not.... When he apologized, your job as his wife was to stay true to your vows, forgive him, and figure out how to move past this mess ya'll in without allowing anger to consume you."

She looked up. "But—"

Ms. Lula interrupted her. "Let me finish."

She placed her elbow on the table and deeply exhaled.

"Breathe hard all you want, but your job is to live the life of Christ before him and allow God to win him over by your actions." Ms. Lula looked over at Joshua.

"And you sir. You've got to stop running from your past. Let me tell you, you can't run from something that'll eventually catch up with you. Don't you know the scripture that says everything hidden will be made known."

He lowered his head.

"Ms. Lula, but it's so much to deal with. I mean, I didn't want to hurt my wife like this."

He shook his head.

"You know, I was a wounded man before I married Janelle, but my pride wouldn't let me admit it."

She shook her head.

"Baby, we all were wounded in some type of way before we found love."

He looked over at his wife and back at Ms. Lula.

"I really love her and besides she's taught me more than she knows. I pay attention to the way she lives even when she thinks I don't."

Ms. Lula looked over at Janelle.

"Baby, he loves you, but he just don't know how to show you. If he didn't love you, he wouldn't be here at my table eating my good food right now."

A tear fell from Janelle's eyes.

"I really want our marriage to work and I guess us pointing fingers at each other to make our actions less than the other, isn't making things any better. I'm sorry."

She pointed to herself.

"I guess I was more hurt than I thought."

She looked over at her husband.

"I assumed that I would be the only one to bring your children into this world and when I found out that you had a daughter, it crushed me. And before I knew it, the old me rose up again."

Ms. Lula popped a bottle of champagne and poured some in her glass.

"Ya'll my entertainment for the night. Let's see how this end."

Janelle shook her head.

"Ms. Lula."

She leaned back, folded her arms, and took a sip from her glass.

"Well, I'm just saying."

He smiled.

"Janelle, I love you more than you know. And when we leave here tonight, I want us to be okay. I want us to be able to learn from this and move forward."

Ms. Lula interjected.

"Is that what ya'll call game or truth?"

He smiled and turned his attention back to his wife.

"It's the truth. Janelle, I'm willing to get counseling for the rest of my issues, but I need you by my side all the way to the end. I'm telling you, I got a lot of issues Janelle."

Ms. Lula mumbled.

"Don't we all."

Janelle tilted her head.

"You say something Ms. Lula?"

She smiled.

"Uh uh, but amen to what he said. Let's be real here. All of your problems won't be gone when you leave here. Ya'll men have got to stop saying stuff that's not true to make a woman happy just because it sounds good. Reality is, more issues gone come, but you gotta be willing to fight for your marriage."

She reached for dessert.

"Now, enough of all that. I'm ready to dig in to this peach cobbler my baby done made for us."

Janelle looked over at Joshua and then back towards Ms. Lula and pointed to both of them.

"Ya'll two a piece of work. Just be plotting behind my back."

Ms. Lula leaned up to the table and intertwined her fingers.

"Baby, let me fill you in on a secret. That's what love looks like. It finds a way to make things work when it doesn't know any other way to penetrate a heart full of unforgiveness, hurt, and anger."

She pointed to Janelle.

"And in your case, silent treatments. Love uses the back door and that back door happens to be me."

After their talk, they enjoyed dessert. About an hour later Ms. Lula took a deep breath.

"It's time for ya'll to go. My job here is done."

Janelle smiled.

"After we clean the kitchen, we'll leave."

Her brows arched as she got up from the table with her champagne glass.

"Looks like ya'll need to get started then."

Joshua laughed.

"Only Ms. Lula."

An hour later, Ms. Lula walked them to the door.

"I enjoyed ya'll, but it's past my bedtime."

Janelle gave her a kiss and reached for her purse and keys.

"We enjoyed you too Ms. Lula. I'll call you in the morning."

Ms. Lula hugged Joshua and leaned her head on the door.

"Janelle."

She looked back.

"Ma'am."

"Don't call me in the morning."

Joshua walked to his car and opened the door.

"Ms. Lula, thank you again."

She smiled.

"You're welcome baby. So, when you gone let me borrow that car?"

He opened the door and got in.

"Whenever you're ready. It's all yours."

She smiled.

"Alright now Ima hold you to that."

"Yes ma'am."

He closed the door and watched Janelle get in her car and let. down her window.

"Good night Ms. Lula. I'll call you and let you know I..."

"I mean when we make it home."

"Alright. Ya'll be careful."

Ms. Lula blew her a kiss

Chapter Forty-Seven

About fifteen minutes later, they arrived home, but Joshua sat in his car. His thoughts drifted to possibility of having a daughter. When he decided to get out of the car, his phone rang.

"Hello..."

He looked up and frowned.

"Look. Do you what you have to do, but I'm not gonna to play these games with you Patrice."

Janelle opened the front door, turned around, and stood in the doorway as he continued.

"From now on, you can reach me through my attorney. I'm not gonna continue to allow you to keep up confusion between me and my wife. She's pregnant and I refuse to let you stress her out."

His ex frowned.

"Oh, so you're protecting the babies your wife is carrying, but you wanted to do away with mine... Really Joshua."

Patrice frowned as he ended the call.

"Hello, hello."

She threw the phone in the chair.

Meanwhile, Joshua walked towards his wife.

"Baby, I'm not gonna to sit back and allow the devil to rip our marriage apart. In the morning, I'll reach out to my attorney and request a paternity test. If Ashley's my daughter, we'll have to figure things out."

He placed his arms around her.

"Baby, I'm sorry that you even have to deal with my past... I promise I'll make it up to you."

She leaned her forehead on his shoulder.

"No need to worry. Just do what you need to do until you get the results. I just hate that this little girl is being pulled into something she had nothing to do with."

She looked at her husband.

"I honestly believe your ex moved because she was afraid to tell you that she didn't go through with the abortion, but at the same time, I'm starting to think that everything she does at this point is because she's angry at the fact that you hurt her. I'm about to get a shower and get ready for bed."

She placed her hand on her stomach.

"Stressing can cost me my unborn children's life. And to be honest, your past isn't even worth it."

He reached for her arm before she could walk away.

"You're right, By the way, on a lighter note, I'm happy Ms. Lula invited me over. Out of all people, I know she has our best interest at heart."

He smiled.

"That lady is something serious. You know she told me I was gone need the gift of speaking in tongues because I didn't have the words to pray for the mess I'm in?"

She laughed.

"That sounds like something she would say."

She walked back over to him and sat on the arm the sofa.

"I didn't even know she watched my mom and dad go through a rough marriage. Talk about generational."

He shook his head.

"I know right. Look Janelle, I don't want our marriage to end in divorce like our parents."

"Me either. So tonight—"

"I vow to no longer sit back and allow the devil to rip our marriage apart. As of tonight, I'm rewriting the script. We gone going to weather the storm. Alright."

She smiled. "Alright."

Later that evening, Janelle lay in Joshua's arms and rested in peace knowing that everything was now completely in God's control.

Chapter Forty-Eight

Two days later, nervousness held Joshua captive as he arrived to the hospital for his paternity test. Fearful of what the results would be, he took a deep breath and exhaled deeply. As Patrice and Ashley walked into the hospital, Ashley walked over and sat in the waiting area. Her mom signed in and walked towards her daughter. Without taking notice of the little girl or her mother, Joshua got up, but before he walked away he answered his phone.

"Good morning Mr. Togglier."

His distinct voice caught Ashley's attention. She looked over at him and tapped her mom on the shoulder and pointed to him.

"Momma, he sounds just like uncle Josh."

Patrice frowned.

"Huh."

She leaned closer to her mom.

"You know... The uncle Josh that called me."

Patrice's eyes grew wide as she leaned back and smiled.

"Oh."

"Is that him momma?"

She tilted her head towards Ashley and forced a smile.

"Baby, you know—"

Before she could say anything else, the nurse walked towards them.

"Patrice and Ashley Shelfree."

They got up and followed the nurse. About fifteen minutes later, Joshua walked back in, in time to hear his name called.

"Mr. Joshua Richards."

As he walked to the back with the nurse, Patrice and Ashley walked past him in almost in slow motion. Ashley pointed to him again.

"Momma, there's that man that sounds like Uncle Josh again."

She smiled and waved at him.

"Excuse me sir."

Her mom froze.

"When you answered your phone, you sounded like my new uncle Josh."

Patrice yanked her and frowned.

"Come on Ashley. Leave the man alone. I'm pretty sure he doesn't want to be bothered."

He was shocked that she remembered his voice. The nurse walked towards him.

"Mr. Joshua Richards."

He turned to her and stared in disbelief that Ashley's features were so strong and resembled him in more ways than one. The nurse reached for the paternity exam as he walked in and sat down.

"Good afternoon Mr. Richards. Today we'll be taking samples from you for your paternity test."

She explained the process; however, he seemed to be in a daze as she spoke. She smiled and snapped her fingers.

"Excuse me... Mr. Richards. Did you land in space yet?"

He looked up and rubbed the back of his neck.

"I'm sorry. I was in deep thought."

"I could see that."

She explained the process once more before beginning.

"Please open your mouth for me to collect the samples."

The nurse reached for the swabs and began. A tear escaped from his eyes.

"I don't mean to probe sir, but are you okay?"

"Yes ma'am. I'm okay."

She took a sticker with his information on it and wrapped it around the container with his samples and smiled.

"It's natural to be nervous about having a paternity test done, but it's for the best. It's always better to know than to be left in the dark wandering what if." She smiled. "We're all done here. You'll receive your results within two to three business days."

"Thank you ma'am, you have a good day."

As he walked through the glass doors at the hospital to leave, Patrice's car caught his attention, but no one was in it. As he got in his car, he slammed the door, leaned back in the seat, and punched the steering wheel causing the horn to blow. The horn caught Ashley's attention as she and her mom walked out of the hospital. She looked up at her mom.

"Momma, who is that man?"

Patrice lowered her head and walked to the car.

"You'll find out soon enough baby."

Ashley looked up as she held her mom's hand.

"What does that mean?"

She responded sternly.

"Get in the car Ashley and stop asking so many questions."

She lowered her head.

"Yes ma'am."

That evening when Joshua returned home, he walked in, sat down his briefcase, and leaned back in the recliner. Janelle yelled out from the kitchen.

"Joshua is that you?"

She walked into the living room and saw him sitting on the sofa in a daze.

"Hey. How did everything go?"

She walked over to the sofa and placed her hand on his shoulder.

"Josh. Please don't shut me out."

"She looks just like me."

She looked up at him.

"How do you know?"

He shook his head.

"I saw her at the hospital when I walked back in from taking the call from my attorney."

Her eyes grew wide.

"Oh. How do you know it was her?"

"Really Janelle. She was with her mom."

He leaned up and rubbed his head.

"She has beautiful caramel skin like my mom, long pretty natural hair like my sister, and when she smiled, I could've sworn I saw dimples like my dad."

He leaned back.

"Not to mention she recognized my voice and asked her mom if I was uncle Josh, but Patrice grabbed her and told her she was pretty sure I didn't want to be bothered."

He shook his head and held up four fingers.

"If she's mine, I've missed out on four years of my daughter's life."

Frustration gripped his voice.

"Who does that?"

She looked at him with sympathy in her eyes.

"Joshua, in her defense. You did ask for an abortion. What did you expect?"

He frowned.

"Janelle, I don't want to hear this from you right now."

She jerked her neck back.

"I can't say that I understand what you're going through. I can only imagine, but it's not fair that one minute you claim to be apologetic for everything you do to me, then on the other hand, you return back to your vomit. This isn't my fault. I'm not the one who got her pregnant, Joshua... And I refuse to let you take your frustration out on me."

She shook her head as he got up and walked towards the front door dangling his keys in her hand.

"There you go running from your problems again."

As he turned around and reached for his keys, she shook her head.

"I'm not gonna keep letting you run from your problems Joshua. Be mad if you want, but I love you too much to keep watching you do this to yourself."

He walked into the bedroom and slammed the door. She deeply exhaled and sat down on the sofa.

"Jesus."

Chapter Forty-Nine

T he next evening, during their women's meeting, Janelle stood behind the podium and smiled.

"Hey ladies... Tonight, our lesson will come from Job chapters 1-42. We will discuss what to do when life takes you on a detour?"

She gathered her thoughts and smiled.

"I typically don't open up too much about my personal life, but I find it necessary tonight. After learning that my husband may possibly have a four-year-old daughter, every emotion possible visited me. I wanted to hate him. I wanted to scream and tell him exactly how I felt."

She chuckled and looked down at the podium.

"I wanted everything to be a dream that he would gently tap me and awaken from, but it was real. I found myself revisiting every lesson that I've taught in our meetings... I almost felt like I failed God because I didn't respond to this unexpected detour the way I thought I would... that's why I feel it necessary to talk about what to do when life takes us on a detour tonight."

Ms. Lula smiled.

"Uh."

Janelle opened her Bible and turned to the book of Job.

"I remember hearing the story of Job and his wife, but the story I always heard was so negative. I couldn't understand what would make her tell her husband to curse God and die."

She held up her finger.

"Until I went back and reread her response completely. Then, I realized that it wasn't until after she lost all of her children at once and watched her husband suffer in misery that she uttered those words."

The ladies listened attentively as she continued.

"But then, I remembered the story of her husband."

She shook her head.

"I always heard about the first two chapters of Job and the last chapter of his blessings, but after reading about his wife, I felt compelled to continue reading. I mean Job was a faithful man, right."

The ladies nodded as she continued.

"At least that's what God said, but somewhere between chapters three and thirty-seven, life took him on a detour and it took a toll on him. He went back and forth with his friends who didn't understand how to comfort him and I could feel his frustration as I read and flipped each page... You know that's what life does to us at times, it takes us on this unexpected detour and when were forced to take a different route, it can bring frustrations that cause us to act out of character. It can even cause us to spew out words we thought we'd never utter just like Jobs wife."

She gestured her hands in circle.

"That's when we feel as if we've failed God or God has failed us, but reality is He never fails us. He comforts, answers, and blesses us as just as Job did."

She pointed to Ms. Lula.

"And ya'll know how silly Ms. Lula is, but when life took me on that detour, she reminded me that forgiveness was powerful and that my husband's past had nothing to do with his love for me."

The young lady behind Ms. Lula nodded.

"I know that's right. Now, why aint nobody ever preached that story to me like that?"

Janelle laughed.

"You know, life can make you see scriptures in a whole new light, but you—"

Ms. Lula interrupted her.

"And that's why we need to know the word for yourself, so we can experience true revelation. We live in a generation where people hear the voice of the internet and not the voice of God. If we don't take the time to sit in the word and hear God for ourselves, we'll continue to be bamboozled by googled messages."

The young lady behind Ms. Lula lifted her hand.

"I have a very serious question."

Janelle looked over at her and smiled.

"Sure, go ahead."

She lowered her head.

"I just don't want to be judged."

Ms. Lula turned around and looked at her.

"Aint nobody." She stopped and pointed to everyone. "I mean nobody, got no business judging you about nothing because every last one of us in here is a hot mess needing Jesus' help. Now, go ahead and say what you gotta say."

The young lady took a deep breath and shook her head.

"Well, my husband talked to me the other day about spicing up our marriage... And he asked me to bring in another woman. I want him to be happy, but I don't think that's the right way."

Ms. Lula shook her head.

"First off, I aint judging you, but that's a detour the devil trying to take you on. Besides, I'm judging that lying spirit that's trying to convince you to jump on board with that mess. I don't know what's wrong with this perverted generation tainting marriages by adding to what God clearly already subtracted from."

She held up two fingers.

"When you was dating, ya'll were two right."

"Yes ma'am."

She pulled one finger down.

"And then, when you got married, you became one."

She held up two more fingers.

"And if you bring another person in, ya'll gone be three and I ain't talking about the Holy Trinity either."

The young she shook her head.

"He only wants to bring one person in and if you subtract two from one that leaves one and when you add one that's two."

Ms. Lula shook her head.

"Child child child. It's three because the one you bringing in, bringing the devil with her."

A young lady in the back of the church laughed out loud.

"Only Ms. Lula could come up with something like that."

Chapter Fifty

T hree days later, Joshua sat in his office finishing work for their next case. Ten minutes later, he received a call. He looked down and realized that it was his attorney and waited a second before answering. He leaned back in his chair.

"Hello."

"Good morning Mr. Richards."

"Good morning."

The attorney reached for the envelope from desk.

"I decided I would read the results once I contacted you. So..."

He cleared his throat.

"Are you ready for this?"

He took a deep breath.

"I'm as ready as I can be."

He opened the envelope and read the results.

"Mr. Richards, are you still there?"

"I'm here. Thank you, Mr. Togglier. Have a blessed day."

"You as well."

He ended the call and walked to his boss's office. He paused, closed his eyes, and took a deep breath before entering.

"Mr. Franklin, I need to take the rest of the day off."

His boss looked at him.

"Is everything okay?"

"It will be."

His boss reached for a folder out of his desk.

"Sure. It's a slow day anyway, so it'll be no problem. On your way out, please hand this to the secretary for me. She knows what it's for."

"Okay."

Before he walked out of the office, he turned back towards his boss holding the folder in his left hand.

"I really appreciate this Mr. Franklin."

He smiled.

"No problem. You have a good day."

"You as well."

As he walked into his office, he reached for his keys, and proceeded to walk to the front of the building. He smiled and handed the secretary the folder.

"Mr. Franklin asked me to give this to you."

She smiled.

"Leaving so soon Mr. Richards?"

"Yes ma'am. I'll be back tomorrow."

"Alright. Have a good day... Oh, and please tell your wife I said hi."

"I sure will."

As he walked to the car, his phone rang.

"Hello."

"Hey Josh. I'm leaving the office a little early and heading back to the house. I'm not feeling my best today."

His brows met.

"You alright?"

She stared at the paper on the desk and reached for her keys.

"I'll be fine."

"I guess I'll see you when you get home. I'm taking the rest of the day off too."

She opened the car door.

"Are you okay?"

"I'm good. I'll see you when you get there."

Her brows arched.

"Okay."

Twenty minutes later, she arrived home to find her husband sitting in complete silence with tears in his eyes. Her brows met as she put her purse down and walked over to sit next to him. She gently placed her hand on his leg.

"Josh, you okay. What happened?"

He shook his head, took a deep breath, and leaned back.

"I got the results today... She's mine. I'm sorry Janelle. I never meant for any of this happen."

Taken back, she forced a smile and wiped the tears from her eyes.

"It's okay. I know you didn't. Remember, it's your past."

He turned to his wife.

"Yeah. But, my past is now a part of my... I mean our future."

She smiled.

"That's not a bad thing you know."

She leaned her head on his shoulder.

"Does she know yet?"

"I'm pretty sure she does. The thing is I lied and told her that I was her uncle. How am I supposed to explain that?"

She glanced over at him.

"The only thing you can do at this point is tell the truth, because if you lie, you're gonna to have to keep telling another lie to cover the next one. So, sit down and have a heart to heart with her in a way she can understand."

She got up from the sofa and looked at him.

"I'm going to lay down if you need me."

"Okay."

He looked at her with sorrowful eyes as she walked towards their bedroom. He turned around.

"Janelle... I'm sorry."

She smiled.

"It's okay."

She walked into the room and sat on her side of the bed as tears slowly escaped from her eyes. She reached down and rubbed her stomach.

"Lord. What am I supposed to do?"

Chapter Fifty-One

T he next day during Janelle's lunch break, she ran into Mrs. Chambers at the market. She walked over to her and smiled.

"Hi. Mrs. Chambers."

She returned a smile.

"Hi Mrs. Richards. How are you today?"

"I'm great and you."

She pointed to her buggy.

"I'm doing well. I just decided to do some last minute shopping on my break. You look almost as if you have a lot on your mind today."

Janelle glanced at the lady walking by and turned her attention back to the counselor.

"Actually, I've wanted to call and talk to you. This whole assignment thing has been challenging. I really want to be in a happy place with my husband again."

She slowly pushed the buggy back to the rack.

"I really want to be there for you and your husband right now, but I have to move out of God's way and allow the both of you to work through this together with His guidance. I know that other counselors wouldn't agree, but my goal is for you to trust God with your marriage."

She smiled.

"And the process that He's taking you through by not being totally dependent upon me. That was the purpose of the workbook from our last session. They're way too many people that hinder growth in marriages by holding couples hand every single step of the way instead of allowing God to guide them."

She forced a smile.

"I understand."

The counselor gestured her hand towards the door.

"Mrs. Richards, please walk to my car with me. I want to give you something to hold on to as you continue to rely on God during this shaky time in your marriage."

Her eyes smiled as she walked out of the store with the counselor.

"I truly thank you for everything."

"You're welcome."

She smiled.

"Helping save marriages is what I love to do because when my marriage was broken and on the way to a divorce, God sent someone to help me. My way of getting back at the enemy, is saving one of the things he delights in tearing apart...Marriages"

She reached into her car, and handed Janelle a tiny jar of mustard seeds.

"Mrs. Richards, all you need to do is trust God. We all have our moments in life where we struggle from time to time with our faith. But one thing is for sure."

She pointed to her.

"Your faith has power. It doesn't have to be big, just the size of one of these seeds. When God sprinkles mist on the grass while you're asleep, it doesn't float back to the sky; therefore, it's your job to trust that God's Words won't return to him void? Now, that's what you call faith. So, stop worrying and do your part. When challenges come, I want you to look at the tiny seeds in this jar and remember the power of your faith."

She leaned over to hug her.

"I truly needed this."

"Hang in there Mrs. Richards. It's only a few more days until our next session."

She smiled.

"And remember to have a wonderful day."

"You as well."

As they walked back in the market, they went opposite direction. After grabbing a few things, Janelle went to the register to check out. As she stood in the line, an older caucasian lady with beautiful white hair turned around.

"Hey sweetie."

She smiled.

"Hi. How are you?"

She pulled out her wallet as the cashier rung up her items and looked back at Janelle with a wide smile.

"I'm doing great."

She excitedly proceeded.

"I turned eighty yesterday. I must say that I'm well for my age."

"Wow. You don't look a day over fifty."

"Well, thank you baby." She looked at Janelle's ring finger. "I see that you're married."

She smiled.

"Yes ma'am."

The cashier listened attentively as if what they were saying was jut for her. The older lady looked at Janelle and smiled.

"Baby enjoy your husband and make sure to show him how much you love him no matter what. My husband passed away last year and I'm learning to live without him. Lord knows I miss him so much."

"Yes ma'am. Thank you. I'm sorry for your loss."

She looked back at Janelle as she paid the cashier.

"Baby, it's not a lost because I was married to my best friend. I miss him, but I know his soul is finally resting. All I can say is enjoy every moment of your marriage because you never know when your time or his time is up."

Her smile faded away.

"Yes ma'am. You have a good day."

"You too baby."

In deep thought from the older lady's words, Janelle walked out of the market, popped the trunk, and placed her groceries in the car. One of the young ladies from her women's meeting called her name and walked towards her.

She smiled. "Hey Janelle."

She returned a smile.

"Hey! I guess I came to the store to early, huh."

She laughed.

"Nope. I came too late. I needed for you to pay for my groceries."

She shook her head and laughed.

"I love your hair. Who did your faux locs?"

The young lady flipped her hair.

"Girl stop... I aint got that kind of money to pay for nobody to do this."

She held up her fingers and wiggled them.

"God gifted these fingers right here to do it."

She tilted her head.

"For free."

Janelle laughed.

"Well, since your hands are so gifted, I have these babies in a few months and I need you to do my hair for the delivery."

The young lady reached for a list from her purse.

"Girl, I got you. I'm not gonna hold you up. Besides, I got some shopping to do."

She smiled.

"Don't buy the store out now."

The young lady laughed.

"Girl... stop playing. My food stamps limited. My refill didn't hit yet."

Janelle shook her head and smiled.

"You so silly. See you at the next meeting."

The young lady waved goodbye as she walked into the store. Janelle got in the car, reached down for her phone, and made a call. Sandra ran from her room and grabbed the phone from the sofa.

"Hello."

Janelle put on her seatbelt.

"Hey. I have a question for you."

She grabbed the remote and turned the television down.

"What's up?"

"If you were in my situation, how would you react to finding out that your husband has a four-year-old daughter that he thought was aborted?"

Sandra shook her head.

"Janelle, as hard is this may be to believe, I would let it go. He can't go back and make the baby go away. So, the best thing for you to do is to find a way to forgive and be more concerned about them babies you have inside of you. The devil is trying to take your focus off of your miracles."

She smiled.

"You're right."

Sandra laughed.

"I know I am. All he wants to happen is for you to stress yourself out and lose the blessings God has given you."

"I figured you would say that."

"Girl, I have to forgive my husband for so much until it's pitiful. Don't get me wrong. I know the pain you feel is real and I could only imagine what's going through your mind right now, but life is too short to sit around silently angry over your husband's past."

She held the phone for a few second.

"Janelle, you still there?"

"I'm here."

"Please don't be upset with me, but my goal as your friend is to try to change the way you think about your husband."

She pulled in the driveway and parked the car.

"I mean, the sad thing is that I'm over a women's group and I need help myself."

Sandra shook her head.

"So... what you're saying is that because you have a title and you lead some ladies that you're not human? So, you're telling me that you're a Christian robot right."

Her eyes widened.

"No."

"Yes, you are and that's not fair. I bet if someone cuts you, you gonna bleed."

She laughed.

"And I guarantee you if you break a leg, you gone holla. You wanna to know why?"

She leaned her head back on the head rest in the car.

"I already know."

"Well, I'm gonna remind you again. It's because you're human. Everybody goes through things in life."

She chuckled.

"No one is exempt from having issues; especially in marriages because baby, life happens to us all. Besides, we all need someone to talk to. Girl pastors and teachers go through things too. The only difference is some are too prideful to be transparent enough to share their reality and that's what messes people up and causes them to feel like they're the only one's going through. You think their invisible from pain, right?"

"Not really."

Sandra walked into her kitchen and reached for the fork on the stove.

"That's the way you make it sound. Girl, don't be fooled thinking that you're supposed to be everything for everyone else and ignore all that you go through for the satisfaction of what others might think."

She flipped the chicken in the pan.

"As your friend, I refuse to sit back and listen to you beat yourself up like that."

Janelle got out of the car and walked around to the trunk.

"You're right."

"Trust me. Forgiving your husband is gonna to be your best weapon. You know, life is too short to hold grudges; especially when you never know when your time or his time is up."

She glanced up.

"Wait, what?"

"Life is too short to—"

"I know what you said. It was an old lady at the market and she said the same thing."

Sandra laughed.

"Girl, you know God be on repeat mode. Ya'll call that confirmation. Besides, I'm pretty sure she was trying to tell you to value the time you have with the one you love because time is something you never get back."

She chuckled.

"You're right. I really need to get me some rest."

Sandra smiled.

"Yep, that sounds about right. I'll call you later."

"Alright. Thank you for talking to me."

"Any time. That's what friends are for right."

She popped the trunk.

"Yep. Love you girl."

Sandra smiled.

"Love you too."

Chapter Fifty-Two

A few days later, Janelle and Joshua sat on the sofa watching the sports center. Hearing her phone ring, she reached and grabbed it from the table.

"Hello."

"Good evening Mrs. Richards."

She recognized the voice and smiled.

"Hi. How are you?"

"I'm doing well and how are the Richards?"

"We're great."

Joshua's brow met as he looked at his wife.

"Your next appointment is Monday at 3:00 p.m. Is that time okay for you all?

She looked over at Joshua.

"Hey. This is Mrs. Chambers office. Do you want to confirm or not for Monday at three?"

He rubbed his chin.

"Yeah, I guess you can confirm it."

She placed the phone back to her ear.

"That time works for us."

The secretary confirmed their appointment.

"We'll see you all then. Have a wonderful day."

"Thank you. You as well."

A couple of hours later, she looked over at her husband.

"Josh, did you ever complete your workbook? You know she's gonna to ask about it."

He shook his head and laughed.

"Nope. What about you?"

"I have like two more lessons to complete and I'll be done."

He reached for the remote.

"All I can do when I get there is tell the truth."

He rubbed his lips with his fingers.

"I mean, it's not like I'm about to complete it all in three days."

She rolled her eyes.

"Did you even look at it?"

"I looked at it."

He shrugged his shoulders.

"That's about it. It was too many personal questions on the first two pages for me and I'd rather leave those things buried in my past. I'm over that stuff."

Frustrated from his comment, she got up from the sofa and mumbled as she walked towards the kitchen.

"I bet you are."

He looked back.

"Did you say something?"

She smirked.

"Not a word."

She proceeded to walk into the kitchen and poured a glass of orange juice. She yelled out.

"Josh."

He turned around.

"Yeah."

"You want some orange juice?"

He turned back towards the television.

"Nah. I'm good."

took a sip as she looked over at the microwave and saw the time and frowned.

"It's already 11:30 p.m."

She walked back into the living room and sat next to her husband. She inhaled and exhaled slower. He looked over at her as she rubbed the top of her stomach.

"You okay?"

She leaned her head up and looked over at him.

"Yeah. I just think I have a little gas."

He turned his nose up.

"Just don't release on me."

"Whatever."

She turned towards him.

"You know, I really hope Ashley likes me."

"Me too."

She reached for his hand and placed it on the top of her belly.

"So, this is what it feels like when two babies are moving at once? Mannn." He leaned over and kissed he on her cheek. "I love you Janelle."

"Love you too."

The following day, they took a stroll through the park holding hands and reminisced on the good old days they had together. Joshua looked over at Janelle.

"How about some ice-cream?"

She noticed the ice-cream truck.

"Sounds good to me. Besides, I wanna try something different anyway."

"Oh Lord, don't try too much."

She chuckled. "Whatever Joshua."

He laughed.

"I'm just saying. You know how your stomach is set up."

Walking over to the ice-cream truck, Janelle decided to try the homemade banana pudding ice-cream while Joshua insisted on the strawberry sundae. As they walked over and watched the ducks in the lake, Janelle reached for her back.

"Josh, I'm really enjoying myself, but my back is killing me right now."

He rubbed her back.

"You ready."

"Yeah."

As they walked to the car, Joshua noticed the time.

"Mannnn it's already 7:00 p.m.?"

She smiled.

"You know time flies by when you're enjoying the one you love."

He reached for her hand.

"I'm about to stop and get some pizza. You want some."

"Nope, I'm good."

They arrived home an hour later and walked into the house. Tired from the day, Janelle yawned and got ready for bed while Joshua sat up eating pizza and watching the sports channel. He looked up and smiled.

"I must say. I out did myself today and I didn't even have to do the assignments."

The next morning, Janelle, showered and got dressed for church. She walked into the kitchen with her phone in her hand, looked up, and saw Joshua standing at the stove in his khaki pants, black polo shirt, and black shoes. Her brows met.

"You about to leave?"

He turned around and reached for a plate.

"Yeah, after we eat breakfast."

"Oh, where you headed to this morning?"

She walked over to the refrigerator, grabbed a bottle of water, and sat at the table playing Candy Crush.

He walked over to the table and handed her, her plate.

"To church with you."

She glanced up at him and smiled.

"Really."

He smiled and kissed her on the forehead.

"Yes. Really."

Chapter Fifty-Three

T he next day, Janelle and Joshua got ready for her doctor's appointment. He walked behind her, placed his arms around her, and smiled.

"I can't wait to meet our babies."

She turned around.

"I know right. I can't believe I'm about to be a mother."

His eyes smiled.

"What!!! I can't believe we're about to have twins."

She giggled.

"Yep, double for our trouble."

He turned around to walk away.

"Alright slowdy poke, hurry and get dressed so we can be on time."

About an hour later she walked in the living room. Joshua turned around.

"Whatttt! You ready?"

She smiled.

"Yep. You ready?"

He got up from the sofa.

"I stay ready."

She shook her head and walked into the kitchen.

"Oh! I see you got jokes, huh."

"I'm just saying. You're always late for everything."

Twenty minutes later, they arrived at the office, signed in, and sat down next to a couple and smiled. The lady sitting next to her forced a smile.

"Congratulations."

Janelle looked over at her.

"Thank you. Same to you."

The lady shook her head.

"No, I'm not pregnant. I wish I could be, but the doctors told me there was no chance that would happen after going through my last ectopic pregnancy, especially, since menopause decided to come immediately after that."

The lady reached and grabbed her husband's hand.

"It would've been our first."

Janelle looked over at Joshua as he sent a message and looked back towards the lady.

"I'm so sorry to hear that, but God always has the last word you know."

The lady frowned.

"No, I don't know. What do you mean by that?"

"My doctor explained to me that due to a childhood accident, I wouldn't be able to have children, but there's something about faith. When you least expect it, it's bound to happen."

She pointed down to her belly.

"I'm a miracle and so are the babies inside of me."

The nurse opened the door.

"Gabrielle Tupor."

The lady got up.

"Thank you and it was nice meeting you."

Janelle smiled.

"Nice to meet you too."

Joshua looked over at Janelle as the lady walked away.

"You so friendly."

She rolled her eyes.

"You should try it."

About ten minutes later, the nurse came to the door.

"Janelle Richards. We're ready for you."

Before the nurse put them in a room she looked over at Janelle and smiled.

"Mrs. Richards, we need a urine sample."

She reached for the cup and walked into the restroom. Three minutes later, she came out and the nurse walked them to room three. She checked Janelle's weight and smiled.

"Mrs. Richards, you've gained ten pounds since your last visit."

She smiled.

"I feel it too."

The nurse reached for a gown.

"When I leave out, take off everything and slide this on."

Janelle reached for the gown. "Thank you."

Joshua scrolled through his phone as his wife got undressed, slipped on the gown, and sat on the examining table.

Minutes later, the doctor and nurse came in and the doctor extended his hand towards Joshua.

"Good morning Mr. Richards."

Joshua firmly shook his hand.

"Good morning."

The doctor looked over at Janelle and patted her on the shoulder.

"Only eight more weeks left before you meet your babies. I know you're excited."

She smiled.

"We're super excited."

He looked over at Joshua.

"So, you're a first-time dad huh? This has to be exciting."

Joshua looked at his wife.

"No sir. I actually have a four-year-old daughter." He lowered his head and fondled his hands.

"Great, then you can teach your wife a thing or two."

The nurse handed the doctor the towel, k-y jelly, and fetoscope.

"Are ya'll ready to hear these strong heartbeats?"

Janelle smiled as she lay back on the examining table and she placed her hand behind her head as the doctor squeezed the jelly on her stomach. He placed the fetoscope on her belly and gently moved it around to find the babies heart beats. Seconds later, the doctor smiled.

"They're they go."

He cleaned her stomach and reached for his gloves.

"Alright, lay back and let's check you."

He placed her feet in the stirrups, checked her, washed his hands, and explained the process of inducing her labor. On his way out, he shook Joshua's hand.

"It was nice seeing you again. Have a wonderful day."

Joshua smiled.

"You as well."

Shortly after arriving home, Joshua walked his wife over to her car and kissed on the forehead.

"I'll see you this evening."

She got in the car.

"Alright. See you then."

Chapter Fifty-Five

The next morning, Janelle remembered they had a counseling session. She reached for her phone to make a call.

"Hello."

"Hey Josh."

He took a sip of his coffee.

"Good morning. I didn't wake you up because I had to leave to meet a deadline."

She twirled her ring around her finger.

"No, it's okay. I actually called to remind you about our counseling session this afternoon at three."

He rubbed his nose.

"Man, I forgot all about that. Can we reschedule?"

She took a deep breath.

"No, I just told you about this Friday."

He leaned back in his chair.

"Alright. I'll be there."

"Joshua please don't forget."

"I won't. I'll see you this afternoon. I love you."

"Love you too."

She got ready and arrived at the church a little after nine and took all the time she needed to print out the programs for pastor Peter. About 11:30 a.m., she received a text.

Hey girl! 😊

She picked up her phone.

Hey, Sandra. What's up?

Sandra smiled.

I'm headed your way. You want to get lunch? 😊

Sure. 😊

Okay. See you then....

Fifteen minutes later, Janelle grabbed her phone when she saw Sandra pull up. She knocked on the pastor's door.

"Hey. I'm about to grab lunch. Do you need anything back?"

He shook his head.

"No thank you."

"Okay. See you later."

As she got in the car, she smiled.

"I guess lunch is on you?"

Sandra laughed.

"Of course girl. I got you."

As they drove off and pulled up to the light, Janelle took notice of the car next to them.

"Isn't that Brian's car?"

Looking over at the car, Sandra was taken back at the young lady sitting on the passenger side smiling. So, she blew the horn, but Brian didn't hear it. As the light turned green, Sandra drove off and took a right turn. Janelle looked over at her with sorrowful eyes.

"You okay."

"I'm fine."

They grabbed their lunch and headed back to the church in complete silence. Janelle looked over at Sandra before getting out of the car.

"Sandra, you know you always tell me that looks can be deceiving."

"You're absolutely right."

Janelle watched as Sandra drove off and walked back into the church. Later that day, she grabbed her things, peeked into the pastor's office, and smiled.

"Hey Pastor."

He cleared his throat.

"Hey."

"I'm leaving for the day. Do you need me to do anything before I leave?"

He reached into his desk.

"Yes. Can you please drop this off at the post office for me?"

She walked into the office and reached for the envelopes.

"Anything else."

He rubbed his head. "No thank you. Just enjoy your day."

She smiled. "You too."

Meanwhile, Sandra arrived at the courthouse and sat in the parking lot fighting back the tears. She took a deep breath, got out of the car, and walked in. She placed her purse and keys on the table for security to check and walked through the security check system. She looked over at the guard.

"Can you please point me to where I can get divorce papers please?"

He pointed.

"Take a right, then it's the second door on the left."

She smiled.

"Thank you."

Later that evening, Sandra arrived home, sat at the table and completed the divorce application. As a tear fell down her face, she grabbed the application from the table, walked into her room, and fell to her knees on the side of her bed.

"God, I don't understand where I went wrong. I've done all that I know is required of me as a wife, but he remains so distant, not to mention the woman in his car. I'm so tired of this."

Before she could finish, Brian arrived home to find her on her knees crying with papers in her hand. His lips parted.

"Sandra."

When she didn't respond. He walked over and sat on the bed.

"Sandra. What happened?"

She looked up with tears in her eyes.

"Really? You happened."

He reached for the papers in her hand.

"Oh. Hell nah. What's this for?"

She wiped her face.

"I saw you in the car with her."

She reached for the paper, but before she grabbed them, he ripped them up.

"That cost me ten dollars."

He coughed up a laugh.

"Well, you better get back on your knees and pray for God to give you a refund."

He stood up and laughed.

"You in here tripping for nothing. Over here letting the devil talk in your head."

She rolled her eyes.

"Who is she?"

He quickly looked at her and smirked.

"Sandra, that was Denise from my job. Her car wouldn't start and I was taking her to her appointment."

She smacked her lips.

"Whatever Brian."

He rubbed his chin.

"Woman, do I look stupid? Why would I ride around town with another woman knowing you live here? Not to mention you got friends that tell everything they see?"

He shook his head and walked towards her.

"Sandra, don't play like this. You know I love you."

Her frown dwindled away.

"I guess Janelle was right. Looks can be deceiving."

She smiled.

"I'm sorry."

He kissed her on the forehead.

"You over here trying to get me in trouble with God."

He looked at her and laughed.

"I got enough I need to repent for... You trippin."

She shook her head and rolled her eyes.

"Whatever. Even when I wanna to hate you, I can't."

"Woman, that's why God sent me to you. Now, can we please go eat. Got me over here nervous and all I wanted to do was come home and surprise my beautiful wife."

He grabbed his phone and keys.

"Girl, I thought I was gone have to ask Josh for they counselor number. Let's go... You buying."

She grabbed her purse.

"Nope... How you gone surprise me and I got to—"

"There you go again, jumping to conclusions and can't take a joke."

He confidently pointed to himself.

"Dinner on me baby."

Sandra's phone rang, it was Janelle.

"Hello."

"Hey! You okay?"

"Yeah, I'm good. I guess looks can be deceiving. We're about to go eat."

"Whatttt! What's the occasion?"

Brian heard her.

"Love is the occasion Janelle."

She laughed.

"Awe. Well ya'll have fun. I'm on my way to our session and I just wanted to check on you. Call me when you get a minute."

Sandra smiled.

"Okay. Be careful."

"You too."

Sandra ended the call and looked over at Brian with a wide smile.

"Thank you, Brian."

"For what."

"Being you."

He laughed.

"I'm telling you girl. God showed out when He created me."

She rolled her eyes.

"Whatever."

Chapter Fifty-Six

Thirty minutes later, Janelle left the post office and arrived to their session. As she walked in, Joshua looked at her and smiled.

"I beat you here huh."

She playfully smiled.

"Whatever."

She looked over at the secretary.

"Good afternoon. You look stunning as usual."

"Thank you, Mrs. Richards. You as well." She took a call, nodded, and looked up at them.

"Mrs. Chambers will be ready for you in few more minutes."

Joshua looked up. "Okay, that's fine."

She pointed her finger towards them.

"Excuse me... Mrs. Chambers wanted me to let you know—"

Before she could warn them, an older couple walked out of Mrs. Chambers office. Mrs. Chambers smiled.

"Have a wonderful day."

The older gentleman looked back and winked his eye.

"I will as long as she act right."

Joshua lifted his head, turned towards Janelle, and laughed. The older gentlemen noticed him.

"Young man, what you laughing for. Stay married this long and you'll see your wife turn into a buzzard too... I'm talking about a buzzard that'll make you clip its wings so it can't fly. And if it can't fly, it'll be too tired to walk. And if it can't walk, it can't eat." He balled up his lips. "Then, it'll croak and dieeee."

Joshua rubbed the left side of his head. He couldn't seem to contain his laughter.

"Yes sir."

The man looked at Janelle.

"What you smiling for? It's your wings..."

He pointed towards Joshua.

"He gone clip and you gone dieeeeee."

The older lady hit her husband with her purse.

"Will you shut up and leave them children alone. I tell you the truth."

She looked over at them and shook her head.

"Don't listen to this clown. He just mad because The Lord done clipped his heavenly wings."

Joshua smiled. "Yes ma'am, but it's okay. We understand."

The older gentleman looked back.

"You understand what? That some women crazy as hell."

The older lady shook her head once more.

"When you told me your last name, I should've done just what it said, paused and thought about it before I said I do. I never thought sexy would turn into stupid."

The older lady playfully pushed her husband and walked away. Joshua jumped up to break his fall.

"I'm pressing charges. Did you see that old hateful buzzard push me?"

The secretary laughed.

"We saw it all Mr. Pause."

He rolled his eyes. "Whatever."

Chapter Fifty-Seven

As the older couple left, the counselor shook her head and gestured for Janelle and Joshua to come back to her office. The Counselor sat down in her tufted chair, crossed her legs, and smiled.

"Good afternoon."

They both smiled.

"Good afternoon."

"I'm sorry. They are the funniest couple I know. I've known them for forever."

She smiled.

"You would think I'd be used to it by now. They've been married for fifty years."

Janelle laughed.

"Actually, I thought it was rather cute myself. I needed that laugh especially not knowing what this session entails of."

Mrs. Chambers reached for her glasses.

"Me too. You know, sometimes they just randomly pop up. It's like they know when I'm not booked."

Joshua laughed.

"So, their stalkers?"

She looked at him and smiled.

"No, actually they're my parents."

His forehead wrinkled.

"I'm sorry."

"No, it's okay. Believe me, after some couples see them and hear my father's same old lame lines, they feel like what they're going through really isn't that bad."

Mrs. Chambers observed the couple and took a sip of her tea.

"So, lets dive head first into this session. I gave you both a workbook to complete during our last session. How did that work for you?"

Janelle looked at her husband and back to the counselor.

"I completed everything except for two lessons."

She looked towards Joshua.

"What about you?"

He laughed and shrugged his shoulders.

"I mean, I didn't even look at it." He held up a finger. "However, I've tried hard to treat my wife the way she should be treated."

The counselor smiled.

"Just as I thought. The reasons for giving you all the workbooks was simply to effectively prove a point, but the only way to prove that point was to make you think that it was an assignment to help your marriage."

She adjusted herself in the chair and continued.

"Mr. Richards, seventy-five percent of the men that receive this work book never complete it because it's considered too much work. It's time consuming and in their minds, not necessary."

She crossed her legs.

"I simply place them in my inconsistent group. Do you follow?"

He shook his head and exhaled profoundly.

"No."

"Simply said, this is a husband who is unwilling to do the work to save his marriage with assumptions that time will erase the mess his marriage is in."

She took a sip of tea, looked at his wife, and continued.

"Mrs. Richards, you're placed in the group of wives who are excited about their marriage getting better; however, somewhere along the way, this group of women allow life's circumstances to distract them; therefore, causing a flood of emotions to dictate to them whether they should give up or continue to fight for their marriage. It's almost like the story in the bible of the seeds that fell onto the ground. The question is, have the lessons you've both learned fell on fertile or harsh stubborn ground? Mrs. Richards, what happened to trigger this?"

She took a deep breath, exhaled, and stared at the clock on the wall. The counselor snapped her finger to get her attention.

"Mrs. Richards, what happened?"

She turned her attention back to the counselor.

"Maybe my husband should tell you."

The counselor looked over at him.

"Mr. Richards, please explain."

He took a deep breath and cleared his throat.

"It's been rough for me."

He looked over at his wife.

"I mean us. I recently found out that my ex never had the abortion we both agreed on."

He sat back on the sofa.

"And now, I have a four-year-old daughter, not to mention that my wife is pregnant with twins."

She removed her glasses from her face.

285

"Mrs. Richards, how did this make you feel?"

She smiled and shook her head.

"It hurt, I mean it really hurt. I'm trying hard not to hold him responsible for his past."

The counselor looked at her with gentle eyes.

"You're absolutely right. You can't hold him responsible for his past or past relationships. You know... there are things from each of our past that need to be addressed in order to eliminate negative cycles that aren't welcome or needed in our life or marriages."

He leaned up.

"But I, don't care about my past. I'm trying to build a future with my wife."

The counselor smirked. "Is that what you've brainwashed yourself into thinking?"

He leaned back.

"I really don't care."

She stared at him.

"I remember you telling me during one of our sessions about your father and the way he treated your mother. Your tone and body language exemplified the pain you felt watching your mother go through this."

She reached for their folder, opened it, and pointed to his statement.

"You even went as far as to say that you didn't want to end up like him. So, if this is the case, how could you not care about your past that's so deeply intertwined in your marriage?"

He glanced over at his wife. The counselor leaned up placing her elbows on her thighs.

"Mr. Richards, for the sake of your marriage, your daughter, and unborn children, are you ready to untangle yourself from the generational behaviors passed down from your father to you and your marriage?"

He rubbed his chin.

"I guess."

"Mr. Richards, this is a very serious matter; therefore, guessing is not an option. You must be all in or all out. Which one do you choose?"

He took a deep breath.

"I'm all in."

She looked at Janelle.

"Mrs. Richards are you ready?"

She smiled.

"I'm ready."

The counselor reached for the silver bowl from her desk filled with folded papers.

"Today, we will start off by digging into the bowls of your past."

He stared as the counselor as she continued.

"Many times, our past has a funny way of digging itself out of the grave we assumed we buried it in. The key word here is assumed, but the things we assumed were dead tend to return with vengeance to assassinate our marriages and our future. The stench of its aroma strikes fear within, but being healed from it brings joy."

She smiled.

"So, Mr. Richards, I'll begin with you."

He moved to the edge of the chair.

"Okay."

She held out the bowl towards him.

"Mix the folded papers in the bowl and pick the one of your choice."

He reached and grabbed a hand full of the papers and dropped them back in the bowl, chuckled, and picked one. The counselor sat back and crossed her legs.

"Now, open the paper and elaborate on the word you picked from your past."

His wife looked over at him waiting to hear his word.

"Mr. Richards, can you please share your word with us."

He rubbed his lips and exhaled deeply.

"My word is trust."

Janelle watched as her husband stared at the word stalling for time.

"Mr. Richards, please elaborate."

He rubbed his forehead

"Ummm. Growing up my dad would always tell me not to trust anyone. Far too often, he would march in the house mad with the world and the first thing he would say was, 'Don't trust nobody. These people out here only out for self.'"

"In other words, he brainwashed you into believing genuine people didn't exist?"

He shifted uncomfortably on the sofa and nodded as his brows arched.

"Correct... He was never faithful to my mom you know and I couldn't understand why because she was a good mother and wife. She always made sure that he didn't have to do anything but come home from work, get a bath, eat, and go to sleep."

He shook his head.

"What man doesn't want that? It was like, after I hit my teenage years, he openly cheated in my presence like he didn't

288

care if she would find out. He continuously reminded me that having another woman on the side was the best thing to do to keep from getting hurt... You know, I think he liked being miserable."

"Mr. Richards, many times we misread the behavior of others for one thing, when it's another. Could it be that your father desired to be happy, but didn't know how?"

Janelle looked at her husband waiting for his response.

He shrugged his shoulders.

"Maybe."

She stares in the eyes.

"Mr. Richards, would you ignore a broken leg?"

He frowned with confusion in his eyes.

"No."

Her brows arched.

"Why?"

He frowned once more.

"Because it could jeopardize me being able to walk."

She slightly tilted her head and smiled.

"Exactly. Your father's misery came from ignoring his past and when you ignore things, they tend to cripple you."

The counselor shook her head with sympathy in her eyes.

"You see, no one desires to be miserable."

She chuckled.

"So many people try hard to be happy, but things from their past causes misery to win... It's like they're trapped and crying for help through their actions because that's the only way they know how."

She held up her finger.

"The question is, what you want for your children? Is this the life you want for your daughter to have with men?"

He glanced at his wife.

"No, I don't."

She gave a gentle smile.

"Then break the cycle. Mr. Richards, some of the behaviors you exhibit comes from your father's past and chances are, he learned them from his father. You see, negative behaviors and unwanted patterns tend to flow from generation to generation, whether good or bad... One's inability to accept the truth, keeps them stagnant and they think that what they're doing is new, but even the Bible says, 'There's nothing new under the sun.'"

She reached for her cup and took a sip of tea and placed the cup back onto the table.

"Mr. Richards, do you follow what I'm saying."

"I do."

"Do you understand that breaking this ugly cycle won't come easy."

His brows arched as he looked over at his wife.

"I understand."

She looked up after taking notes.

"No matter how hard it gets, your motivation will be that you're fighting for your children to have a better life than you. The twins that your wife is carrying are blank canvases... Be careful what you paint on their futures. On the other hand, your daughters canvas isn't blank anymore because the painting for her began five years ago."

His brows furrowed.

"But she's four."

"As I said, the painting began five years ago while she was in the wound. The first stroke came when you rejected her not even realizing that she would be the one to sooth your heart just as she did when you finally had the chance to see her pretty little face at the hospital."

Taken back, a tear fell from his eyes. The counselor continued.

"Mr. Richards, it's time to forgive yourself so that you can finally paint a beautiful ending with your daughter... It's not too late."

He rubbed his hands back and forth on his thighs as tears fell down his face. His wife reached for his hand to comfort him as tears fell from his eyes.

"Mr. Richards, I know today's session is hard, but you're fighting for something way more rewarding than you know and that's a happy family."

He placed his hand on his nose and sniffled as she continued.

"We're all born free, but as we get older, we tend to allow our past to enslave us. The question is, why do we give it so much power when God's word is there with the keys to unlock us from all of the bondage we're in by renewing our minds and overcoming our past?"

Janelle glanced over at her husband as the counselor stood up and slid her chair closer to them.

"Mr. Richards, I would like to continue knocking on the doors of your past because I feel that you're leaving out crucial information that's blocking your breakthrough."

He rubbed his eyes, inhaled, and exhaled deeply. He looked up and rubbed his chin.

"I wasted so many years hating my father not even thinking for one moment that maybe he didn't understand how his behavior affected me. I can't even go back and hug him and tell him that I'm sorry."

The counselor looked at him as he shook his head.

"Mr. Richards, what happed to your father?"

He cleared his throat and looked away.

"I was on my way to the store after work and as I turned to get on the main highway and got to the light, I saw an ambulance pass by. Ten minutes later, I got to the store and my mom called."

"What did she say?"

He shook his head as tears formed in his eyes once more.

"She said that my dad had passed away."

The counselor handed him a box of Kleenex.

"I'm sorry and I know this is so hard for you right now, but you have to allow yourself to be free from all of this pain you have bottled up on the inside."

He lowered his head.

"Mom said he went in the room after eating and took a nap, but he never woke up. You know, that's a peaceful way to go."

She looked at him with gentle eyes and smiled.

"You see, there's beauty in all of your pain. You just had to find it. Your father didn't suffer in death. He simply went to sleep and now he's waiting for the day he'll see you again."

She looked over at Janelle. "Is it okay for me to comfort your husband?"

"Yes ma'am."

The counselor gestured for him to stand up. She placed her hands on his shoulders and smiled.

"You're going to be okay."

She pulled him towards her to comfort him and smiled at Janelle. She stepped back and sat down as he rubbed the tears from his face and sat down next to his wife. Mrs. Chambers sat down and crossed her legs.

"Today's session was necessary for the healing process of your marriage to begin and I know it was tough." She smiled. "But it gave you the closure that your heart has always searched for."

She got up, walked over to her desk, scanned through the calendar, and looked up.

She looked up. "Mr. and Mrs. Richards, I have an opening for this Friday at 5:00 p.m.... Are you up for it?"

Janelle looked over at her husband. "That's fine."

The counselor walked them to the door and smiled.

"Have a great day." She placed her hand on Joshua's back. "God is about to paint a new picture for you."

He smiled. "You have a good day as well."

Chapter Fifty-Eight

S hortly after arriving home, Joshua walked into the
kitchen. He looked over at his wife and smiled.
"You cooking or I'm making my famous veggie burgers?"

She pointed to him.

"You're making your famous veggie burgers."

He laughed and reached into the refrigerator, and
grabbed the portabella mushroom caps.

"It's like that?"

"Pretty much."

"You want chips or my homemade fries?"

She leaned against the island.

"Fries."

"So, can I get some freshly squeezed lemonade with
that too?"

He looked up.

"Now you pushing it. Let me guess, you want me to cut
up the onions too, right?"

She gave a flirty smile.

"Yes... Spoil me. I'm in desperate need of it."

After cleaning the kitchen, Joshua fluffed the pillows
while Janelle showered and ready for bed. She walked in
the room and looked over at him.

"Good night Joshua."

He opened his eyes.

"Good night."

But, it would be a sleepless night for him as Mrs. Chambers words taunted him.

The painting of her canvas began in the womb when you rejected her.

Shaken by the thoughts of his daughter, he got up, walked into the living room, and mumbled. "I don't get it. How could I mess up that bad?"

Janelle woke up from his absence, walked in the living room, and gently placed her hand on his shoulder.

"Josh, you okay?"

He looked back at his wife and turned around as she walked around the sofa. Sitting next to him, she leaned her head on his shoulder.

"Josh... it's okay. I understand today was rough, but the beautiful thing is that you left with closure from your past." She looked at him. "Now, you can start over and paint a beautiful canvas for Ashely and our children so God can make all things new."

He smiled.

"You're right. I got to stop being so negative."

She laughed and mimicked the counselors father.

"Pretty much. So, we clipping you're daddy ugly ways? So, they can dieeeeeeee."

He laughed as they got up, placed his arms around his wife, went back to bed, and fell asleep holding her in his arms.

The next morning, he called Patrice to talk things over with her. He smiled when she answered.

"Hi Patrice."

"Good morning Joshua."

"Look Patrice, I'm sorry that I haven't been there for you and Ashley and I want to make things right."

She held the phone in silence.

"Patrice."

"I'm here."

"I know you may hate me right now and you have every right to, but I need for you to understand that I would've been there for Ashley had I known you didn't follow through with the abortion. When I proposed to you, I really meant it, but I was also still in love with my ex and when you told me that you were pregnant, I panicked."

She adjusted herself in her chair as he continued.

"Look, I'm really sorry and I honestly don't know how to take you being so quiet right now. Can you please forgive me?"

She exhaled.

"Joshua, all I ever wanted was closure and you just gave me the one thing I needed. An apology and answers to questions I've had for so long."

He rubbed his neck.

"You have no clue how relieved I am. Family means everything to me and Ashley being a part of my life completes the puzzle. My wife is so excited to get to know her."

He chuckled.

"She even went as far as to fix a room for her."

He could hear Patrice's smile through the phone when she responded.

"Ashley would love that and she loves going to the park and to get ice-cream."

Tears fell from her eyes.

"Joshua, thank you."

"For what?"

"Not turning your back on her."

He paused as if thinking.

"Hey Patrice, is it okay if I take her to the park next week?"

She smiled.

"Sure. She would love that. Oh, and I've already told her you were her father and I took full responsibility for you saying you were her uncle... She just wouldn't stop questioning me about the whole hospital thing. She understands, but she's ready to finally get to know you."

He smiled.

"Thank you Patrice. Either me or my wife will call you next week."

She smiled. "Okay."

Chapter Fifty-Nine

T he end of the week came swiftly. That morning Joshua sat on the side of the bed, reached over, and shook his wife.

"Hey."

She rolled over.

"Yeah."

"Are you working today?"

She rubbed her eyes.

"Yeah, why?"

He got up and walked into their closet.

"Because it's seven o'clock."

She got up and walked to the bathroom.

"I'm up. I got first bids on the shower."

"It's all good. At least when you get out, I'll have clean fresh breath, while you got a clean body and bad breath."

She got in the shower.

"Whatever. Looks like Brian rubbing off on you."

He walked into the bathroom and reached to rub the steam off the mirror to brush his teeth.

"You know he cheating on his wife, right."

With wide eyes, she peeked out of the shower.

"What?"

He shook his head.

"I'm just playing."

She rolled her eyes.

"You play too much."

Minutes later, Joshua laughed and handed her the mouthwash as she walked over to the sink in her robe.

"Yep, go ahead and get your breath right while I get my shower."

He blew his breath in the air.

"My breath is fresh and clean."

She untwisted her hair and fluffed it with the tips of her fingers.

"Have you called Ashley today?"

He got in the shower.

"I haven't. I'm actually taking her on a play date today."

"I bet she's excited."

She walked out of the closet and smiled.

"Hey, I'm about to cook breakfast and don't forget about our session today at five."

"I won't."

He reached for his towel, got out of the shower, and looked at her.

"You know, pregnancy looks good on you, right?"

Her eyes smiled.

"Thank you."

After getting ready for work, he walked in the kitchen over to his wife, gave her a kiss, ate, and grabbed his things.

"I'll see you at five."

Realizing that he left his phone, he ran back in, but Janelle was already standing at the door. He gave her a kiss as she handed him the phone.

"Thank you. I'll see you later."

"Alright."

He got back in the car and left for work. Later that day, he picked Ashley up from school to take her to the park. She walked to the car in her school uniform and smiled as she got in.

"Hey."

He looked at her and smiled.

"Don't you look cute today."

"Thank you.

Minutes later, they arrived at the park. He smiled as she got out of the car and ran to the swings.

"Daddy, come on."

His heart melted from hearing daddy for the first time. Her laughter gave him pure enjoyment as he pushed her in the swing.

"Hey, you ready to go to the ice-cream shop?"

She smiled.

"Yes sir."

Chapter Sixty

T he next day, Janelle arrived to their counseling session and rushed into the office.

Breathing heavily, she smiled.

"Good evening. I'm sorry, traffic is horrible today."

The secretary smiled.

"I hope it calms down before I leave."

The secretary noticed Janelle looking for her husband and pointed towards the door to her right.

"Your husband just walked into the restroom before you arrived."

She smiled.

"Okay. Thank you."

Before she could sit down, the counselor came to the door.

"Mrs. Richards, are you ready?"

She looked towards the restroom and hesitated. The counselor interrupted her thoughts and looked towards the secretary.

"When Mr. Richards comes out, please send him right in."

"Yes ma'am."

Before Mrs. Richards could close the door, Joshua reached for the door knob.

"So, y'all just going to start without me, right?"

She walked over to her chair, sat down, and chuckled.

"Now why would we do that?"

He sat down next to his wife.

"Champion of late huh."

He laughed as she rolled her eyes while the counselor reached for the silver bowl.

"Well, we won't waste any time."

She held the bowl towards her.

"Mrs. Richards, today we'll start with you. In our last session, your husband was asked to pick a word from the silver bowl, so today you'll do the same."

Janelle nodded as she continued.

"After you have chosen your word, you will elaborate on how it affected you in the past up until now."

She smiled.

"Are you ready?"

Joshua glanced over at his wife as she picked a word from the bowl. He anxiously watched as she slowly opened the paper. Briefly looking up in a daze.

"My word is absence."

She thought for a few seconds and leaned back on the sofa glancing towards the window lost in her memories.

"After my mom passed, the one thing I desired with all of my heart was the presence of my father, but he was never there."

She turned her attention back to the counselor.

"I couldn't wrap my mind around how a father could do that to an innocent child. Someone once told me that I was being unrealistic in waiting for the day he would grace me with his presence... Even if it were only for a moment, but I beg to differ. How is that unrealistic? He's my father."

She shook her head.

"Isn't that what fathers do? In my mind, she was telling me that fathers only take the time to lay and play and later run away from their responsibilities."

She closed her eyes, exhaled deeply, glanced over at her husband, and back to the counselor.

"It was bad enough that I had to grow up without my mother. Don't get me wrong, I appreciate Ms. Lula and I love her so much for being there, but there's nothing like your own and she understands that."

As she blinked, tears flowed down her face. The counselor's brows creased as she reached for the box of Kleenex from her desk and handed it to her.

"Mrs. Richards, if you would like to stop, we can but, if you're comfortable please look at your husband and explain to him how this has affected your marriage."

Janelle reached for a kleenex from the box and gently wiped the tears from her eyes. She shifted her body towards him as her left knee rested on the sofa and reached for his hand.

"Joshua, whenever you're distant and your love isn't present, it reminds me of my father and frustrates the heck out of me. I know it's not your fault, but it hurts when a woman has experienced so much rejection from the one man she loved only to have to experience it with her husband all over again. I try hard not to allow it to affect me, but it seemed to have intensified since the pregnancy. I find myself wasting so much time letting my past dictate to me how I should feel instead of using that time to enjoy you and the pregnancy. And for that, I'm sorry."

The counselor looked at her husband.

"It makes you think doesn't it Mr. Richards. I pray that what you've heard your wife say helps you to understand her and the importance of your presence in your daughter's life."

She placed her glasses on the table next to her.

"You see, all pain from our past has a purpose. What your wife is going through affects you in more ways than you know. Her pain was designed to teach you what not to do to your daughter."

She turned her attention back to Janelle.

"I won't ask you any questions during this session; however, I will revisit this during our next session to eliminate any further stress."

She lifted her finger, took a sip of her water, and looked towards them. She placed her hand on her chest.

"I'm sorry. My throat was parched."

She placed the water on the table next to her.

"Mrs. Richards, you mentioned the time you've wasted in your marriage and it leads up to my next thought. Today, I will pose a question for you both that will lead to your assignment for the week. If you're serious about making everything work in your marriage, then you must be held accountable for time."

Joshua's forehead wrinkled as she continued.

"With only 24 hours in a day, how much time do you invest in your marriage?... How many times a day do you stubbornly ignore the needs of your spouse? These questions are vital for your marriage. You must be willing to take the time every other hour in a day to document how many times you thought positive thoughts of your spouse, how many times thinking of them made you smile, & how much time and effort you actually put into making things work. Even if it's sending a thoughtful text or simply a smiling emoji to let your spouse know that you're thinking of them. In the beginning, you'll need to set an alarm in your phone to remind you of this assignment. Do you follow?"

Janelle nodded and smiled at the counselor.

"I understand."

The counselor looked over at Joshua.

"And you Mr. Richards?"

He smiled.

"I got it."

The counselor smiled.

"It's crucial for you both to remain persistent in keeping up with this assignment. Before long, it will become a part of your daily routine without the reminder of an alarm because it will be embedded within your thoughts and hearts... But wait, for every hour, minute, or second you spend being negative; you must use the letter (X) to represent those thoughts and actions. Once you've completed the assignment for that day, calculate your (X's) and then calculate your positive thoughts and gestures at the bottom of the worksheet."

She crossed her legs and held up her hand holding her thumb and pointing finger together.

"This assignment is designed to mold consistency within in your marriage and to hold you accountable for your actions. If you're never aware of how much time you've wasted in a day being angry, bitter, and unwilling to submit to forgiveness and the love that gently taps on your hearts, you'll never know what needs to be corrected."

Joshua grinned.

"I feel like I'm back in school."

The counselor chuckled.

"Yes, the school of rebuilding your marriage. You see, the number one thing that I've observed in countless marriages as well as yours, is that many of you have daddy issues."

She deeply respired.

"One of my main jobs as a marriage counselor is to make sure your relationship with **The Father** is restored through **truth**. That truth is, that **He loves you** both so much, **but** you **must** be **willing** to **completely open your hearts to His love once again** with childlike **faith**, so that He can heal the damaged done by your earthly dads."

Joshua's eyes grew wide.

"Wow! That was deep."

She reached for the two folders with the assignments from her desk, handed them the folders to them and smiled.

"Do you think you can handle this assignment?"

Janelle smiled.

"I can handle it."

"And you Mr. Richards?"

"Sure."

"Well, it looks like we're done for the day."

She got up and walked over to the calendar on her desk. "How about the same day of the week, but this time at four?"

They looked at each other and back towards the counselor.

"Sure, that's fine."

She lifted her finger.

"Oh, before you leave, there's one more thing with your assignment. Even if you have two hours, two minutes, or even two seconds left in a day, please don't end it with (X's). She walked towards the door and smiled. "Well, we're done for the day I'll see you all next week.

Chapter Sixty-One

T he next morning, Janelle received a call from an unfamiliar
number.

She looked down at her phone and hesitated to answer.

"Hello."

"Hi Janelle."

She took a deep breath and sat down.

"Hi. How are you?"

"I'm sorry to bother you, but I was wondering if we could meet
somewhere in about an hour."

"May I ask why?"

"I really need to talk to you, but I would rather meet face to face.
Just you and I."

Janelle shook her head.

"I guess" She looked down and rubbed her stomach. "How
about Betty's Jeans soul food café down the street?"

"That'll be fine with me."

The mistress caller walked towards the car.

"Oh, and lunch is on me."

"Okay. I'll see you then."

Janelle wondered what the meeting was about not knowing the
motive of the meeting, caused negativity to arrest her thoughts. She
softly whispered.

"If Joshua has screwed up this time, I'm done."

She got up, grabbed her purse, and walked to the car. As she started the car, the radio personality was opening with his daily encouragement.

"What's up out there ya'll. It's your boy Cam J here on 97.8 radio where we bring you music that keeps your hands lifted and your heads bobbin to the best praise, worship, and gospel rap out here. But, before I play this next song, I want to provoke your thoughts just a little bit with Proverbs 4:23. It says, 'be careful what you think because your thoughts control your life.' You know I always say, if your thoughts aint right, shut'em down. Be safe out there in this traffic ya'll. Aight let's kick this lunch hour off with —"

She turned down the radio as she pulled up at Betty Jeans soul food café. She looked up and saw Patrice standing on the sidewalk. She gave a slight smile, got out of the car, and walked towards her.

"Hi Patrice."

She smiled.

"Thanks for meeting me. Wow, you look stunning. Not to mention, you're really starting to show."

Janelle rubbed her belly.

"I know right. How's Ashley?"

"Oh, she's doing great. She's with my mom this week to give me the time needed to prepare for the move."

She forced a smile.

"Oh."

The hostess walked over to them.

"Good afternoon."

She lifted two fingers.

"A table for two, right?"

Patrice smiled.

"Yes."

They followed the hostess to the table next to the window and sat down. A young lady with long black curly hair walked over and smiled.

"Good afternoon, my name is Anna and I'll be your waitress for today. Can I get you something to drink?"

Janelle placed her phone on the table.

"Sure. Lemon water for me please."

The waitress looked over at Patrice and smiled.

"What about you?"

She scanned the drinks on the menu.

"Ummm. Let me get your homemade lemonade."

"I'll be right back with your drinks."

She looked up at Patrice and slightly tilted her head.

"Sooo... May I ask what this lunch meeting is about?"

Patrice crossed her legs under the table and leaned back in her chair.

"Yeah, about that. I'm glad you asked." She exhaled. "I spoke with Joshua the other day about Ashley and afterwards, you were on my mind."

Janelle's stomach knotted as she held it together. The waitress walked back over with their drinks and placed them on the table.

"Are you all ready to order?"

Janelle looked down at the menu and pointed.

"I would like to have your tomato sandwich with your special spread and a bowl of homemade vegetable soup."

Patrice's eyes grew wide.

"You must be hungry.... She serves big bowls of that vegetable soup, but for a good price that is."

Janelle laughed.

"She really does. What I don't eat now, I can save for later."

Patrice scanned the menu.

"Okay. Ummmm I'll have your deep-fried chicken meal with potato salad, and kidney beans."

The waitress took down their orders.

"Your lunch will be out shortly."

Patrice took a sip of her lemonade.

"Oh, my God. This lemonade is the best."

Janelle folded her arms and looked at her.

"Janelle, I'm sorry for stalling. Look..."

She took a deep as she leaned towards the table.

"I haven't been the best person to deal with, so, please forgive me for hating you over something you had nothing to do with. I despised the fact that you had the opportunity to marry the man I was so in love with."

Janelle's brows met as she continued.

"Not to mention that I was a good fiancé to him and the fact that he cheated on me after all I did for him, made me bitter. I should never have blamed you and I wish I could take it all back, but I can't. Besides, I learned so much from you."

Janelle tilted her head.

"How?"

"Well, for one when I tried my best to make you angry, you remained calm and let's not even forget how you apologized for something your husband did to me."

She shook her head.

"At first, I didn't know how to take you. I honestly thought you were being sarcastic because Joshua's the king of sarcasm, but then I realized you were just being yourself. Believe it or not, I was sorry for my attitude towards you about a while ago, but I didn't know how to say it to you personally."

Janelle took a sip of her water as Patrice continued.

"It's not fair that you and your unborn children pay for the way I was treated when I learned that I was pregnant with Ashley. His ex didn't seem to care that I was pregnant and neither did he. Before I knew it, he was asking me to have an abortion. Soooo, I figured I would go along with it. When we got to the clinic, I figured why should I abort my child because he wasn't ready to be a father or stop kicking it with his ex." She lowered her head.

"So, I moved away. It was the most stressful pregnancy ever that sent me into early labor and demanded a C-section in which I have the scar to remind of his unfaithfulness and him even asking me for an abortion... Honestly, I don't want that for you. I want this scar to have a new meaning of forgiveness for me so that I can get over everything."

Janelle looked over at Patrice with sympathy in her eyes.

"No, I'm sorry."

She shook her head.

"I didn't know all of that."

Patrice shrugged her shoulders.

"It's okay, but thank you for understanding. I just want what you have because it's beautiful."

She gave Patrice a confusing stare.

"What do you mean?"

She rushed to explain.

"No, not like that. I mean your heart is so kind even when people with the wrong motives demands your heart to hate."

She laughed.

"Patrice, only Jesus can give you that. I really need for you to understand that I'm not perfect. I can only do that with God's help. I mess up a lot you know."

The waitress walked over with their food and placed it on the table.

"If you need anything, please press the button on your table and it will buzz me."

Patrice smiled.

"Uh, Ms. Betty moving on up in technology with this café, huh?"

The waitress laughed.

"She is and it works wonders because it gives her customers the privacy needed while they eat and me time to do the silverware."

She smiled.

"Don't forget to buzz me when you need me."

Janelle smiled and turned her attention back to Patrice. "As I was saying, I was a little hesitant about coming because I didn't know why you wanted to meet, but I'm glad I did. It's not for me to hate or dislike you. My job is to love you through your pain. I know that Josh hurt you, but what I will say is that every broken relationship leaves a lesson behind and a few answers. I honestly believe that my husband loved you the best way he knew how at the time, but later realized he messed up."

She took a sip of water.

"What I do know is, that you deserve to be loved by a man who will love you back and be the reflection of Christ that you need. But he'll never find you as long as you continue to hide behind the hurt of a man that God never intended to be your husband."

Patrice slightly tilted her head and continued to listen.

"I don't mean that in any disrespectful way."

Patrice relaxed her face.

"Besides Patrice, our children deserve to be raised together in peace as they grow up together. I'm pretty sure Ashley would be happy to know that she'll be a big sister."

Patrice wiped the tear from her eyes.

"Janelle, thank you."

Janelle smiled and handed her a napkin.

"Anytime. So, where are you moving to?"

She smiled.

"I actually found a house three doors down from you."

Janelle turned her head quickly.

"Okay."

Patrice bit into a piece of her chicken and covered her mouth as she spoke.

"Well, you did say that we would be raising them together. I'm just waiting to close on everything. I should know something by the first of next week."

She lifted her hands.

"This chicken is good. I'm telling you, God works in mysterious ways."

Janelle placed her hand on her chin.

"Wow. I'm truly happy for you. I'll be praying that everything works out."

Patrice smiled.

"Janelle, that means a lot coming from you."

Chapter Sixty-Two

A week later, Janelle and Joshua arrived to their counseling session. The secretary walked out of the restroom, sat down at her desk, and smiled.

"Mrs. Richards, you look like you could pop any day now."

She smiled.

"Only a few more weeks and they'll make their debut. By the way, I love your hair."

The secretary smiled.

"Thank you."

She turned to the computer and began typing. A few moments later, her phone rang. After hanging up with the counselor, she looked up.

"Mrs. Chambers is ready for you."

As they walked into the counselor's office, Janelle smiled.

"Good afternoon Mrs. Chambers."

She looked up.

"Good afternoon. You both look nice today."

Joshua smiled.

"Thank you."

She walked over to her chair and sat down. Wasting no time, she sat down, and took a sip of tea.

"Mrs. Richards, let's pick up where we left off last week. I avoided asking too many questions during our last session because I didn't want to stress you or the babies in any way. So, are you ready to continue?"

She smiled.

"Yes ma'am."

The counselor opened her notebook.

"Your word was absence and it reminded you of your father, but it also reminded you of time. Have you ever taken the time to speak with your father in regards to the way his absence has affected you?"

She looked down.

"I mean I've tried before, but."

She shrugged her shoulders.

"When he refused to accept responsibility for his actions, it frustrated me. So... I stop trying."

The counselor observed her husband and took down some notes. She looked back up.

"If you don't mind me asking, how did he avoid accepting the way he made you feel?"

She shifted uncomfortably.

"I mean, he would ask, why I felt the need to bring up the past and he would say, 'God forgave me, so, why can't you.'"

Joshua looked at his wife waiting for her to continue.

She exhaled deeply.

"I tried to explain to him that I needed closure."

She shook her head. "I just needed to understand why."

The counselor crossed her legs.

"Mrs. Richards, some parents just aren't willing to give us the answers that we need to hear... Because they're in denial of what they've done. Most of the time they use God forgave me as a means to avoid."

She shook her head.

"Responsibility."

"So, how do I deal with having no closure?"

"Mrs. Richards, the best way to deal with this is to trust God, forgive, learn from it, be the best mother you can be to your children, and pray that God would one day soften your fathers heart. Even if he never says I'm sorry, don't allow your heart to wax cold."

She looked over at Joshua.

"Mr. Richards, do you understand now how your wife's past has a direct impact on your life?"

"Yes ma'am. I didn't understand during our last session, but I get it now."

He shook his head.

"My wife is a strong woman and I'm proud of her for dealing with her past, but it used to annoy the heck out of me. I guess it was meant to show me issues within myself that I was blinded to because of denial."

The counselor took a sip of her tea and placed the cup back on the table next to her.

"As I always say, everything has a purpose."

She briefly paused and smiled.

"The thing that irritates us the most are the things God uses to get our attention. But in reality, there's a lesson in it, but that's only if we're willing to see it."

She reached for the picture frame from her desk and turned it towards them.

"I grew up watching my parents love and hate one another, but before the night would end, they would always end up lovie dubbie towards one another. They taught us to never go to bed angry with anyone because you never knew if it would be the last breath. I never understood it until I got older. They were living examples of the scripture that says, don't let the sun go down on your anger."

She smiled.

"One day when they decided to come to a session with me, I took advantage of it and asked a question. I looked at my father and asked what did he get out of aggravating my mother. His response left me speechless."

She laughed.

"He said, 'If I didn't argue with your mom at least twice a week, how was I supposed to makeup with her and make more of you.'"

Janelle and Joshua looked at each other and laughed as she continued.

"I'm pretty sure he was joking, but then again... That's my dad for you. The moral of this story is to always understand and value time with one another. Their life motivated me to create the assignment that I gave the both of you. The counseling sessions we've had were designed to help you to understand the importance of dealing with your past because it does have a direct impact on your spouse and your future whether good or bad."

She reached into her folder and pulled out two certificates and sat them on her lap. She held up her finger.

"One more thing. How has your assignments been going?"

Joshua smiled.

"I actually liked the assignment because it held me accountable for the time I spent with my wife and for. After so many X's, I realized that a lot of our issues stemmed from me."

The counselor nodded and smiled.

"I'm so proud of your growth. Not many men acknowledge their part because of pride and because they're too busy blaming others, especially their wives."

She looked over at Janelle.

"How about you?"

Janelle adjusted herself on the sofa.

"I learned that I looked for my husband to show me attention and to be the first to show love and affection while I ignored his needs for the same thing. I thought keeping the house together was good enough until I saw all the X's I had at the end of the day and in doing so, I realized that I withheld the very thing I needed and wanted from him and that was love and attention."

She exhaled deeply.

"I realized that we had become so comfortable in our marriage to the point that we neglected one another and I omitted the fact that home was my first ministry."

The counselor smiled.

"The enemy tends to wait until you're comfortable with one another, then, he reminds you of the negative things your spouse does instead of the good. That in turn distracts you from the love you have for one another and the future that God has in store for you."

She smiled.

"I'm so glad that you understand now, that home is your first ministry."

As she handed them the certificates, Joshua looked at his wife and back to the counselor.

"May I ask what this is?" He laughed.

"Is it another assignment?"

The counselor smiled.

"No, it's not an assignment. It's your certificates for successfully completing your courses here at ND Counseling 101 where our goal is to save marriages."

"So, this is it?"

The counselor stood up and walked over to her desk and sat down.

"Yes... this is it. You see, my last assignment is always the marriage investment charts. When couples understand the value of time and keeping God first in their marriage, my job is done. Then, it's time for me to move out of God's way and on to my next assignment."

She smiled.

"You two are going to be just fine. Believe me, if this were not the case, you wouldn't have a certificate of completion in your hands."

Janelle smiled and looked over at her husband as he shook his head.

"I was just starting to like you."

Mrs. Chambers smiled, walked over, and shook their hands. "Thank you for using ND counseling 101 where you did the work to save your marriage. Remember, always allow God to lead you and be the glue to hold your marriage and family together."

Janelle smiled as she and Joshua walked out of the office.

"Again, thank you Mrs. Chambers."

As they were leaving the secretary caught Janelle's attention and smiled.

"I have something for you."

Janelle's brows met.

"Okay."

She smiled as Joshua walked out of the office to the car. The secretary reached down by her desk and gave her a gift bag and smiled.

"Open it when you get in your car."

"Awe, thank you. It was so nice meeting you."

The secretary put down her pen.

"It was nice meeting you too. I take it that you've completed the course."

She smiled.

"We have and it was worth our time."

The secretary turned back towards her computer.

"Have a great day."

She opened the door.

"You as well."

She anxiously walked to the car to see what was in the bag. She got in the car and pulled out two onesies that read miracles happen and created through faith, four adorable outfits with shoes to match, and a card that read.

*Though life brought challenges your way, God designed you to endure until the end. Although, fear and dread presented doubt, **your faith** although small allowed things to happen for your good. Your marriage was on the chopping board, but you survived and that gives us joy. Watching the growth in your marriage was worth our while. Remember, no matter the trials that come your way,* $\mathcal{A}lways$ $\mathcal{S}tand$ in $\mathcal{F}aith.$

Your Truly,

Mrs. Chambers

& The Staff of ND Counseling 101

Chapter Sixty-Three

A few weeks later, Janelle was awakened out of her sleep. She slowly sat up on the side of her bed, inhaled, and exhaled deeply every few seconds. She reached for her lower back.

"Joshua."

She paused, inhaled slowly, and exhaled deeply blowing air from her mouth.

"Joshua."

He rolled over and saw her sitting on the side of the bed.

"Babe, you okay."

"No, I think I'm in labor."

He got up, reached for the phone, and called the hospital.

"Clara B. Medical Center, how may I help you."

He panicked.

"I think my wife is in labor."

"Hold on please, I'll connect you to labor and delivery."

He looked over at his wife.

"Babe. You need me to do anything."

She frowned.

"Yes... get me to the hospital."

He lifted his hand and shrugged his shoulder.

"Their connecting me—"

She interrupted him and deeply exhaled.

"Joshua... get me to the hospital."

He ended the call, put on his shoes, grabbed her labor bag, and her house shoes to slide on her feet. Before he could slide her shoe on the other foot, her water broke. He ran to the bathroom closet and grabbed some towels, an old dress, and a pair of under wear. Tears flowed down her face as he cleaned her up and helped get her changed. He sat next her rubbing her lower back.

"Janelle, please don't go in labor here. I don't know nothing about delivering babies."

She leaned her head back holding her lower back taking quick short breaths.

"Joshua, please get me to the car."

He grabbed the bag and keys, reached his hand behind her back, and helped her up.

"Come on babe."

As they walked to the door, she stopped, inhaled, and exhaled deeply blowing air from her mouth. He helped her into the car and mumbled to himself as he ran around to the driver's side.

"I know the doctor said they weren't inducing her until next week."

As he got in the car and drove off, he made a call.

"Hello."

"Ms. Lula."

She rubbed her eyes and looked at the clock.

"Joshua, you better be dying waking me up out of my sleep this time of the morning."

He turned to get on the highway.

"Janelle's in labor. Can you meet us at the hospital?"

She got up and rubbed her eyes once more.

"Give me thirty minutes. I'm on my way. Take care of my babies now."

"Yes ma'am."

A few moments later, Ms. Lula got up and got ready to head to the hospital. Meanwhile on the way to the hospital, Janelle reached for the door handle to brace herself for the next contraction. She inhaled and blew air from her mouth once more. Joshua looked over at his wife with sympathetic eyes.

"Babe, you okay."

She frowned and looked over at him with tears in her eyes.

"No, I'm in pain."

Ten minutes later, they arrived at the hospital and she was ready to push. With no time to check her in, they helped her into the wheel chair and took her straight to labor and delivery. By the time she could put on the gown, she inhaled, exhaled deeply, and pushed. The nurses called for the doctor to come immediately. Within two minutes, he walked into the room, checked her, and found that she was already crowning. He looked over at Janelle.

"I'm Dr. Phillips. You've already begun crowning and it's too late for an epidural. Soooo... let's deliver these babies."

Joshua reached for his wife's hand.

"Baby, I'm right here."

The doctor smiled and placed his gloves on his hands.

"Mrs. Richards, give me a big push when you feel the next contraction."

She took a deep breath and exhaled as she pushed. The nurses counted as she pushed.

"10,9,8,7,6,5,4,3,2,1!"

The doctor gently wiggled the baby's shoulder and looked up.

"Two more big push Mrs. Richards."

Joshua helped lean his wife up.

"Push baby."

He peeked down to look in the mirror they had in place for him to see the birth of his babies.

"You got this Janelle."

After two last pushes, the nurse lay a towel on her chest as the baby was coming out. Joshua glanced at the time. It was 3:20 a.m. The nurse reached down to grab the baby and lay him on her chest for Joshua to clip the umbilical cord.

"It's a boy."

Ten minutes later, Janelle finally delivered her baby girl. Tears slowly slid down his face as he clipped the chord.

"Baby, you did it."

He kissed her on the forehead as they removed the after birth and cleaned her and the babies up. He walked over to the babies and smiled with tears in his eyes.

"Hey there ya'll. I'm your dad."

Ten minutes later, Ms. Lula arrived and walked over to the babies and smiled.

"Looka here. My baby done gave me some grandbabies. No inducing needed. God had other plans for ya'll."

She turned to Janelle with a smirk.

"Lord, she looks just like your mother."

She shook her head. "Uh huh and he looks like his father."

Janelle lay in the bed holding her baby girl while Joshua sat in the sleeper chair holding his son. The next morning, Joshua heard someone talking and looked over at the door. Seconds later, the door opened and Brian walked in smiling.

"Good morning Janelle."

She smiled.

"Hey Brian."

He looked at Joshua.

"Man, my boy got twins."

He looked down at baby Jordan.

"Dang, he look just like you."

Joshua smiled.

"Don't hate man... and he got a dimple."

Sandra walked over to Janelle with a gift bag in her hands and smiled at baby Marceya.

"Oh, my God Janelle, she's beautiful."

Two days later, Janelle and Joshua returned home with the babies. Meanwhile, Patrice and Ashley walked hand in hand up the street. Ashley swung the gift bag while her mother carried the flowers. They walked up to the door and Ashley rang the doorbell. Joshua lay Marceya down and kissed her on her forehead.

"Just a second."

He walked to the living room and opened the door. Standing with a big smile, Patrice looked at Joshua.

"Congratulations."

Ashley smiled.

"Congratulations dad."

She looked at her mom.

"I'm a big sister now."

Patrice walked in and smiled as Janelle sat on the sofa. She handed her the flowers.

"Congratulations."

Twenty minutes later, Joshua's mom and sister arrived. They walked in and admired the twins.

"Look at my grandbabies."

His sister looked over at Janelle.

"Can I please take a pic? I promise, I won't post it."

Janelle smiled. "Alright, but don't post my baby on nothing."

Ashley walked over and gave Janelle a kiss.

"Ms. Janelle."

She smiled.

"I'm a big sister now."

She held up two fingers.

"And I got two mommas."

Joshua's mom snatched her head in Joshua's direction. He lowered his head and looked back up.

"Ashley."

She looked over at him.

"Sir."

"Come here for a minute... I have someone for you to meet."

Patrice sat in the recliner with a smile holding Jordan and watched closely as Ashley walked towards her father.

"Hey baby."

He pointed to his mother.

"This is your grandma Marcelle."

His mother smiled.

"Hi little princess."

She looked at Joshua and back to Ashley. "You're so big."

Ashley smiled and gave her a hug. Meanwhile, Joshua's sister cut her eyes over at him and back towards Patrice. She smirked as her brows arched.

He pointed to his sister.

"And this is your auntie."

His sister smiled.

"Hey. She a cutie pie."

Ashley walked back over to the sofa with Janelle and Marceya. Patrice nodded and smiled as a tear escaped from her eyes knowing that they were finally one big happy family.

THE END!!!

1 Peter 3:1, 7

Vs. 1 In the same way, you wives should yield to your husbands. Then, if some husbands do not obey God's teachings, they will be persuaded to believe without anyone's saying a word to them. They will be persuaded by the way their wives live. Vs. 7 In the same way, you husbands should live with your wives in an understanding way, since they are weaker than you. But show them respect, because God gives them the same blessing he gives you-the grace that gives true life. Do this so that nothing will stop your prayers. (NCV)

About the Author

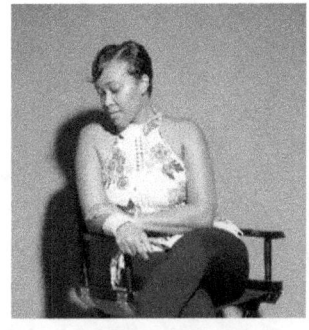

As I am introduced to the world, my dedication to the art of writing is made known. A hidden jewel finally polished to be show cased to the world. I am **Lakisha G. Louissaint**, an author, screenwriter, upcoming producer & director, mother, and wife. Although, these are things that I do, they are not who I am. I am an **imperfect** being created by God, striving to live the life of Christ before the world. I strive to help parents of children with Autism because it directly impacts my life through my son; therefore, be on the lookout for my next upcoming book based on a life raising a child with Autism. Title yet unknown. Learn more about me at

www.IamLakisha.com **Instagram:** iamlakisha1 **Photo Credits:** Michael Moorer https://www.michaelmoorerphotography.com/

www.ingramcontent.com/pod-product-compliance
Lightning Source LLC
Chambersburg PA
CBHW071203020726
47502CB00002B/526

* 9 7 8 0 9 9 9 2 1 1 6 0 1 *